Praise for True Blue

"A real treasure full of action, excitement, and intrigue!"

Jack Haughton

'Imagination –There are two worlds,
the world that we can measure with line and rule, and
the world that we feel with our hearts and imagination.'

A quote from Leigh Hunt - Leaves of Gold

"This quote is particularly fitting for D Stuart White's True Blue. A delightful read with sensitivity to his characters that provides a fitting background story - a must-read!"

Penny McCready

"True Blue sequel to Tall Air is a five-star yarn with surprising twists and enduring white-hot action as two missions during WWII form the nexus of a future worldwide holocaust."

Publisher

"True Blue is a wonderful, cohesive blend of fact and fiction that puts the reader in the cockpit before, during, and after a battle. It is a well-woven storyline with many twists. Each turn of the page reveals more insightful clues. Or are they well-placed illusions to challenge your perceptions? You must read this exciting, fast-paced story to find out."

Tom Combs – author FLIGHT LINE

"You will love this one if you like intrigue-packed espionage. Those words you bring to the page are so carefully chosen, words that make people forget about their struggles and concerns. You transform people. You take them places. Thank you for carrying me along."

Al Cisneros – Blue Angels 75-76

"True Blue is a tangled web of military intrigue, friendship, and honor.

White is totally up to snuff with the glory and the irreverence of military aviation in True Blue. He has done remarkable work devising a storyline that steps up the pace in his Tall Air sequel. He places the reader squarely in the cockpit with Mathew Stone flying not only the A-4 Skyhawk, the F-4 Phantom and even flying left wing for the Blue Angels!

But the strength of the book is its story. It is diligently researched, skillfully told, and just plausible enough to keep you turning the pages. Mathe's reunion with his father is the most vital part of the book and his best prose.

You'll enjoy this book!"

D D Smith, Author- Above Average: Naval Aviation the Hard Way

TRUE BLUE

POW/MIAs - "We have solid evidence" that hundreds of captive Americans were held back by the Chinese and North Koreans, possibly as leverage to gain a China seat on the U.N. Security Council.

A Top American Commander - Korean Conflict

Espionage - "Several administrations have continuously been concerned over what US officials render active intelligence gathering, aided by Chinese diplomats. These concerns were the classified lethal and nonlethal weapons systems standardized in American and offshore universities across the nation since the sixties."

UPI

TRUE BLUE

An Epic of Espionage, Friendship, Heroism and family.

D Stuart White

TRUE BLUE

D Stuart White

Trenton, Georgia

This book is a work of fiction inspired by true stories—reflections of several aviators. But the names, characters, places, and events are the products of the author's imagination and have been reimagined for dramatic purposes. Any resemblance to actual events, locales, organizations, or persons, living or dead, is entirely coincidental. Historical details have been drawn from various published sources throughout the book and are intended only to provide a sense of authenticity from factual representations. Nothing is intended or should be interpreted as expressing or representing the views of the U.S. Navy or other departments or agencies of any governmental body. Although unable to trace all references for permission to quote, I have included many names and am grateful for their contributions.

An *Imprint* of 

FIRST premium printing: 2023
First softcover printed by BookLocker.com, Inc. Trenton, Georgia,

Knighthawk Publisher's books may be published for educational business or promotional sales by portraying the Knighthawk logo as a trademark of Knighthawk Publications. For information, please email wa2dsw@gmail.com.

Library of Congress Cataloging-in-Publication Data
White, D Stuart, 1945 True Blue
Library of Congress Control Number: 2022922179

Paperback ISBN 978-1-958878-33-0
EBook ISBN: 979-8-218-08436-3

Printed on acid-free paper.

Cast of Characters

Captain Mathew (Māthe) Stone (USMC) is the son of William and Elizabeth Stone of Lancaster, PA. He grew up on a farm and lived there until he was nine. Elizabeth took her son to Michigan to be near his grandparents after her husband went MIA in WWII.

He resembles his handsome father to a tee. His new home is next door to Jonathon Finley (AKA Finn), who would become his lifelong best friend.

Mathe is an authority-challenging maverick with a good heart, high moral fiber, and intelligent as hell. He is willing to sacrifice himself for the right choices as his life and family find him dogged by the need to fill the hole in his heart for his lost father. His father's specter is the imprint of Mathew's vision of his future.

Since childhood, **Lieutenant Jonathon Finley** has been fair-haired, quick, and happy-go-lucky-outgoing but eager and ferocious.

Born in Michigan, he plays hockey and loves adventures in Northern Michigan. As Mathe's best friend, competitor, and confidant, he challenges him at every turn and helps him see who he has and will become. They are just what the other needs—a two-headed coin,

Admiral Jamie McCready – A hard-core military lifer and Mathe's mentor enigma but consistently his superior. He has spent most of his military career carrying painful secrets and a boatload of guilt for the loss of Mathe's dad.

Samantha Louise McKenzie (Rusty) - Mathe's lady is bright, fun, and red-haired with green eyes and a fireball. She is a robust and hardcore king nurse and Maddy's best friend. However, her free-spirited ways find the rules of conduct as an officer's friend brutal to square at times.

Madeline Ann Harper (Maddy) - Jonathon Finley's long-term girlfriend and wife. She is a grade-school teacher and a spunky "get it done" type—no challenge too great…even Finn, who she loves dearly.

Chi Dung Thai - A Vietnamese pilot trainee and friend of Mathe who comes under suspicion for engaging in espionage.

Dan (Mudskunk) O'Shea - A squadron mate on the Raleigh who recovers from a severe combat injury and rejoins Mathe in the Blue Angels.

Admiral (Iron-Ass) Clifford Gillespie - The string puller with a wide net of political threads in the Pentagon and throughout the navy.

Lieutenant Colonel McVey – A staunch by-the-book Marine with a colossal ego and volatile temper. He appears to be the inescapable agent of Mathe's downfall and a grinding professional and emotional challenge.

Lieutenant Al "Taco" Chavez - This future Blue Angel is a seasoned aviator with the skill and courage to fly the A-4, then the F-4 into combat in the Vietnam conflict and survive. As a member of the "Death Angels," he registered the squadron's first MiG kill.

Lieutenant William Stone - Mathew Stone's father, reported as MIA on a WWII mission in the South Pacific.

Ensign Michael "Buttend" Jolly - A nugget on his first cruise with RIO air skills beyond his fleet experience.

Elizabeth Stone - Mathew's mother—is a heartbroken woman, trying daily to cope with her inner demons and doing her best to grapple with her husband's loss in WWII.

Marshal "Pappy" Coulter - Admiral McCready's Army Air Corp buddy, suspected of passing "The Coin" to McCready.

Lt David E Finley - Jonathon's Dad and WWII B-29 pilot. He is a father, teacher, and war hero who Mathe idolizes but to Finn is just "Dad." Their hero is responsible for Mathe and Jonathon's need for military understanding, and it is this need that causes their fighter pilot imprinting to occur.

Grandpa Pettibone – Cartoon character and curmudgeon who shares lessons learned from naval aviation misadventures to keep aviators from learning the hard way.

Contents

Cast of Characters 9
One – Gun Fighter 15
Two – The Coin Flip 22
Three – Misplaced Anger 29
Four – Burgeoning Respect 34
Five – Promises Made 48
Six – Survival 54
Seven – Okinawa Tragedy 62
Eight – A Son's Pride 69
Nine – Squirrel Cage Penance 74
Ten – More Than A Specter 85
Eleven – Hopes and Dreams 90
Twelve – Big-Tuna 99
Thirteen – Trust and Respect 107
Fourteen – Egg Man Drops One 115
Fifteen – Lost Souls 130
Sixteen – Playing At Not Playing The Game 144
Seventeen – MIA 152
Eighteen – Treachery 162
Nineteen – Convulsive Cultures 171
Twenty – The Awakening 174
Twenty–One – Masked Anxiety 177
Twenty–Two – Guilt 182
Twenty–Three – Operational 192
Twenty–Four – Into The Dragons Claw 196
Twenty–Five – The Operator– Living The Lie 208
Twenty–Six – Red Ice 227

Twenty–Seven – Decisions 233
Twenty–Eight – A Foot In The Bucket 235
Twenty–Nine – The Duck Conductor 238
Thirty – A Boys Hero Found 247
Thirty–One – Disillusionment 250
Thirty–Two – Razor Blade Allegiances 253
Thirty–Three – Pensacola Beach 261
Acknowledgments 264
The Laws Of The Navy 269
D Stuart White's Articles, Editorials, Posts – LinkedIn 275

One

Gun Fighter

OKINAWA
SPRING, NINETEEN FORTY-FIVE

There comes a time for pilots—a moment when you step into the cockpit and the flight—when everything becomes perfect.
And you realize it is more than just your time. Then all you have is the question—who am I?
Maybe it's the familiarity of what you're doing, perhaps a display of ego, or the realization that you're doing what was meant to be.
But, in the back of your mind, the emergency always hovers—the one you hope you can handle without missing a beat. It will be automatic, you tell yourself—but maybe not. The fear is always on your shoulder—that it could happen to you.
It seeps in—your realization that it could all slip away instantly at any time in your young life.

Lieutenant Jamison McCready and Lieutenant William Stone are in a section of two, sweeping over the Okinawa chain of islands, hunting their enemy.

Their search takes their eyes out of the cockpit—alternately scanning the sky through lofty building cumulus cells for enemy aircraft, then down to the rich multicolored blues and greens of the sun-drenched twinkling seawater far below. Beautiful craggy islands and tips of coral outcroppings separate this far-flung chain of Japanese target opportunities. But, the air today will become their battleground.

Stone straightens up as he squints in his search for life among the tiny lonely atolls—rimmed with their volcanic circles in the bright blue of the Pacific.

Straining to catch hidden wakes that would tell of possible motored sea activity below by the "Nips" have been unproductive.

Their powerful Corsair F4Us are actual fighter bombers. Those in "Fighting Three's" flight today who have flown its predecessor, the F6F Hellcat, understood the F4U Corsair's superiority.

They flew on in tense silence, both appreciating the newness of their aircraft's crisp, responsive handling after being ordered to strip their planes of needless equipment on this mission to lighten their weight. Their reach was farther into their enemies' world with smaller bomb loads and increased fuel.

Contrail condensation periodically streamed from their wingtips as they dive to lower altitudes on the suspected enemy. But returning to their hunting altitude always provides some welcome relief from the heat below. Heavy humidity levels and a 90-plus degree temperature in their wartime tropics pressure cooker were constant. The longer distances between the Okinawa topography and home base—small sand rock outcroppings in the island chain—required different fuel conservation and planning than their recent Soloman Islands bombing experience. Their assignment as fighter cover was welcomed from their repetitious roles as bombers as their raison d'être was getting tiresome.

The two men flew on in anticipation of a possible engagement with reported Japanese Zekes and Vals that had been overflying the area. They would need every advantage today. But unfortunately, McCready and Stone have no idea of the impending brutal battle that waits as they approach the town of Naha from seaward on the southernmost Okinawa Island.

Suddenly they find themselves fighting for their lives.

McCready peers over at Stone, and without warning, his wingtip abruptly rises as he pulls hard away from the flight—*something is up, and it is not good.*

He quickly catches the tracers flashing by Stone's canopy, and his sudden descent tells the story as shells continue to pass under his aircraft and behind his wing.

"Sweet Jesus!"

I kick full right rudder (crab) to turn the nose away from the forward motion of his fighter briefly for a quick look behind.

"Where did those Zeros come from?" I shout. "How the hell did they surprise us?" As our enemy streaks past my canopy, I follow both down. The fight is on. Trailing the Zero, I scheme for the shot that will save one of "Fighting Threes" best.

Realizing I am now a *gunfighter*—a new and exciting but uncomfortable role—gives me a chance to stand out from the intensive ground attack missions we had been flying.

We were trained to initiate a fight at a superior altitude against the Zero and carry enough speed to 'boot out' in case things didn't go our way.

And, oh, by the way—'the Zero cannot turn right'—were their instructional words.

I see my chance for a shot as I continue my pursuit of Bill with the Zero-in trail behind him. The Jap turns aggressively, right following Bill's maneuvers to escape.

"My chance? Ha, no right turn my ass!"

While pulling the trigger for a perfect deflection shot, the Jap disengages from Bill, half-roles his aircraft inverted, and executes a descending half-loop. His split-S maneuver is quick and effective as he jumps on my tail—and begins pounding away with his 20 mm on both of us. *How'd I get caught—this is not happening.*

It's time to get the heck out of here, but is it too late? My Corsair shudders from hits to my wing and engine as I tighten the right turn while trying to outturn the Jap, who stays with me and cuts inside my diving turn.

Glancing at the sky, looking for help above, Bill breaks away, and I notice the confused melee between my squadron mates and their enemy. I am now alone as his bullets chew up my aircraft. Steepening my dive, trying the few options I know to shake my opponent, 20mm bullets jackhammer my armored seat, and continue taking chunks out of my right wing.

With another glance down at where my wing joins my fuselage, the damage to the oil cooler and several bullet holes in the engine cowl dictate the obvious.

This is not good.

With another scan, my rising temperature and pressure gauge readings tell all—confirming the damage. To make matters worse, the prop will not cycle—*a shot-up prop governor—GREAT!*

Just a matter of time now!

Stan, my crew chief back on the boat, will not be happy with me. My airplane was now full of holes.

Whoever proffered that a Zero could not turn right had better rethink their position because I was finding out the hard way. Then, thankfully, the pounding stops as tracers from Bill's F4U fly off my port wing as he reenters the fight. My wingman had lured the Jap into focusing on just me, and he got in a quick burst in his intersecting flight path. The "Thatch Weave" tactical maneuver we had practiced worked, and he might have saved my bacon.

Not all of the Nip's seasoned aviators had bought it earlier in the war. This guy is good! How had he survived a Kamikaze role or not been killed outright—like some of their best Japanese fighter pilots earlier in the war?

I turned again and saw Al Wood. Seeing our plight, he followed us, searching for a shot at the Jap. The four swastikas painted on Al's aircraft from our Mediterranean combat two months earlier probably caught the Jap's attention. Lucky for us, the Zero breaks off the engagement and heads home. However, he was experienced and motivated, and Bill and I had paid the price.

Suddenly Bill pulls up beside me—just off my wing with flames swirling out of his engine cowling and enveloping the side of his fighter.

"Bill, you're on fire," I yelled—but I got no answer.

Bill catches my glance and kisses me off with his hand signal and a quick tap of his helmet—then points to me to take the lead. Unfortunately, both of our fighters are in real trouble.

Might his gesture be our last communication? As we both struggle to keep our Corsairs flying, he breaks away in a semi-controlled spiraling dive to the ocean. Oh God, oh no, not Bill!

I catch my breath while trying to control my anger and distress—holding onto a fleeting hope that he will pull out for a successful ditch in the sea or find land. I pray he will make it back, even as I see his smoking spiral.

Fixing his approximate position, I again refocus on flying the airplane, calling out to him several more times but getting no answer.

In what feels like a second chance, I finally succumbed to the realization that I am also going down. And again, temperatures and pressures pegged in the red tell the real story—can't coax the throttle and prop controls anymore, as the heat and humidity have finally caught up.

Adrenaline is only going to take me so far today. Trying to justify my predicament, *I know I'll be a puddle of Jell-O in short order if I don't get out of the Corsair—one way or the other. But, if I survive—an ocean dip might feel great. So, Jamie, concentrate on landing or ditching this crippled bird now,* I tell myself.

After further tightening my harness, I rolled back the canopy for some ram air and caught the immediate sea scent rush—solid and refreshing. While trying to level the wings, I noticed the fluttering metal blowing in the wind from a partially attached aileron trying to separate itself from the wing. My rapidly decaying airspeed now catches my attention, along with the loss of lateral control. Scanning the sky once more, searching for help, I broadcast my location and plight, but the sky is empty blue—I am alone. It saddens me as I realize that Stone shot the Jap off my tail and saved my life—but he might have lost his own.

I've got to keep flying as long as possible with the airspeed above eighty knots. There—off the nose to right—a tiny atoll. Waves curling onto a small lagoon beach caught my eye—it looks like it has enough room to make a gear-down landing possible.

My sink rate is critical as the variable pitch prop will not bite the air. I've got to maintain control and stretch the glide. Keep the nose down—no buffet/stall indications yet—just 300 yards to go.

A fully oil-covered windscreen forces my head out of the cockpit. Boy, did this bird have a snout. I can hardly see over the engine nacelle.

Descending 150 yards now looks like 500—getting heavy on the controls.

I hope "Whistling Death," the Jap’s name for the mighty Corsair, only half fits today.

Almost over the beach—time to dirty her up with the gear and flaps and hold enough airspeed to hit the atoll—Hold 77 knots, or it's all over, Jamie. Don’t lose it now—we’ve almost made it!

Two

The Coin Flip

OFF THE COAST OF NORTH VIETNAM – NINETEEN SEVENTY-THREE

It had been hours since the MiG shoot down by Commander Al Chavez—the division A-4 flight lead on the mission. Captain Mathew (Māthe) Stone, William Stone's son, returned to the carrier USS Raleigh (CVA-23), flying a helicopter gunship—after the loss of both his and squadron mate Lieutenant Jonathon (Finn) Finley's A-4s on the mission. Mathe flew back aboard, flying a hijacked Marine Huey from Lieutenant Colonel McVey's squadron at the Marble Mountain Marine Airbase (Da Nang East Airfield), Vietnam.

It was a practical substitute for the A-4 I had launched from Raleigh's flight deck. After my ejection, I left it on Marble's base perimeter. The mission had started as a ground attack run but turned into an unauthorized rescue mission—and it was all so fresh in my head.

There was my squadron mate and best friend, Lieutenant Jonathon Finley, bloodied and sprawled out across the flight deck behind me as I muscled the Huey upward out of the fog bank to the safety of cloudless blue. I was now an ambulance driver and scared shitless! Glancing back, he was barely hanging onto life.

"Hay, hay, stay with me, Finn. Damn, Finn, hang with me. We're almost home. Hang on, pal," I yelled.

Turning back again quickly to gain complete control of the Huey, I yelled, "Talk to me, Finn! Tell me about Maddy."

Trying to be heard above the machine's drumbeat, “Not now, buddy, not now—stay awake.”

Thankfully I called “feet wet” (departing land for water) at our egress point as the coast flashed beneath us on our escape. The USS Raleigh had picked us up on radar and gave me the steer to the ship. Flipping on the TACAN (tactical air navigation system), I tuned to the ship's frequency and waited for the radio navigation needle to stabilize on our inbound bearing to the ship. Of course, scooting over the wave tops at 200 feet with no real flight time in the Huey was a concern. Still, it only grabbed part of my attention. While driving the ADF (automatic direction finder) needle, I struggled to hold the inbound course to the ship as I glanced back at my friend's lifeless, limp body rolling with the chopper’s motion.

They were ready for us after I declared an emergency, and I was given the command to land—and Raleigh took us aboard. With my limited Huey flight time, I miraculously set her down on the aft flight deck. Then, with a quick system and engine shut down, I staggered out of the cockpit, trying to control myself. I hadn’t realized how intense my back pain was from my ejection just off the perimeter of the Marble until now. Ejections were violent, and my body ached from my collarbones to my toes, but my concern for Finn had over road all. It was killing me as I tried to bend over the gurney that held my friend—mentally willing him back to life from his semi-conscious state. But, of course, my pain was nothing compared to the beating Finn had taken from his ejection, let alone the possible AK round(s) and shrapnel that had penetrated his body. His short stay in the north had been rough.

I brushed off the corpsman's pesky interdiction while trying to hold onto a grimacing counterfeit pain-free mythical hero warrior. Hovering over Finn, both of us looking like total crap, I struggled as the medics strapped him tight for the short trip to medical below deck.

I had to let go of the deck personal cart as the white shirt wheeled my best pal Finn away—without me in tow as I glanced back at the flight deck of the Huey—all that blood.

Brushing another bothersome arm grab aside, I yelled, “He’s the best man I know. Fix him, doc!”

I dragged him to the shot-up helo in the North’s swampy feces-ridden rice paddy, praying and pleading with his partially conscious body to survive. But, with the stench of blood and swamp all over him, I couldn’t let him go. Jesus, what a day!

Not of my choosing—it had been a rescue story built for some Hollywood scriptwriter. But the results were a bit unexpected. I didn’t recognize it at the time, but Taco’s shootdown of the MiG, plus the rescue, provided the entire crew of the carrier Raleigh with a shot of positive adrenaline. It seemed to help some that day to set aside the pressures of our operational grind—for a short time.

They worked hard and needed something to get excited about. Finally, Finn and I were back, and Chavez had taken down the squadron’s first MiG. Each alone would have called for a celebration. But, with Finn in the capable hands of the ship’s doctors, I wanted to let go of a challenging day. The mayhem in the ready room and throughout the ship was epic. I knew it wouldn’t last long, for I would now be entering another flack zone, the ship’s command structure—indeed, some real shit.

And again, I felt a tug on my arm and turned to see the corpsman—looking severe as a root canal and possibly his message just as foreboding.

"Sir, you're ordered to the captain's quarters to speak with Admiral McCready—please come with me," said the young sailor.

Turning aside, "What—the admiral?" *Great, here we go.*

"Sailor, I must stop by the squadron's ready room before meeting the Admiral. Are you familiar with the location?"

"Yes, sir, I know your squadron, the Talons, right?"

I just had to stop and check things out—these events didn't happen that often and I couldn't help myself. I'm already in serious trouble, so what difference is five more minutes?

Moving down the passageway to the Talon's victory party, I could hear the celebration growing in intensity—fitting the moment. As I stepped through the hatch, I was enveloped in the squadron's pilots' righteous post-strike whoop-up. With his well-groomed handlebar mustache, Chavez was getting his share of the appreciation for his MiG kill, and to my embarrassment, I was immediately showered with smiles of admiration. I tried my best to escape with forced cool, but my brothers would have no part of it, and I was swept up and enveloped in the celebration—not for long, though. McCready was waiting for me.

From the very moment I stepped into his quarters, you could see that the Admiral was irritated. I could smell it in the air. What was I expecting, Ruffles and Flourishes? Instead, our discussion was an inquisition—a come-to-Jesus moment with Admiral Jamison "One Ton" McCready. Speaking to an Admiral for the first time was stressful, especially today.

But I caught the whispered word that somehow one of MAG-16's Hueys flew off his base without authorization, and the CO, Lieutenant Colonel McVey, was pissed.

I was confident that my actions were justified and correct, even with the potential wrath undoubtedly coming from Marble Mountain by one highly irritated Marine Lieutenant Colonel—yeah, my ball and chain.

Captain D R Matthews

Ch-46 Marble Mountain, Vietnam - 1969

Lt. Daniel Heming

LCDR Kinney - Served on board 4 carriers, during WWII and the Korean conflict. He flew the following aircraft: F4F4, F4U, F9F5, F2, F2P, C45, CD3, F9F6 and C1A/TFs.

Grumman F9F Panther

A McDonnell Douglas F2H Banshee

My mind instantly returned to the picture of a miserable, short, lump-chested, ramrod-straight Marine officer with the standard high and tight close-cropped gray peppered hair. My first run-in with McVey a few years ago made me smile and simultaneously cringe. But, at the time, I felt that this dickhead, would do whatever it took to succeed in the Corps, which had often included trampling on his men for his benefit—and that picture probably hadn't changed.

I was stationed at Marble Mountain just southeast of Da Nang as a helo driver of the CH-46 (Phrog) Sea Knight for the Marine Corps two years prior. At one point, Lieutenant Colonel McVey, my boss, jumped me after a mission for dinged rotor blades while trying to squeeze into a hot LZ to rescue some of our troops. His meanness and vitriol were on full display, and yes, I was a little aggressive with him as I pushed back, but I told him forcefully, 'I was doing my job.'

Some things never change. McVey had probably totally lost it again after my rescue of Finn. When he heard my name mentioned, I'm sure he went into full vent—or maybe not. You just never knew about the service life of your career after such a caper, but two times? Trying to convince myself, I thought—*I've been here before, so what's the sweat—I was alive, and my buddy Finn now had a chance to live. I sure hoped he would make it. I'm ok, even if my career might be over.*

McVey was probably calling for my ass in stir—permanently—as the shit now was surely rolling downhill toward me.

If it were not for all the good memories of Academy graduates that helped me succeed in the training command, I would have done a better job on him the first time. I wasn't sure if he was just another rank-climbing ring knocker. But with an attitude like that—he just had to be. However, he never wore the ring; maybe I was wrong—I hoped.

I had been trained to depersonalize the horror that might occur in battle—as it eventually did on that mission. But I could never shut down the panic that rose within and locked me up in saving Finn that day.

The brutal reality and concern for my pal drove me into unfamiliar petrifying fear. I had killed people face to face that day, and it would haunt me for years. Yet, there was no immediate shock, just a realization that I was beyond upset by this regrettable lasting human/religious ingrained deficiency—killing—now face to face.

I wondered if I would overcome the event—to know the complete pure satisfaction, importance, and pride of belonging to this group of warriors and assisting Finn's survival.

But today, little did I know of the intense conversations occurring between the Pentagon, various naval intelligence offices, in-country, and COMNAVFORV (Commander, Naval Forces Vietnam). These conversations would seriously impact what was left of my career as a naval aviator.

Three

Misplaced Anger

ABOARD THE RALEIGH (CVA-23)
A SHORT TIME LATER

Admiral Jamison McCready picked up the phone and was surprised to hear Admiral Gillespie's voice. It was highly irregular for receipt of a direct call from the Pentagon.

"Admiral, I have a message from my boss about a recent strike from the Raleigh into the North and that a highly irregular rescue operation occurred. Do I understand that Captain Mathew Stone was involved in the rescue?"

"Well, yes, sir. He rescued Lieutenant Jonathon Finley, who had been captured."

"Yes, we have been reviewing Captain Stone's jacket—competent but seems to carry himself with a certain flair—a disdain for authority?

"Yes, sir, just like his Dad, Lieutenant William Stone, but he is a solid performer. Did you know his Dad, Bill Stone? He also flew in our day—maybe from Wake Island—CVE 65?"

"I didn't know him personally, but I sure know of him, so I want to talk to you. But I know you are busy doing some house cleaning with a certain colonel from Marble Mountain. So I will not detain you now but will be in contact soon," and he abruptly hung up the phone."

McCready hustled out of his stateroom to meet Stone for his post-strike review. He was amazed that Gillespie knew anything about this. *Word sure travels fast these days.* Yes, it had to be McVey. He sure has a thing about Mathew. *Yes, news of the mission had traveled far and wide in this community. Surely—McVey again?*

McCready's post-strike review with Captain Stone had told him a lot, and he was internally proud of his young aviator. He then proceeded to the First Blood Drawn Celebration in the Talon's ready room. But, his thoughts were interrupted in the passageway by a communications officer. He was told that a request by a second helicopter to come aboard had been radioed. It was a ship from Marble Mountain, and the Captain thought he should be notified. *Could it be?* He abruptly turned in the hatchway and headed for Raleigh's bridge.

A second ship from Marble, probably the Colonel—how does he do it? Mathew has only been on board for a few hours.

McVey announced his approach to the ship, and his words fit with the emotional harangue they had heard coming directly from Marble Mountain all afternoon—the loss of one of his choppers. Not one mention of concern for the downed pilots' status—flown back in their aircraft. Without a real overhead time and landing clearance, McVey came aboard and stepped out of the chopper—hell-bent on taking a piece out of someone. The bull was raging. His face and posture told me all I needed to know from the bridge.

I hurried to sickbay before heading to my quarters. *McVey can wait.* I caught Captain Stone standing beside an empty bed, awaiting Lt. Finley's return from surgery with concern written all over his face.

"Captain, how are your wounds?" The admiral said with a softened but commanding voice.

Stone turned to attention with a grimace.

"Fine, sir—just a little sore."

"After your wounds are thoroughly checked, I want you to go immediately to your quarters and not leave them until I give you the OK, do you understand?"

"Yes, sir, but..."

"No buts, Captain, that's an order."

I was more worried about Mathew's short temper and past behavior in previous confrontations with McVey. But McVey had no surprises for me up his sleeve today.

The deck crew escorted McVey directly to my temporary office—the captain's stateroom—he must have thought. The surprise on his face upon meeting an admiral and not the captain or, better yet, the CAG (Carrier Air Group Commander) was epic. As I stood before him with an icy mask, I knew he had no chance today to display the raw displeasure and the bullying as noted in our first meeting years ago. It took a lot of arm twisting then to save Mathew's career.

It was more than too bad that McVey had not fully honored his oath as an officer—taking full responsibility for all related to his command. I sensed he would do anything to get ahead in his career. But unfortunately, McVey was more concerned about his welfare and career than those under his command.

I suspected he had limited loyalty among his men at Marble. He ruled by absolute tyranny with extreme anger and no compassion—his way or the highway method of command—berating junior officers and enlisted men in front of each other.

Occasionally it seemed he might do the right thing eventually—but only when supervised and cornered like a rat. As one southern senator once said, "today, he was in rare form—like he found a hair in his biscuit." As he sat in front of me, vibrating, searching for the right words, I knew it was now my turn. I found the sweat rolling out of him refreshing. It was good to watch him struggle to rein it in.

In the end, the give and take were not crucial. He voiced his displeasure over the actions of one of our pilots—but what could he say to an Admiral? It was not about the theft of a helicopter but the wounded ego of a man who was not entirely in command.

He suddenly rose, and a flood of words, earnest frustrated expletives, ripped across the desk toward me. It concerned a young Marine aviator, and I felt my cheeks crimsoning—but I was more than ready. Then, finally, he paused, struggling to rein in his temper again, and retook his seat.

"You're a little too senior for that kind of talk, aren't you, Colonel, or is that your standard operating procedure?"

After a brief but intense stare-down, I railed without slamming my fist against the desktop and rechecked myself. Finally, I told him what was what and to take leave of my ship ASAP.

I sat on the bridge as the CAG called out, "Sir, blades turning," as McVey's ship rose, dipped a nose to accelerate forward, and departed from the boat to the west. I tried to maintain the calm composure required by my rank, but my grin was hard to hide.

The following day two pilots returned from Marble Mountain to fly their aircraft back and found a colorful new surprise awaiting them on Raleigh's flight deck.

Our crew's expressions of mocking ridicule—only reserved for those pilots that mistakenly landed on the wrong carrier were inscribed all over their bird.

McVey's Huey was painted with numerous epitaphs and expressions of intense ridicule, pity, and slander—written and signed in disjointed words and images of false sympathy about the Marines' loss of an aircraft—on every surface of the chopper. I knew McVey's consternation would be louder than a Montana moose call when he saw his Huey again, and his men would probably pay the price.

The stunt only heightened the fabulous high each of Raleigh's crew had felt. I am sure this day will live on in the ship's lore and each sailor's heart for years.

It was even more critical because the whole country was tearing itself apart over our conflict in Asia. So it was a rare and exceptional day on our floating island. And yes, I would shoulder Stone's missteps again if I had to, for it fulfilled a long-ago promise and was the right thing to do for him, not to mention the loyalty it could help build in my command.

Four

Burgeoning Respect

USS RALEIGH (CVA-23)
A SHORT TIME LATER

Word finally reached Mathe that Lieutenant Finley's wounds were severe—that he would survive and be transferred when stabilized.

Mathe was greatly relieved to hear that Finn was out of surgery and improving. After McCready released him from his JO (junior officer) jailhouse, he hustled back to surgery for a chat.

At sickbay, he was greeted by on second-class petty officer and what looked like a horizontal mummy, with an arm and a leg hanging akimbo from an overhead sling above the bed. The medic was scurrying about confirming the mummy's vitals. Finn was encased in a sea of gauze and plaster—up one leg and midsection with a partially wrapped head. They had covered his head with only his mouth and two eyes barely visible.

Holy Shit!

I was shocked and stunned at what I saw but smiled to cover my fears as I moved closer to Finn's bedside. He was struggling to stay awake as the drugs tightened their grip.

"What the hell happened to you, Finn?"

He tried to smile, but his face couldn't quite make a greeting work. His middle finger worked just fine, though.

"Hey, GAW...good to see you, "Rock," he slowly mumbled.

"If I haven't thanked you already—I can't remember if I did. These drugs are making me a complete moron. I could have been eating rice for the rest of my miserable life or had no life if you had not found me. I now realize what you did and the price you might pay for doing it. But you saved my life. Thank you!"

I stared at Finn with thoughts of our lifelong past. We had been in these situations all our lives, with him pulling me out of more jams than I could count. There always had been plenty of "shut-up" in this guy,

I smiled, nodded with relief, and blurted out.

"Nah, nothing you wouldn't have done for me or anyone else—no biggie."

"Come on, Mathe, not like this one—it's your time for the big one—you know the ribbon I'm talking about—blue with white stars."

"No, Pal, Chavez can take it for the team—it's his down of the MiG."

The conversation stalled as I caught his encased body move uncomfortably, collecting himself with a wince from the pain of his injuries.

"Mathe, I heard about a flap with that colonel from Marble. It hasn't jeopardized your chances for Blues selection. Have you heard from them yet?"

"Yea, that's Colonel McVey. A fly on the wall told me McVey and Admiral McCready had a little discussion about our event, and it wasn't pretty. The dustup emanating from Admiral McCready's stateroom probably was heard throughout the ship. I'm sure it was directed at McVey. The Admiral's temper was ramped up. Word is they were in there blistering the air for a while. I don't think he respects McVey very much."

"Do you know what they said?"

"Well, let's say McVey might be looking for a new career. You can't blow that kind of grief in on an admiral and expect to get away with it—especially if you're a Marine."

I smiled, thinking about my past discussion with the Colonel a year ago—maybe similar? *But will I escape the noose this time?*

"Finn, please do not pass this along. I thought you deserved to know, and as for the Blues—who knows? My application was forwarded a year ago."

"Safe with me, pal. I can barely talk, let alone remember what you just said—good drugs."

I couldn't help but laugh.

"Thanks, Finn. I haven't heard anything yet. So please don't fret about my Blues application. I might have screwed the pooch on that one, but no matter, you're here, and that's what counts."

"They'll call you. I know it. It is meant to be—one of us has to get there, and you're on deck!"

"So what's the verdict? You still look like crap."

"Thanks! Don't you like the mummy suit? Actually, it could be a lot worse—like on a corpse."

"The eye will heal just fine—no problem—will see the enemy for a little eunuch payback in a few days. I am missing one key feature, but they tell me it doesn't matter."

"Really, like what, your brain?"

"No asshole—one nut."

I winced for a moment, remembering the blood, and caught his half-smile. I couldn't help myself as I fell apart.

"God, Finn, the jokes will be off the charts—especially with your buddies in the JO bunkroom. You'll need a new handle, for sure. Like, hmm…"One and Done," or "The Ball Master, as I laughed so hard, tears ran down my face." But Finn did not find any of it very funny.

"When you're done, perhaps you'll tell me why you're here unless it's just for entertainment or some sick form of punishment."

"Sorry, Finn! I was so sure you were belly up. It's a relief—but maybe not for Maddy. But let's look at it another way. You're still here. You're her lucky bag. You might have been lost, but you are found. One nut—traded for your life—is not a bad deal. You might have just bought your life for this little loss."

"Mathe, they tell me one works just fine, so maybe we can drop this subject."

"Ok, Finn, you're the one in the rack. Wiping the tears off my face, I realized I had one more thing to tell him. By the way, after the McVey dustup, I did meet with McCready."

"Oh, shit, I bet that was fun."

"You know, it was completely different than I expected. I thought I'd be keelhauled by noon, but it wasn't even mentioned—all very bizarre—a lot I don't understand. Before you take your afternoon beauty sleep, do you remember a guy in primary named Chi Dung Thai?"

"Not sure, but what the hell—why?"

Again I caught Finn struggling to stay awake as the drugs took their grip. He was slowly sinking—now almost half asleep. *So I guess this will have to wait.*

"Well, Chi, ahh, it can keep. It'll save for another time."

"O, O…K… See ya?"

"You bet, Finn."

I turned to leave, concerned but determined to drive some humor into him while flipping him off. But he was almost gone as I caught his try for a half-smile.

Half-awake, Finn watched his buddy disappear through the hatch and thought to himself—*pal, being shit hot could bite you in the ass at any moment—I'm proud of you, though, but I hope you remember you're only as good as your last landing. I owe you my life, buddy,* and then drifted off to sleep.

Needing some air, I found my way to the flight deck. Stepping out of the hatchway, I heard Admiral McCready's voice.

"Captain!"

Oh shit, now what?

I turned to face him—THE ADMIRAL—and gave him my full attention.

"Sir, yes, sir."

I stared at the admiral expecting the worst—maybe things had changed. Maybe the shit did hit the fan? Maybe my flying career was over. But, instead, McCready just stared back, knowingly with those steely eyes.

Something was up.

"Follow me," was all he said. And I followed him below deck—my mind racing.

Maybe McVey had convinced him I should be in the brig.

My nerves improved as I followed him down a ladder to the main hanger deck. It had been forty-two hours since our last meeting—enough time for anything to happen.

Everything was moving too fast—two lost Talon jets, the first MiG shoot down, my rescue of Lieutenant Finley, a post-strike inquisition with the admiral and each of my bosses, and the emotional relief of Finn's likely recovery. And then the wild post-kill celebration in the Talon's ready room had only increased my energy suck. It had taken its emotional toll—not to mention the bruising my body underwent during and after the ejection at Marble. I wasn't sure I could keep it together for one more discussion.

He suddenly turned, and I almost ran into him. He opened his hand, and a shiny silver coin rose into the air leaving the Admiral's fingertips.

It sparkled as it rose from the glare of the hanger bay overhead lights. I reached for it in mid-air but was surprised I missed it—and it hit the deck.

Out of nowhere, I remembered something about not letting a coin drop to the floor. Then, of course, I would have to buy the house a drink—a Navy tradition, I think—something like that.

We both reached for the coin at our feet. The admiral smirked knowingly and subtly deferred to my grab.

A glance at the coin instantly told me almost everything. It was a two-headed coin like the one that Finn's Dad had harped on throughout our childhood.

He had said something about Finn and me becoming a two-headed coin and never winning and something about wrong paths taken. I didn't understand, but I respected the intensity with which his message was delivered and the true hero worship I felt for him as a B-29 pilot/war fighter.

I inspected the etched squadron emblem and motto on its face as it rested in my open palm. It was almost too much for me to comprehend—for it represented another time and war. Yet, I suddenly wanted to return it to the admiral to get it out of my hand. It brought up many questions, memories, and the responsibility it might hold for me.

As I held the coin, Admiral McCready grabbed my shoulder. I looked up and found "One Ton" McCready's smile. Very reassuring but unusual!

McCready pointed to a small open office just off the carrier's garage. Still physically spent from the mission events and coming off the adrenaline rush, I followed the Admiral in silence, dreading his next move.

As McCready led Mathe across the hangar bay deck, he had to chuckle as he recalled his meeting with Lieutenant Colonel McVey, Mathe's prior CO and nemesis, on the deck of the Raleigh.

"Captain, let's chat—and hold onto that coin. The nature of your assignment here will probably change as word spreads about your recent mission, and I think I owe you a heads-up. Besides, I have a story to tell you."

Change, what change—swabbing the deck, peeling potatoes—what? A story, God? I hope I can stay awake.

I followed, and we found our way into the small office after I stumbled over the lip of a repair mat under the wing of the Intruder. My head was spinning with new questions that butted up against my insecurity. *It looks like I will not get promoted soon, or maybe worse.*

"Sit, Captain."

"Yes, sir." *Oh crap, here it comes.*

I sat sagging attention in the chair while trying to ignore the pain in my back from my ejection, which required a new position in the chair every few minutes. Even so, I was all ears. The office was small, airless, with no escape hatch, and probably soundproof and, in my case, most likely bulletproof.

Yep, he could shoot me, and no one would know. I struggled to center up. It had been a roller coaster of shit, and I felt like I was losing it.

Get it together, Mathew!

The admiral was silent as he took his time to speak, pondering his words with his young aviator. He knew Mathe was more skilled—possibly more worthy than most fighting men in his fraternity. It wasn't his bombing grades or trap scores. It was more than that. It was his pure resolve to try to save his squadron mate—putting Lieutenant Finley's safety, at all costs, ahead of his own. He had firmly positioned himself above his peers, and he hoped the citation he had recommended for him would help his future growth.

"Mathew, the word was relayed today from CINCPAC Headquarters staff that they want to clear the air with you concerning your mission. But before we begin."

Seeing hesitation as he seemed to grope for the right words, I braced.

Mathew's Imprinting

"It's about your Dad—Lieutenant William Stone."

My dad, what is he saying? What does he know about my dad?

"My dad, sir?"

I saw the tension in the Admiral's face and gulped as my mind raced and my stomach knotted even tighter. It was now getting personal with an Admiral whom I hardly knew. *What the hell is going on?* He had referenced him before with no additional info. Yet, he had hesitated in choosing not to discuss his knowledge of my dad in his quarters—after the "Talons" shoot down and the save of Lieutenant Finley.

"You see, I knew your dad and your mom, for that matter, well—years before you were born—even before WWII and Korea. We were all good friends and our common bond—like you and Lieutenant Finley. It was aviation—and it brought a lasting friendship.

You know, Captain, I know you. You might not think I do—but I do," he said, with a smile etched across his face again.

"We have similar backgrounds, except separated by geography and time. I could never compete with your wild/ribald youthful adventures. They are probably still legend in some circles in your hometown. But, my youth wasn't like yours."

How the hell did he know about that, I wondered.

"Farming was challenging, rewarding, but demanding. We just worked—all the time. Your mom and dad grew up a few miles from each other, and we all went to the same school—we had a lot in common and spent time together.

I stayed in touch with your mom after your dad went MIA. She shared your youthful antics with me and was concerned about your behavior and future."

Wow, my mom never told me anything! Where is he going with this?

"Thank goodness Lieutenant Finley's Dad provided well-needed guidance to you and Finn. He probably steered you into choosing a side—taking a stand, joining the military, and all that it represents in the confusion of our sixties times.

You seemed to see clearly through it all, and here you are—right or wrong. I took the same stand, but it wasn't as hard to do with so much plain and simple evil before our eyes. I'm sure you haven't looked back negatively on your decisions—I certainly haven't.

Your dad and I pulled off the same adventures she told me about you—some of those youthful exploits you are known for. But nothing compared to yours.

Covering my forehead with my hand and looking into my lap, I cringed at remembering many episodes I would rather have forgotten.

We once dragged an outhouse down our hometown's main street—right thru the middle of town behind our car. We had borrowed it from a local farm, and we thought that was big time—but you!"

Giving me no time to speak, he went on.

"We had rules growing up, and we stuck to them. We mostly had chores, school work, church, and more chores. What little spare time we had with friends was spent doing simple things—the swimming hole in summer, picnics, ice skating in the winter, and hayrides probably sound boring, but it was great. We were taught to respect women—keep them at arm's length." He smiles. "Hard sometimes."

You grew up with a whole different set of ideas. There was a lot of freedom and rebelliousness—things were looser—and more outspoken. Women are different now, not quiet wallflowers waiting to be asked to dance. If they want to dance, the ladies of your generation, get out there and do it."

Where is he going with all this? I don't need a birds-and-bees chat now. I'm confused.

"And you know, I think that's a good thing. They hate this war at home. See no reason for it—burn their underwear and draft cards and peacefully protest. Sometimes I agree with them. Your mom would have loved being a flower child. I kept track of her, you know."

He turns and stares at me as his body stiffens in his chair—as though some daydream is over.

"Upside down times they are—but I hate to admit, maybe not."

Are you kidding me—he' in and she' in—a sex life discussion?

"Oh yes, I checked in with your mom periodically during your early years and beyond. It broke my heart to see her going downhill.

I was good friends with your dad—just a pair of Pennsylvania farm boys. Being part of war never crossed our minds—until it had to. Your parents were destined for each other—everyone knew that. Elizabeth was beautiful, fun, and intelligent. She never knew how I felt about her. She only had eyes for your dad."

Surprisingly, an admiral was talking to me during such a critical time in his career. Sure I just had saved my pal, but this was going a little overboard.

I'm sure he had better things to do than to spend time with me. His challenges had to be huge—directing his command and more in his war. It was unfortunate that most in command these days were continually devalued and compromised by the micromanaged incompetency of our political leaders.

And yet, with all his challenges and problems, he was taking time to treat me with some humanity and respect—befriending a junior officer under his command during, I am sure, some pretty frustrating times for him. But it was his time. My eyes widened, and my jaw dropped slightly lower in astonishment as the Admiral went on.

"Mathew, I wanted to talk a little more about your dad and me during our time as bomber pilots back in another war. I assume you might be interested."

As if I could say no. My dad, my mom? I was all ears now.

"Yes, sir!"

"Before I give you a little background, I want to tell you a little story about that coin in your pocket."

Wait, one story at a time—my background, mom and dad, McVey, and the coin—my head was spinning.

The Coin

"Do you have any idea about the traditions of the coin?"

"No, sir."

"If you are ever challenged by someone to see your coin in a drinking establishment—like the older one in your hand—you are supposed to show it to them, and they show you theirs. If you are caught without yours, you owe them a drink, but if you have yours, they owe you a drink for challenging you. If you drop your coin on the floor—you buy the house a round—as simple as that. Surely you have heard of this tradition?"

"Kind of, sir."

"Are you superstitious?"

Mathe hesitated. *Where is this going now?*

"No, Sir, I don't think so."

"Which is it, Mathew? Sailors have always put great faith in fortune-tellers' imagined and actual predictions. Phantoms abound in a sailor's life. They may be exaggerations from life's extraordinary adventures at sea—either observed or inferred."

"Well, OK, yes, sir."

"Rumor has it that a coin passed from a WWI aviator was deemed responsible for untold good luck in the aviation community but held enough bad luck for a few superstitious aviators.

It initially saved the life of this WWI pilot after his bailout. He could not convince the partisans of his real allied identity. They held him as a prisoner and condemned him to death the next day by firing squad. He remembered the coin given to him by his squadron commander, pulled it from his flight jacket, and presented it to confirm his identity. A life saved by the coin alone!

I remember the many instances of fellow pilots I knew with their talismans, tokens, and rituals. One guy had his hung around his neck.

And yes, (with a wink) possibly the exact coin you hold. It has been passed from one deserving aviator to another with mixed but definite outcomes over the years. It is my responsibility to move it forward with another. In time, I will give you a deep dive into the history of the one in your pocket, so don't lose it—it might hold some significance for you in the future." He said with a knowing smile, "if you are superstitious at all."

In time we separated from the hanger bay office, I again sought solace on the flight deck—just off the bow of the empty deck. As I pondered the mission into the north, the rising seascape and clouds dictated the warning of an impending storm. Again, it occurred to me that saving someone's life meant they belonged to you. Maybe they just owe you for the physical and emotional pain and fear suffered with the rescue. But I knew this irrational thought was overridden by someone else.

As I steadied myself against the increasing pitch and roll of the deck, the squall line approaching off the bow caught my attention again. Rooted to the deck against the impending storm in silence, I realized how tired I was—bone tired. The kind of tiredness that comes from a good back alley fight—picking up more than my fair share of the physical damage inflicted. I tried to rid my mind of my meeting with McCready. The slap of ocean moisture breaking the deck felt refreshing on my face and awakened me to thoughts of my concern for Finn. A quartering gust of wind from the approaching squall line suddenly threw me off balance. As I caught myself, I was, for some reason, reminded that I might not have anything to do with Finns' rescue. *I'm not a man of faith, but I know he exists. How could we have survived being attacked on that Vietnam plateau? Yet, someone was looking after us.*

And suddenly, out of character, I turned to face the entire length of the ship's deck, rooted my feet firmly against the wind at my back, with a true sailor's standard back deck lean. Then, with bent knees, one foot offset behind the other, and a definite wind-starched pants crease, I quietly took a posture of acceptance and thanked God for our survival.

Five

Promises Made

USS RALEIGH
NEXT DAY

Meeting again, I wanted to launch into the guilt and grief I felt about the tragic loss of Mathew's dad while trying to mask my pain for both of us.

Instead, I felt a complete description of my relationship with Bill Stone, Mathew's dad, as a budding naval aviator, perhaps more important than the rest of the story. I could see Mathew was eager for more—tired as he was.

Relationships/Remembrances

"Moving on, Captain, I enlisted in 1941 to set myself up to become a pilot in the navy. From a young age, I was fascinated with flight, and with the war in Europe growing—I saw my opportunity—from small-town farm boy to a military pilot. Your father also enlisted in naval air right around the same time.

Pearl Harbor changed everything for us, and before we knew it, we found ourselves in flight training down in Pensacola.

We were roommates, and one night in the bachelor officers' quarters, we found ourselves studying flight procedures and writing letters home after battling the trusty SNJ, our advanced navy trainer, over auxiliary outlying field Foley most of the day.

I looked over at your father. He was reading one of the many letters from your mom. His head suddenly drooped as sadness spread across his face—but he stayed silent. I looked away, not wanting to invade his feelings.

He suddenly turned to me." 'Jamie, you've got to promise me you'll keep your eyes on Elizabeth—if the worst happens. She's not as strong as she seems.'

'What are you talking about, Stone?'

'Just in case, just in case,' he said.

'Check,' I finally understood what he was trying to say.

The worst happens?

'Bill, but you shouldn't have any concerns. Nothing is going to happen to you.'

"I returned to the quiet of the room with my new, somewhat unwanted, and unknown responsibility and pondered our futures and how we would handle air combat.

Captain, I have had many assignments in my naval career, and I am thankful for the recognition and challenges they all offered. I followed your career closely—it wasn't because of my fondness for your mother and father. You didn't fit the mold of officers and enlisted men I have enjoyed serving with. It's just that I have not been able to accommodate your peg in the hole. You are different."

McCready's images of officers he had known materialized in his mind. *Those who were clever and lazy were fit for high command with the nerve to deal with all situations, those who were clever and industrious were best for high staff appointment, but those who were stupid and industrious were the ones to look out for. They were the ones to be removed as soon as possible from the equation. And for some reason, the stupid and lazy who could be used—popped forward. But unfortunately, none of them fit Mathew's persona.*

"I have worked with and observed the best and worst navy-ready room posers, junior officers, commanding officers, and execs. In my assignments, I think I have seen it all. You might say you probably have run into a few already—like a certain Marine colonel."

My eyes widened upon hearing his reference to McVey.

"And I have to say—you just never seemed to fit; the careerist, the poor decision-maker, the little man striving for attention. You know the 'humph'—that pose or sound that sends the message, I'm bigger than all of this, so leave me alone. And don't forget the ones that tell you they have been there, seen that, and have gotten the T-shirt types—you know—the don't screw with me types. The list goes on, but you get the idea.

And thank God for that because it made it easier to follow your mom's direction and keep an eye on you while you serve.

Therefore, I had chosen to jump in periodically when I thought it was discreetly needed to keep your career from derailing. But, unfortunately, the posers I have mentioned have made train wrecks of many good men's naval careers.

Captain, did you ever wonder how and why you were assigned to fly attack aircraft in VA-33 after your run-in with McVey a few years ago as a CH-46 helo driver at Marble? At the time, I understood that you did your best to destroy your career and yourself.

It was challenging to reassign you to an attack squadron—let alone for the navy to accept my training recommendations. So I had to call in some favors. They were resisted by command but insisted upon by me. I wanted you to get up to speed to fly navy jets for a little more dynamic payback than your old seat provided. It was a highly improbable transition that was frowned upon by our superior officers in the training command."

'He will never hack it,' they said, "but you were successful, and here we are."

What was the admiral talking about—I earned the right to fly the A-4. What is this some personal respect and feeling—befriending a junior officer? I don't get it. What does he know about my time at Marble Mountain or McVey?

I could hardly keep it together—beyond stunned. *But, was I in control, or was it an illusion—were they my career choices—will my decisions make a difference—now, with a two-star as my mentor—wow! But, maybe—this is cool—perhaps he will help take me where I am destined.*

"Well, Sir—I didn't know, but—thank you!" Not knowing what more to say while trying to control my emotions and act appreciative—I fidgeted with the coin now in my pocket. Then, finally, the reality that I might not be as good as I thought or have incomplete control hit home—hard!

"Captain, I have one more issue to discuss with you."

I sat up a little straighter. *More?*

The Admiral fixed his gaze—eye to eye and asked an utterly off-the-subject question.

Chi Dung Thai

"Do you remember the Naval Air Training Command students cross-trained for active duty for their own country's air force?"

"Ah, yes, sir. A few Vietnamese students come primarily to mind.

They were the brunt of a lot of jokes. Flight communications always seemed to be a problem for them, you know, the language thing—you could never expect they would end up being where you thought they would be in the air or on the ground—it became quite a problem for those in the tower and their instructors giving them directions—much confusion, many close calls."

"Yes, do you remember any of the students by name?"

I hesitated.

"Well, yes sir—Lieutenant Chi something, no, maybe like Dung Thai—Chi Dung Thai—was that his name, I think, not sure I can remember anymore, why sir?"

"Please, tell me all you can remember about him."

"Well, sir, he was the only Vietnamese pilot I befriended, and he ended up being our roommate in the bachelor officers' quarters—a real quiet guy—but he enjoyed all the pilot banter—you know all that who is the better pilot stuff. I liked him because he worked hard and kept his head down. Is there a problem, sir?"

"Thanks, Captain, just curious. I had heard the same stories. Getting back to my story, Captain, I started as an enlisted sailor at the Great Lakes Naval Training Center. It was 'bluejacket' time that taught me to understand the mindset of young sailors. They had backgrounds much like mine. Yes, Mathew, I am in some circles called a 'Mustang' because of my prior-enlisted status. However, I would like to think that my relationships with my men, learned from those early experiences as a sailor, were the cause of our squadron's recognized superior performance in fleet collateral duty assignments and more.

Coming from an 80-acre farm and attending a small school, my life was all about caring for the farm's hogs, chickens, cows, horses, and crops—long, backbreaking days, maybe like your dad, Captain. But I just wanted to fly. Becoming a navy pilot was like pie in the sky. I'd have to measure up. But I knew I could do it.

My parents, Izzy and Eva McCready were always with me in my mind and heart. They were my rock to help me meet my many new career challenges—probably like your mom, Lieutenant Finley, and Finn's dad.

In time (1944), we found ourselves in the Mediterranean fighting the Germans. Your dad and I were flying the F6F Hellcat from the USS Tulagi. Let me tell you some sea stories about your dad and me."

Six

Survival

Under the cool dimness of the ready room's riveted sun of combat: the savage and partisan overtones of leather and tobacco meddle with the stark silence of excitement and trepidation. The sweat-soaked energy, a prelude to the impending ferocity, seeps as fawn grimaces shimmer along with the smoke of cigars and the barrels of guns. And then the warrior's exhilaration quiets, and spirits dampen as thoughts of past lost warriors drift quietly through the room.

"Mathew, it was nineteen forty-four in the Western Mediterranean. I sat in the cockpit of the F6F on that hot, muggy, still-dark morning. A strong wind wrapped the deck as we prepared for the first launch of the day in the Mediterranean. My fatigue from the blistering pace of our operations, the early morning, and the cockpit bathed in flight deck red lighting conspired to marginalize my concentration. As a result, I had trouble focusing in the dark-adapted light and realized I had to dig a little deeper for today's launch.

And then came the bull horn command," 'Pilots, start your engines.'

I smiled. *Holy shit—déjà vu—here we go again, just like the stories Finn's dad used to tell us about his time in the big war flying B-29s. I love war stories. Bring them on, Admiral. I'm all ears.*

"Sitting in the cockpit of my F6F Hellcat and waiting for the deck crew to pull the propeller through a few rotations to clear the cylinders, I energized the cartridge starter and, with a bang, brought the mixture to full rich as the engine turned over. My anticipation for our launch grew as the bang echoed from my starting cartridge and bounced off the other aircraft on the USS Tulagi's flight deck. That same explosive echo repeated from multiple aircraft readying for the morning launch. It was like an explosion of very noisy fireflies followed by the belching surge of flaming engine exhausts from each plane, blowing clouds of white and blue exhaust down the deck. Finally, the ship quivered as the fox flag shot up into the two-block position, and she found her launch course.

It was the moment that brought everything into focus. My mind and the instruments in front of me were energized. After being waved forward, I unfolded the wings in preparation for my launch off the deck.

With wing hinges in position, I pulled the D ring to lock them and waited for my repositioning signal.

Hellcat Launch

After six months of constant training, we felt we were ready for anything the Germans would throw at us in the "Med." Accordingly, in our early morning preparations, we proceeded past the Straits of Gibraltar with a full moon hanging over our task force. On the north passage of the strait, the ship took advantage of the tides. The prevailing winds out of the east did not require a large carrier to turn into the wind.

We coordinated with the fleet of big gunships (USS Nevada, Arkansas, Texas, Quincy, Omaha, and Tuscaloosa) to provide spotting support this morning. The scuttlebutt was—'to prepare for something big.'

Our squadron's primary task was not fun. We patrolled low and slow over a set of coordinates while looking for any activity to target. We did it well but disliked it intensely. The frequent loitering to more precisely redirect the ship's big guns fire unnerved many in our squadron. It was tedious and dangerous—from shell fire close to our aircraft. In addition, we often picked up rows of holes in the wing and fuselage from small arms fire at low altitudes.

The call to 'get high,' to not get hit, often preceded a salvo of 16" shells from our ships. At first, it was terrific to watch, but then it quickly turned unnerving, seeing fired shells flying into our designated targets. It was frightening when one of my squadron mates was instantly vaporized by a direct hit from one of these 16-inch guns.

The Med proved reasonably navigable but held frequent unpredictable storms concentrated in the western Mediterranean and northern shores. The azure waters from 5,000 ft did not tell the whole story. The mountains held suffocating heat and unpredictable sea winds and sand—unsuitable for planes or pilots.

I was in the first plane formation. I followed the skipper and LT. Hershman, his wingmen, coming off the deck.

CAG led us—five sections of F6F Hellcats on a strike into the Italian mountains northeast of Cape Negre. Your dad and I were on a railhead reconnaissance as bombers. After our first few attacks on the railroad junction, we were vectored to another target in the south of France. I pulled the throttle back to a max range, settling into combat spread. My muscles ached from today's sortie, the cramped cockpit, and the fact that the enemy was hunting us. I rolled my shoulders to loosen the tension and strain from our bombing runs. Pulling the canopy back and unclipping my oxygen mask brought some relief as I grabbed my Lucky Strikes and lit up.

Your dad saw my actions off my starboard wing but stayed focused and vigilant while I did my post-strike thing to decompress.

Complacency was not in your dad's lexicon of behaviors. He was a complete professional and had the uncanny ability to withdraw from all emotional attachments to concentrate fully and entirely on every second of every mission—at times beyond what others thought prudent. He always sought perfection in his flying—while others just worked within their capabilities so they didn't bust it. As a result, he was constantly squeezing as much energy and performance out of himself and each aircraft he flew. We often looked to his leadership when it hit the fan.

Naval flight provided all we needed. We were action-driven, adrenaline-grabbing, above-average intelligence males who needed an approved legitimization of our warrior spirit. Safety was a term we would gladly redefine from its civilian definition.

Operation Dragoon-Southern France

Being diverted to Southern France made us part of Operation Dragoon. It was developed to protect the flank of the Allied Normandy advance into Germany. It was just a few hundred reconnaissance and interdiction sorties against German rolling stock and strikes in support of U.S. Army troops landing in southern France.

There we were, a flight of F6Fs cruising over the Med, stroking throttles repeatedly with throttle tensioning that never seemed to hold the required setting. We eyeballed the sky for Germans that never seemed to show, monitoring temps and pressure for variance while being refreshed by the cold altitude air against the heat of the blazing sun through the canopy.

One quick scan of the instruments and the sky above told me I was not alone.

The small black dot didn't grab my attention immediately until it suddenly moved across my field of vision. Was this welcome allied air support or one of the few German He 111 bombers we were told to watch for?

A wayward fly flew the needle on my ADF (Automatic Direction Finder) better than I did. Besides providing a needed gut check, this stowaway battle buddy gave me a welcome bit of humor and some support. My thoughts moved to the book, "God is My…" well, you know the title. I named him Louie and wondered how he would take our impending combat. I now had my little copilot—a welcome friend in a day that would probably be filled with destruction and horror.

I caught your dad's hand signal to prepare for our bombing run, which brought me back to the real world and the business of preparing myself and the aircraft for whatever came next.

Our approach to the second target was through beautiful cumulus clouds with streaming sunshine followed by broken clouds with a low overcast. With the target finally in sight, we closed up in right echelon, preparing for the preplanned diving roll-in. Each pilot began toggling switches to arm their rockets or bombs.

Don't screw up,—I told myself—as I armed up—careful to set the pipper (center bead of a ring gunsight) mill setting for the eventual 45-degree dive with a 9,000-foot release prior to roll in. I looked at your dad with his head down, momentarily concentrating on confirming his armament for the bomb and the strafing run to come.

After the roll with the belly of my airplane pointing to the sky, I looked over the canopy rail while pulling hard to stay with the flight. Everyone was hanging in their straps, working their butts off. My flurry of effort included; kicking the rudder, compensating for aircraft drift, and keeping separation from those ahead as we passed between cloud layers. I eyeballed the flack bursts at various altitudes while re-adjusting power settings and re-confirming the arming-up checks. Flinching at the close bursts of flack that seemed just above my canopy, I continued reconfirming the target location. Then while wiping the stinging sweat out of my eyes, I aligned the pipper for release. Seeing my group strung out in front of me was a good feeling. However, with the sudden change of altitude, flack bursts, and the altimeter unwinding, I unconsciously tried to get as small as possible to keep safe as my shoulders found my ears.

Then bomb release and pull-up were followed by jinking while trying to keep the aircraft from the inevitable stall shudder as we grabbed for altitude in the join-up. Finally, I wrapped up the F6F to quickly rendezvous with the returning strike group 5 miles off my port wingtip. We were fortunate that no one got bagged as the flight lead took us back to the boat. While looking back on the target—secondary explosions and fires told of our success.

Unexpectantly, without a hand signal or radio call warning, your dad banked hard away from our formation, giving chase to two Heinkel He 111 heavy bombers he'd spotted. Conflicted about whether I should follow, I watched his direct lineup give him a pure trail shot as he pumped.50 caliber bullets into the German and knocked him out of the sky. Ensign Wood also broke off and headed southbound to follow the splitter.

On the way back to the boat, the excitement was contagious. Intermittent hooting and hollering over the radio echoed our victories. Back onboard the Tulagi, your dad provided the play-by-play of his shoot down of the two Ju-52 transports, while Wood received credit for two Heinkel bombers. Not too shabby for a spotter squadron's first tangle with the enemy.

My vision of war as a naval officer certainly did not fit the image of death and destruction we wrought on the German troops in southern France—terrifying deeds to protect our loved ones back home—I justified. As a result, I felt little consequence for the French civilians below but grew to understand their gratitude and appreciation for our work. I am sure your dad felt the same way as we compared notes between missions.

Eventually, numbness found its way into our squadron from fatigue and the sight of our bombs and guns killing up close. The loss of friends only added to the emotional drain as we gutted it out until our naval squadrons were of no further use in the allied European effort.

After fifteen days of a heightened state of German destruction and death, we were ready for a break. Our work had demoralized the Germans. We took them apart, one tank, rail line, vehicle, and ship at a time. Our unrelenting harassment of motorized columns and the impact of naval gunfire turned their retreat into a rout.

Little did we know that our European efforts would be recognized for many years by the French population, specifically the town of Pennautier. The townspeople realized that our Hellcats played a big part in completely wiping out the German presence in their city and countryside. In future years, remembrance ceremonies for seven navy pilots will be held. In addition, a tablet in marble stands in the town square with each pilot's name—your dad's and mine included. It is engraved as an homage and thank you from the townspeople for hunting and chasing away the 'German Wolves.'

After months in the "Med," our ships and aircraft were redirected for combat against the Japanese in the Pacific—a whole new ball game."

Seven
Okinawa Tragedy

"Captain, let me continue describing our efforts during WWII in the Pacific Theater. Several months later, after our transfer from the Med, the squadron proceeded into the Pacific onboard the USS Wake Island (CVE 65). We had just transitioned to flying the F4U Corsair, and the increased performance given by the "Whistling Death" bent-winged bird was welcome."

F4U Patrol

I smiled and remembered stories about those that flew the F4U and said, "Not like the challenge offered by the earlier Grumman Wildcat—with its hangar ground loops with chocks installed, sir?" The admiral did not smile.

"During this time, Japanese suicide attacks had been picking up, and we kept a wary eye out for them. Our patrols were continuous as our small task force passed through the Surigao Straits near Leyte Island. Then, while circling offshore in preparation for another strafing run on a Jap naval installation, I caught a glimpse of a glistening metallic dot through the windscreen.

It couldn't be my winged cockpit buddy Louie from the Med—now in full glistening armor. No—the pack of Zeros grew in size as I called out their high and low positions. The flight lead heard my call and turned into the onslaught. They came directly at us—Vals (carrier-borne Jap dive bomber) and Oscars with more Zeros in high cover.

As they passed through our section at speed, it was evident that ramming us was their option, if not the intention. I quickly wheeled and got a solid deflection shot on a Val, which, for some reason, took its time burning. As I poured more lead onto the burning bomber, the sound of metal hitting my aircraft registered. I broke the engagement and dove to increase energy for speed protection. The Zero did not follow me, and I chuckled at such a quick victory. Bomber turned fighter pilot in a day—my, my!

But the realization that our enemy had nothing to lose in our aerial engagements and would seek to take their own lives along with mine was sobering. This variable now brought a new dimension to our fight in the air, and I wondered how our tactics would change to fight this new menace. We were in a gunfight, and the winner would take all! But unfortunately, this fight never materialized as our low-fuel states and the overwhelming enemy odds against us drove us home.

Gratefully back aboard, we received new orders for Okinawa and more of the same. You know, Okinawa, one of those tiny dots on the map West of Iwo Jima?"

Bad Day over Okinawa

"On that fateful day, your dad and I were on a sweep of Japanese-held islands looking for targets of opportunity. Our flight of four was at 5,000 feet, at around 390 knots.

Lt William Candler - Served on board 4 carriers, during WWII, in the Mediterranean and the Pacific Theaters of war - multiple spotting and bombing / strafing raids and campaigns over Luzon, Okinawa, Iwo Jima, France and Italy.

Grumman F-4F Wildcat

F4U Corsair

ENS Al Wood and **LTJG Ed Olszewski** after each scored a double victory, Pacific theater WWII.

Our job was to destroy ground/sea targets and Japanese island ports. With deeper penetrations into the Jap's airspace while probing their strengths and weaknesses, we would kill them whenever we found them. They were a scourge and caused our task force much suffering. When we found them, we punished them at will. Today we were explicitly tasked to intercept the onslaught of Kamikaze continually attacking our fleet.

I continued my scan of the cockpit and the surrounding sky and suddenly caught the engine's RPM drop. Had I unconsciously bumped the throttle (PCL) or the propeller control during the monotony of our patrol on our return leg to the base, or was the engine sending me a signal? I coaxed the throttle and prop back to my original max endurance setting and tried to settle in again as I caught Ensign Heming's aircraft off my wing. Our trusty nugget hung on my right wing with unwavering strength for a new guy. He hung tight, even in a loose spread formation from what seemed like abject fear. It might have been his untested navigation skills and the possibility that he might lose the flight and not find his way home. I rechecked his position, and his rock-steady Corsair mimicked my aircraft's every movement in our section.

Watching him brought a smile to my face. I remember my new guy days, new, exciting and terrifying. I pulled off my soggy sweat-soaked leather glove and wiped the stinging sweat from my eyes again.

To starboard lay one of the larger islands in the Okinawa chain. The weather was excellent except for the string of cumulonimbus off the far southwestern horizon with its skirt of falling rain. A few miles below, I caught our radar picket line coastal convoy etching a sharp white wake in the blue Pacific. That day, our fighter director was on board the destroyer Morrison (PD-560) just off the coast of the southernmost island of Okinawa. The call from the Morrison was startling—it was now on. We were suddenly vectored on a CAP (combat air patrol) intercept to another incoming flight of Kamikaze A6Ms and Zero-Sen type 0 aircraft. They were coming in waves.

The Japanese willingness to sacrifice themselves instilled fear in us and those in the destroyer picket crews. They attacked from dawn to dusk, but we knew we could only slow them down, not stop them.

I took their vector into a flight of Mitsubishi AGMs just as the ship suddenly opened up. Pushing the throttle forward, I caught the engine note change key from baritone to tenor. These shells were armed with variably timed proximity fuses. As a result, they didn't have to hit a target directly to damage or destroy an enemy. Occasionally, friendly fire shell fragments unintentionally hit our aircraft with sad results.

My scrotum began to constrict tighter against my body as my heart beat faster, and beads of sweat traveled down my spine. I had to push my fear aside and prepare for the fight.

Pushing over in pursuit, my excitement rose with the rising wale of the slipstream through the gun ports. But today, I learned the hard way as my wing opened up from shrapnel with a soft whoomp—damage from the Morrison's shells meant for the Japs. Damn, why couldn't they hold their fire until we finished our job? In my head, I envisioned a ball of burning fuel, oil, and exploding machine gun rounds in a pyrotechnic display of showering sparks and flame—serving as my demise. Fear can mess with your mind, as you know, Mathew. Judging the strain on my fighter from the increased angle of attack, the aircraft's wale, and the fast-approaching airspeed maneuvering limit, I pulled the stick back, too far back, with all my strength. She almost stalled as I relaxed the pitch to keep her flying. Partial flight control authority gave me temporary confidence to stay in the fight while the aircraft hung on the prop, clawing for altitude. *Jesus, those goddamn gunners!*

The fight was epic. Amazingly, without any losses, your dad shepherded us home. He fought off each Jap that attacked our flight. I lagged, struggling to keep my Corsair flying.

"Yes, your dad should have been a Marine like you. He could endure the mental and emotional strain and the pace of work during that war—more so than most I knew. Yet, his spirit and grit far surpassed most, and I can't say enough how proud I am to serve with him.

The Japs your dad gunned that day could not compete with his fiery onslaught. He was extreme in his intensity, and our squadron loved him for it. Yet, he stood tall and rigid in his actions, thoughts, and deeds and will never be forgotten. We stretched our anxieties to excel in combat and meet his expectations—to stay alive that day. His fear, if he had any, never showed. On the contrary, he was as solid as they come."

"Having flown together, sir, I appreciate you telling me about him. It means a lot. I wish I had known him."

Again McCready hesitated as his guilty conscience would not yet allow him to tell Mathew about his final mission with his dad later that year.

"He would have been proud of you, son—maybe a bit concerned but proud. But, unfortunately, you have a problem with your temper."

"Yes, sir, I am aware of that. I think a lot was from anger when I went home for mom's funeral. I found his metals in a box at the top of her closet. She never mentioned them or much of anything to me. So all I knew was that he was MIA."

"Yes, well, broken hearts take time to heal."

There was a knock on the stateroom door, taking us both out of our thoughts.

"Sir, sorry to interrupt. I have been holding your calls as you requested, but this one—well—I thought it was too important to miss. Would you like to take it on the bridge?"

"Thank you. Please tell whoever it is. I'll be there shortly."

"Aye, aye, sir."

He looks at me with a preoccupied glance. *Must be something big.*

"Captain, time to wrap this up. Life and times go on. I have told you much, but there is a great deal more that you need to know—some of it hard to hear and hard for me to say.

You are dismissed, Mathew. We will meet again soon, so get some rest."

"Yes, sir."

McCready watches Mathe leave his office before picking up the phone to check for missed messages, *possibly a blowback from McVey.*

Damn, so much like Bill. It isn't very comforting. I have so much more to tell him—sad, ugly truths. I hope he can handle it.

Eight

A Son's Pride

USS RALEIGH – ADMIRAL'S STATEROOM
SHORT TIME LATER

"Thank you, sir. I appreciate your history with my father and your shared stories."

"Mathew, to a man, each squadron member respected your dad completely.

He spoke concisely and efficiently with each of us. But, when he talked to the squadron, consideration or empathy wasn't what your dad wanted. I always felt that he needed a pledge of 100% from each man. I can imagine his opinion of the "moonbeam" children of your sixties—floating from the real to infinity and back in a cloud of ganja and who knows what else. You can probably verify the change that took place in our society. I'm sure MSU was quite a place when you were there. And then a sea change in behavior and rules."

In silence, I nodded, quietly embarrassed for the behaviors of my generation—so different when you compare both.

"Yes, sir, you're right. But, unfortunately, the times smelled of laziness and self-serving apathy with only a few willing to stand tall."

"Yes, our parents also let us run hard, in the "normal" risky way for boys during our time—the thirties. But, they knew that more growth and learning come from taking risks and missteps. I know you are familiar with these—situations that could lead to a quick trip to a hospital emergency ward. But, there were no drugs or false worlds for us, just a zest for sometimes risky explorations and acceptance and sharing of experiences.

The risks we took in our youth were dangerous and not easily understood by many. But in pushing things, we were smart enough to know when enough was enough—most of the time. The world was wide open but with enough rules to keep our young minds in line. Our common sense and introjected parental values saved many from actual harm—it was a marvelous time."

I hesitated to tell him that he had just described my youthful universe—much the same.

"Coming from similar communities, your dad and I were essentially carbon copies of each other except for some recognizable physical differences."

I smiled again in understanding. *This sounds like a familiar refrain*—thinking of my youth with Finn.

"I always liked the fact that you always knew where you stood with your dad. He knew no middle ground or a gray area. For him, there were only missions, objectives, and facts.

True Blue

So, just *like* a Marine, he took care of me that day in Okinawa—a Marine in navy blue. I knew he would give up everything to care for his squadron mates, and I also knew I'd do the same for him. But I worried about how I would handle that day. I would have to make that life-and-death decision for him. He was a true ass-kicker in our brotherhood of flying warriors. The message he gave the Jap fighter pilots that day, and many preceding, was that this is our side of the street, and if you threaten my boys—your life will get much shorter.

We always sensed that he belonged to something greater that would outlive his mortality. So all of us held onto his flame—the fire that would allow us to survive. We knew our mutual success and losses over the war years would depend on him. His loss that day cut deeply into each flyer's soul. Yet, we were as staunchly loyal to each other as he was genuine with us—*True Blue* he was.

He was a natural fighter pilot, and I'm sure his courage was partly driven by the fear of losing the one thing he likely valued more highly than life—his reputation as a man among men. Yet he carried a perverse pride in serving.

I don't want to belabor this, but I can't help it. His strength of character displayed itself in unrelenting poised friendliness. As a true individualist, he was obedient to the rules, and we learned from his ability to suffer the discipline of our early training and the pain of war as a "well-bread beast" that disappears to stomach his hurt in silence.

You're as territorial, aggressive, and tenacious as your dad—it's a shame that you didn't get a chance to grow up with him and learn the many lessons he was holding for you.

Mathew, you have shown some of these attributes and attitudes during your career, both good and bad. I have always felt my responsibility to help you maintain this edge in the topsy-turvy world of naval aviation.

He nailed our squadron colors to the mast before every mission, and we pressed ahead without ever looking back—never to surrender. He was like our strict wizened admiral—you might remember his name, "Bull" Halsey. And like Halsey, your dad lived "Bull's" mantra completely—'Kill Japs and kill more Japs until they are erased from this world—no quarter.' Yes, he was a Marine posing as a navy lieutenant. And he might have been more of a Marine than you are at this stage in your career."

My heart filled, and I swelled with pride at the admiral's words and smiled, even as I immediately bristled at the challenge thrown my way by the admiral. I could not take my off eyes off McCready. I wanted to hear more about my father to bath in his life story and strength. I hoped McCready's description of dad would never end. I could tell he meant every word, and so he continued.

"You know, I like Marines because being a Marine is serious business. Not to take away from our side of the fence, but marines are not in a social club or a fraternal organization. They are a brotherhood of warriors—nothing more, nothing less, pure and simple—all in the ass-kicking business, and unfortunately, these days—business is good."

I could see McCready emotionally felt the excitement and pain of his words—as I felt.

The impact of our mutual loss might mean that neither of us will be able to accept his defeat in different ways. He then changed the subject. I guess there wasn't much more to say. I could see him living his experiences again to survive that savage day many years ago.

"Getting back to my story—it kills me to say this, but that was the last time I saw your dad, and there was nothing I could do. I held onto the fleeting hope that he would pull out for a successful ditching in the sea or find land—that he would make it back." But he was reported as missing in action, and there was nothing we could do about it except fly continual sweeps of the sector, which turned up negative. So we die when we must for each other—he did keep the trust." Silence preceded McCready's uneasy shift in his chair—his concern conflicted about continuing his story.

I sensed something more was deeply bothering him—a deep fear of what transpired that day or just the painful memory—I didn't know.

Nine
Squirrel Cage Penance

PENTAGON
NINETEEN SEVENTY-THREE

Take heed in your manner of speaking
That the language ye use may be sound,
"Impossible" may not be found.

McCready was ushered into Admiral Gillespie's office and stood in front of his massive desk.

My reassignment to the Pentagon—fresh from my fleet flag responsibilities, seemed natural in my evolution of command. Before, I had visited the Pentagon for tactical insider threat training but had never been formally assigned an operational role.

My new boss was a three-star Admiral named Clifford Gillespie. Even though most privately referred to Gillespie as "Iron Ass Junior," I did not want to become the brunt of this nickname. Years ago, I remembered him in the fleet as "Bull Gillespie"—some things never change. His grade A Brillo padded, four-button way of speaking his mind caused high-pressure frontal weather systems to turn into low, paint to peel from the side of ships, and ulcers to appear instantly. He was old school—without a doubt. And, yes, even my cat Dingel II felt his scourge when he heard his name. Dingel II would disappear for days. But, yes, he did look tougher than a hard-boiled owl, I thought.

Upon arriving at the "Squirrel Cage," my initial assignment was to address the human factors that impacted my new department's security inefficiencies.

I accepted the responsibility and soldiered forward without any illusion that the Pentagon's consolidation/unification of cross-service communication architecture would ever occur. On the contrary, I surmised it would take years to complete. Thousands of network administrators with different chains of command, standards, and protocols saw to that. But, as always, people were the weak link, which was my strength.

In my new world, with its share of natural and quasi-administrative crises, the environment was telling on my stomach. There was no physical combat or real immediate life and death decisions like in my recent past—just career conflict, dismissal, or demotion for the most minute detail or protocol missed—or communication errantly passed.

How could 23,000 workers go wrong in "Fort Fumble?" But, on the other hand, maybe there was a reason for using 666 toilet paper rolls daily.

So, my job became one of managing ethos— attitudes, expectations, and aspirations—getting beyond just focusing on the tech piece of the puzzle. Instead, it was about the culture and how to man, train, and equip this small part of the organization.

Did this new department possess only a superficial awareness of its vulnerabilities—by design? It offered a roaring opportunity to cut through the administrative goo. Of course, true excellence was way off, but I had a vision for those responsible and how to get them there.

I had passed the capabilities test in my initial interviews as it appeared that my superiors were looking for a high-level administrator— and I was confident they had found one.

Reading thru my file disclosed past command reports and measures that indicated some noted strengths and weaknesses. I guess I can live with them.

■"His strengths were his integrity and ability to own up with no "sins of omission" and no shortcuts plus solid accountability. He stood out among many.

■"He also displayed the ability to gain a depth of knowledge. When McCready recognizes something wrong, he handles it effectively with a questioning attitude."

Yes, it was not an easy task for me in a formal rank structure in my early days, but I felt I had cultivated a solid approach over the years.

■"His inborn knack for stating directions while establishing the appropriate atmosphere for formality is legendary. Cutting the small talk and personal familiarity were strong traits of the "Barker" and later "One Ton." His early flight deck commands gave him the label that brought the heat down on most if attention was not paid.

■"Admiral McCready believes skipped step errors and inattention compromised establishing the appropriate gravity needed to run a functioning department efficiently."

Even with a firm grasp of what ailed my department, I struggled initially. I had been thru a tough week of indoctrination about the legal and ethical why's and hows of work-life in "Fort Fumble."

As I waited in Admiral Gillespie's office for my boss to arrive, I wondered what was next. I missed line responsibilities and was concerned about how long I could hold it together in this new assignment—a job I accepted with reservation at the tail end of my career.

Orders were orders while weighing the discomfort and uncertainty of my new responsibilities against the lost freedoms of command at sea.

I must be getting old.

Thinking back over the years—I missed the challenge, privilege, and intense pleasure of joining that dance of ferocity and compassion that was naval aviation.

The honor of it all seemed sadly lacking among the men who scurried about their essential work as they fought the internal verbal battles, mind games, and backstabs within this five-walled monster. But, I found elements of those I worked with that I liked and held on tight to maintain my drive.

As I waited for our meeting, I caught the wall placard inscribed in an Old English font—"Iron Ass Junior," given to him by another admiral and fellow academy graduate.

It brought back the memory of a poem I had read and studied early in my career.

Admiral Hopwood's poem (The Laws of The Navy) had grounded me for years. It was my footing, providing one of the vertebrae in the backbone of my naval decision-making process—just maybe the whole spine. It provided a process reminder—an all-encompassing and timeless moral lesson for my career:

As the wave washes clear at the hawse pipe,
Washes aft and is lost in the wake;
So shalt thou drop astern all unheeded,
Such time as these laws ye forsake.

Take heed in your manner of speaking
That the language ye use may be sound,

In the list of the words of your choosing
"Impossible" may not be found.
Now, these are the Laws of the Navy,
And many and mighty are they.
But the hull and the deck and the keel
And the truck of the law is -- **OBEY**.

Gillespie's door opened after a light tap. "Admiral Gillespie will join you in a few minutes," his aide announced. I nodded as the yeoman backed out quietly.

"Iron Ass Junior's" office was a naval history lesson—of his career written in blood and way more than impressive. I would know him now as "boss."*As if I needed one at this stage in my career!*

I wondered why the name had stuck for so many years. But unfortunately, the answer I pondered was almost assuredly right around the corner.

I tried to identify with the many framed awards, pictures, and aircraft the admiral had flown—mementos and memories from a colorful aviation career—all very impressive and quite over the top. But then, the admiral suddenly burst thru the office door. Exploded would be a more apt description.

He was agitated and expectant as he grumbled to himself. Finally, he glanced at me and moved toward his desk. Gillespie's service had certainly aged this man. I thought he looked old but handsome with a tailor-made uniform, styled hair, etc. The lines etched on his face told a story of the years and challenges he had faced. His demeanor did not hint at weakness—a superior attitude and behavior. He took his seat before me, reached out to press the office intercom button, and asked for two coffees.

"Admiral, reporting as ordered," I announced, standing at half-seasoned attention.

"Jamie, pull up a chair. Good to see you."

I sat uncomfortably, looking at an imperious, almost unfriendly stare.

Urgency oozed out of every pore, and it looked like he was not about to waste time with small talk. Gillespie congratulated me on my successful career in the fleet and welcomed me to the Pentagon.

"I was given word from my superiors that there is a matter of urgency that I think you might be well equipped to handle—in addition to your ongoing duties."

Stiffening in my chair as the obligatory steaming cups of coffee arrived on a tray—no words of thanks were uttered, just silent steps in and out.

"Black or cream with sugar?"

"Black is fine, sir."

"Jamie, I'm about to involve you in reports and rumors of a certain WWII aviator who has been seen periodically for decades. We reported him missing in action during that war in the Pacific. You might remember your squadron mate Lieutenant Stone. He, too, was shot down on the same mission. You remember the one that you crash-landed on that small Okinawa atoll."

God, how could I forget that day but reported to be still alive? "Yes, sir."

I was stunned to hear this news as the admiral's words hung in the air. I recalled that day like I knew the back of my hand. And then felt a wave of trepidation as I remembered the MIA report. The truth and circumstances surrounding the actual events of the loss of Stone only drove my guilt deeper.

"Sir, are you telling me there is a chance Stone is still alive?"

"Assuming the legitimacy to these sightings—our confirmation efforts to identify this American's exact location have consistently come up empty. But a recent report in the AP, nearly 30 years after his disappearance, has energized the press to seek answers from the government. How that got out, I can only guess. However, he was reported as MIA, not KIA—so yes, it is possible, albeit faint.

We have noted these nagging sightings for years, but they were never corroborated after we reported him missing. So, there have been no real signs that Lieutenant Stone is alive, just these pesky sightings of an "American." A few years back, the exception was an American veteran's death report. So we were frankly astonished when hearing of this new report.

The U.S. Government remains committed to bringing this "American" home if we can confirm these reports. New evidence has been growing that this "American" military officer, a POW, is alive in Asia. So I must add that any suggestion that we've abandoned him is simply incorrect. We have raised the issue at the highest level while pursuing him through intermediaries.

Over the years, the Vietnamese, Chinese, and Japanese have repeatedly denied involvement in his disappearance or wear bouts. Nevertheless, many in this and other governments believe Lieutenant Stone is dead.

Technically this case has been closed, but it co-insides with the direct objective of your next assignment. So I'm asking you to watch for this American serviceman as you pursue *another individual*—your primary assignment—why we are meeting today!

Most importantly, we are searching for a former Vietnamese pilot named Chi Dung Thai. Chi cross-trained and graduated from the Naval

Air Training Command in 1969. He was a South Vietnamese Air Force pilot training under our command. We understand Chi befriended or had a close association with one of our student naval aviators at the time—one you have supported in some prior sticky situations. Captain Matthew Stone, Lieutenant William Stone's son, is that naval aviator. "

McCready's eyes widened as he readjusted his seat posture—all ears as the reality of the assignment sunk in.

"Chi's past before joining the Vietnamese Air Force is our concern. We know him now to be a worldwide threat. We need to find out what we are up against. We think that Chi Dung Thai and this American, possibly Lieutenant William Stone, might be bound somehow—a nexus, maybe a link between them, even if the American's identity is verified as our MIA. This must be clarified."

I froze. *Did he say Lieutenant Stone or Captain Stone—and this Vietnamese guy? Together? How can that be—and why?*

"Are you with me, Admiral?"

"Yes, sir."

"Sir, Wait, did you mean the American—my old shipmate Lieutenant Stone may be alive after being shot down by the Japanese during WWII? And that he may have something to do with Chi?"

McCready searched the Admiral's face for the truth and didn't sense any evasion.

"Not sure, not that we can verify now."

"But, sir, what if it turns out to be him? What are our intentions on getting him out?"

"Let's take one step at a time, Admiral, and confirm his existence first. Yes, one step at a time."

Admiral Gillespie leaned forward and looked McCready directly in the eye. Then, with a renewed stiffness in his posture that punctuated a boundary in his voice, he spoke in a firm but subdued tone.

"Listen, Admiral, I'm not happy with this outcome either, but we have this mission directly from the CNO. This is what the President wants.

Our next step is predicated on your identification of Chi and the "American" and dependent on his circumstance or the nature of a possible relationship."

After a brief pause, Gillespie sat back in his chair and took a call. At the same time, I rubbernecked the admiral's office walls again while digesting this improbable information—so many questions.

I fought to put a lid on my emotions. But instead, my jaw grew tighter—then tighter, as my frustration, confusion, and pain began to grow. I tried to recall any information about Chi. But instead, confusion and frustration reigned concerning Dung or whomever. Memories of my squadron mate Lieutenant Stone raced through my head.

Possibly alive? Incredible!

I was in shock and having difficulty digesting this reality as I looked up and caught Gillespie's stare. While he hung up the phone, he reached into his lower credenza drawer. Then, pulling out a massive bottle of his favorite—Dingle Irish Whiskey—he proceeded to pour two fingers into his mug while checking the wall clock.

Well, at least we have one thing in common. For some strange reason, thoughts of my pet cat Dingle II popped into my head. So naturally, I welcomed the admiral's gesture as I was somewhat of a connoisseur—of cat's and Dingle's name association with single malt Irish whiskey.

"Want some?"

"Yes, sir, I think I will."

Admiral Gillespie poured three fingers into my coffee mug, and we sat silently for a moment. I had too many questions, and the possibility that my old friend might still be alive floored me.

"Sir, can you tell me about Chi Dung's background and the real objectives behind this assignment?"

The silence from Gillespie told me he probably was trying to decide how much to divulge.

"Sir, is "The American" the real driver or just a sidebar in this assignment?

Gillespie pushed his hand, palm up, across the desk in the air—his signal to stop.

"I cannot give you any more information, Admiral. All I can tell you is that your assignment is vitally important."

"But, sir, why is Chi so important? Or is it Stone?"

"Admiral, that is classified. I think that is enough for today."

I nodded as "Iron Ass" suddenly pulled a classified folder from his top desk drawer.

"What we have discussed today is confidential. You will get a full brief tomorrow morning at 07:30 in this office. Your questions will be answered, so please review this file for our meeting and have your questions ready by then.

I have a question for you, Jamison, or concern about Captain Stone. We have picked up a strong vibe over his lack of respect for authority during his career. Can you confirm these reports? Is he disrespectful, Admiral McCready—you know the face—the behavior?"

"Yes, I do, but no, sir, he is not outwardly. But he will express strong opinions if the subject crosses his sense of right and wrong."

"Ok then. You are dismissed."

"Sir, thank you for your confidence."

I tossed back the whiskey, stood up, and exited the office—more confused and excited about an assignment than any in my career.

While walking the hallway back to my office, Gillespie's post-meeting words echoed, 'Admiral, as we discussed, Stone's son might be the perfect candidate to meet your field challenges. So, your assignment is to turn your Captain into one of us quickly. There will be no personality tests, admissions committees, psychologists, and indeed no participation by Captain Stone in actual ops. You know the drill. As a trained naval aviator, he should be familiar with compressed timelines. Just firehose him in our craft's short course, so he has a chance to succeed where so many others failed before him. Yes, his pipeline to more responsibility has been very familiar to him. But to become an operator in this time frame, his new environs will require much of your pilot, maybe more than he can handle. Nevertheless, his success or failure is your responsibility—so make it so! Have I made myself clear, Admiral?'

I smiled, realizing all the limitations and training constraints Mathew would be held. But I also knew he was a very smart grinder and chuckled again as I opened the door to my office.

Rigorous field training as a special agent might be the perfect fit for Captain Mathew Stone—infiltrating the CCP and weakening their system—maybe not!

Ten

More Than A Specter

SHORT TIME LATER

"Uncharted the rocks that surround thee,
Take heed that the channels thou learn,
Lest thy name serve
to buoy for another
That shoal the "Court-Martial Return."

I poured over every word of the classified documents I had signed for. I knew that formal diplomatic relations had recently been established between the US and the PRC (People's Republic of China) with the United States Liaison Office (USLO) office in Beijing—a counterpart PRC office in Washington.

As I read through the documents, I muttered with repressed rage. *But, of course, it won't work,* as I pushed away from the desk to pour another scotch.

"I have never lied for my government, and I won't do it now," trying to justify what I had been told to keep secret—never to divulge the whole story. My inner battle over this imposed muzzling had me tied in knots for years.

I refuse to do it. I may have withheld info, but I have never lied.

The possibility that my squadron mate from a long-ago war was alive opened my dread for the day of its possible confirmation—for I knew then I would finally have to tell all after holding it for too many years. But, my conscience demanded the truth be told, and I would eventually have to face my guilt and fess up to everything.

I was puzzled at the extent of the investigation into the whereabouts of my long-lost friend as I poured through the confidential file (classified) on Lieutenant William Stone, WWII navy pilot, and its companion Chi file.

The same unanswered questions kept popping up.

They wouldn't let me tell the complete truth of our last mission together. The fact that he possibly was alive—was classified and never mentioned. *And they couldn't rescue Bill in all this time—just amazing.* And I'm just hearing about it—now!

He read through the "Americans," or was it LT William Stone's file notations, sightings, dates, and circumstances surrounding his captivity.

The next day Admirals McCready and Gillespie listened to intelligence analysts' overviews of the American and Chi Dung Thai's history and suspected whereabouts. They were two separate case studies that, even at first glance, seemed not to be linked. But the analyst's surmised otherwise.

"Gentlemen, it was reported in the early years of the American's confinement that the sightings were the work of fifth columnists," analysts commented. This group of individuals was trying to undermine our nation with their report clandestinely.

I piped in immediately.

"What, how so—would you care to explain?"

"Well, during this time, we identified foreign powers—and sadly, some within our government trying to undermine the US. But unfortunately, we were never able to reach a solid conclusion because confirmation of these reports always proved inconclusive. But over time, and I mean years, these continued reports created a lot of embarrassing governmental second-guessing—internal political flaps and false starts.

But, most importantly, they all pointed to circumstantial evidence that an American was alive—and the American could be Lieutenant Stone.

It is still unclear why our continued probing for answers has been so elusive. How could this MIA undermine our position in the world?"

What the hell is this guy talking about—did he just double-talk me?

"I can imagine a foreign power colluding to hold on to one of our own, an American intelligence officer and naval aviator, over that time?"

A what? Bill, an intelligence officer? I don't think so. He was a naval aviator, not a spy. It's just unfathomable, and for all these years? Did they think he could be held and used as a bargaining chip in negotiations with Washington? Instead, our government seems to have created a story of unyielding deniability concerning Stone's affiliations.

"We don't know whether he was trafficked for financial gain and passed from country to country to leverage his knowledge. Pressure to not release or acknowledge his existence might have grown in time. But, with an eventual discovery and unmasking of an American—that surely would be forthcoming—they would have had to pay a high political international price.

Abduction records and other documents have surfaced since the last reported sightings against the political talking points of our government's officials. They suggest that Americans reported as MIAs had been held in Vietnam, China, and Korea. Over the years, based on these documents, we conducted an investigation. Even though crucial factions within the US Government continued to deny any direct knowledge of American captives and possibly Stone's existence or even a relationship with his work in the ONI (Office of Naval Intelligence), we discovered it was true."

He worked for the ONI, and someone covered it up. Unbelievable, but why?

"The universal story from most governmental authorities we questioned has been, 'We've never heard of Lieutenant Stone or who he is—we don't know. If he is an American,' we have no news of his existence. Nevertheless, we are willing to help, and all the intelligence services in the region can come together to gather information about him to find his possible whereabouts. And we're willing to cooperate."

McCready sat stone-eyed as he bore angry holes into the analyst's story. *More unyielding deniability.*

"So, the real question is he 'The American,' still alive, and why was he exchanged perpetually over these years? This tenet is still suspect, in our opinion. Only the FBI has commented in the last five years. Their investigators believe, and I quote, 'Stone is not dead.' He is still alive and being held in China despite public statements from US officials."

The briefing ended, leaving me at a loss for words. Finally, I rose from my chair along with Gillespie.

Gillespie thanked the analyst for his review on the "American" and Chi, then turned and asked me to follow as he left the conference room. Then, stepping into the hallway, Gillespie turned again and, in a whisper, gave me further uncorroborated information.

"Admiral, you will not find what I am about to tell you documented anywhere in this building nor ever spoken about by any government official. So, it will behoove you to keep this last bit of information between us—formally, you do not need to know!"

"I understand, sir."

Our conversation lasted five minutes and this "hair on fire" moment only deepened my fears. However, our assignment's urgency was more than an ankle-biter, as Admiral Gillespie described a situation of high confidentiality.

"Sir, are we dealing with a game-changing weapon?" And again, Gillespie waved me off in stone-cold silence. Then, in parting words, "So, Admiral, get Captain Stone up to speed quickly!"

"I'm on it, sir."

And we separated.

Eleven
Hopes and Dreams

TWO MONTHS PRIOR

O thou, when thou nearest promotion,
And the gilded peak is nigh,
Give heed to words and thine actions,
Lest others be wearied thereby.

Mathe picked up the phone.

"Yes, commander, I recognized your voice," He knew the voice on the other end, and instantly his heart rate jumped. *Oh God, this is it. I have been waiting for this one my whole life.*

Commander Len Butros, the Blue Angel's squadron commander—the "Boss" in Blues parlance, introduced himself again.

"How are you and the Talons doing, Stone?"

Before Mathe could answer, Butros jumped right back in.

"Mathew, your application to join the Blue Angels Flight Demonstration Team has been thoroughly reviewed."

Mathe expectantly drew a pause. His tone was much more formal than in their past discussions. *Crap, this doesn't sound good.*

"You possess many of the characteristics and skills to be successful as a member of the Team—the traits we look for in a successful Blue Angel." And then he paused—a little longer than average.

"And your achievements and professionalism in naval aviation are well documented. We wish you success in your future career endeavors.

But before I get to additional questions—at this time, we have a problem."

Mathe swallowed hard—*uh oh*! Boutros's short controlled professional manner with pauses was killing him.

I could think of one or two past adventures that might make this whole thing go South.

Come on, Commander, please get to it.

"Problem, sir?"

"Just a second, Stone. I have a small interruption I need to remedy."

"Yes, sir."

Mathe thought he heard other voices in the background.

He was beginning to feel this opportunity slowly slipping through his fingers—*was this the kiss-off?* His skin began to glisten. Well, at least I'll know one way or the other.

I recalled similar feelings of angst during a T-28 night cross-country hop flight. I remembered the pressure of a complete electrical failure at weather minimums coming into the South Weymouth Naval Air Station, visiting a friend in Boston. After a letdown from a high-altitude fix, the emergency generator warning light flashed on in front of me—and then boom, the lights went out, and I mean everything in the aircraft—total electrical failure.

The pressure mounted as I tried to address this emergency. As a result, I couldn't talk, couldn't see, and couldn't navigate to the airport. Compounding the problem, at the same time, I was sweating my low fuel state light (bingo fuel) caused by my poor preflight weather and fuel usage estimate planning. All this occurred while slightly hungover from the previous night's revelry in the bar at Beaufort, MCAS. Yes, I had gone bingo (minimum fuel state) along with my aircraft. Without a generator, I could not request a GCA (ground-controlled approach) from Weymouth to pull my bacon out of this emergency. In addition, the pressure on my bladder had exceeded its capacity from the previous night's party—compounding the problem. I relieved myself in the under-seat relief tube, and while trying to stow the tube, my friend became stuck to the cold tube edge!

It was a total wrestling match in the cockpit, with one hand moving from the throttle to the stick and then back to the cock, trying not to lose more skin from my friend. Luckily, I was flying in a section (two aircraft) that night, and I flew his wing right to touchdown. Nevertheless, the flight gave new meaning to "skin of my teeth" moments.

There were moments, and then the really BIG moments in naval aviation. This was one of them. Commander Butros's following words would be one of them.

Mathe thought back to the interviews and his naval officer record as his mouth quickly dried into a sticky saliva goo. His hand holding the phone seemed to have a new twitch—a nervous tic unnoticed before. Maybe his recent shenanigans with Colonel McVey tripped him up? His interviews and flying abilities were good—not outstanding. Yet, he felt he had bonded with the Team during their social events.

What am I missing? Could it have been the reception with wives and personnel from the squadron? I knew I was under the microscope at that affair. It was just another test to see if I had the social graces in mixed company—their deeper dive into my personality. I knew that each team member had critiqued my interpersonal and social skills—and I thought I had passed the test—except for a fumbled drink and an errant fart at one of the gatherings. I looked for the pieces I'd dropped along the way.

So what had gone wrong? All the boxes were checked—I thought. Maybe it was my aggressiveness—which periodically flared throughout my career had been my undoing. Surely my propensity to get into bar fights, which never got reported, caught up with me—jeopardizing my chances to join this elite group—Nah, this is the navy!

"Sorry for the wait, Captain. You still there?"

"Oh yes, I'm here."

I shivered with expectation.

"Captain, the entire Team stands in front of my desk and has something to tell you. This is a review so that you will grow in the future."

There was another long hesitation over the phone as Matt's hopes sank. Then, "oh shit,"—he muffled to himself.

"Gentlemen," he heard Butros call out. "Do we want Captain Stone to join the Team?"

In unison, they answered in a roaring, rolling shout that Mathe thought could be heard on Raleigh's flight deck above.

"Hell No—HELL NO!" Then, just as loud, the ominous few seconds of silence. Then, "You can't join the fraternity—but WELCOME ABOARD ASS HOLE," they shouted in unison. Their good-natured laughter and backslaps in the background told the story and brought a massive smile as I almost peed myself. The Team seemed just as excited about my acceptance as I was as the hoots and hollers died.

Damn! I whispered under my breath. *I've been accepted—a rookie again, OUTSTANDING—just another chance to prove myself. Now I have to get my act together, seriously!*

"Okay, gentlemen, clear out—I need a word with Captain Stone," Butros commanded. In the background, I heard; foot shuffling, laughter, rude comments, and then the quiet.

Butros now had my full attention.

In a more personal tone, "Yes, you have been accepted into next year's Team—one of two to join us soon in Pensacola.

Your formal orders will arrive in the next week for a two-year commitment. They will describe an initial fifteen to sixteen weeks of training, including approximately one hundred and twenty flights to reach our first live demonstration—where you will relearn how to fly.

We look forward to your arrival in Pensacola for training in December so we can prepare for the season opener in March. You will fly left-wing first as number three, then transition to slot in your second year. It will go by quickly, so enjoy the ride, Matthew—see you soon. Any questions?"

"No, sir, thank you again for your confidence."

"Don't mention it, Stone. You have spent years honing your skills and your more than 1280 tactical jet hours hold some pretty interesting highlights—you have earned the right for some "metal sharpening."

"Thank you, sir!"

I smiled with rising anticipation with this first test passed. I knew it would be a huge gut check—nothing more demanding in naval aviation than honing your skills to the precision required to fly with this Team.

Intimidating—you bet, and a newbie again—wow!

I've got to call Rusty and tell Finn—right away.

But Commander Butros's words, 'Some pretty interesting highlights,' kept reverberating.

How much did he know or care about my run-in with McVey? Thoughts of that day returned with amazing clarity.

Vietnam—Finn had punched out of his A-4 and was captured. I also ejected and "borrowed" the Huey to rescue Finn.

The stark contrast between that frightening day against all the positives that had transpired for me was astonishing. But, even so, I was concerned about the visibility my run-in with McVey had caused.

I have got to let that jerk McVey go. He is old news—I have to get my head out of the past for this new opportunity. I just have to!

If you add up the Navy Cross just awarded by the Admiral for the rescue mission and this new opportunity with the Blues—things are looking up. Time to make that call!

I smiled at the thought of the award—proud but apprehensive at the same time—remembering an earlier time, a simpler time in my Marine naval aviation journey, and the excitement I felt. But then, it was a time of nonstop hustle with all comforts stripped away. We were poked, shouted at, slapped around, and ordered without control over our lives.

— · —

Reveille woke me from my sleep coma as a new aviation officer candidate. We were all in various states of acceptance and tolerance for what was thrown at us, and the dream of navy wings was stronger for most. Early morning starlight was fading that December morning. But, I was here, at Pensacola Naval Air Station, in the panhandle with the gulf less than a click away. It might be Florida, but it felt cold. Yet, I could smell the salt air bringing a hint of early morning warmth and a distinctive unfamiliar mix, a smell that I did not recognize—no sign of the sun yet.

We rushed to form up on the grinder in our march to 04:30 chow from the INDOC building. For most, the excitement of this new world reverberated with expectation even with the morning's lack of sleep.

But unfortunately, not all candidates echoed my path, the one I had dreamed about for years. Unfortunately, the price was more than they were willing to pay.

Newly Minted Ensigns with Big Fast Dreams.

— · —

I finally reached the pinnacle—acceptance into the "The Team." It was worth the ride—all of it. And what a ride!

Finn is going to lose his shit! Both of us had dreamed about being Blue Angels.

But first, Rusty.

I quickly dialed her number, and she answered.

"Hey, Rusty, it's Mathe.

Rusty paused. "You have got to be kidding me, Mathe! It must be serious. You never call me."

"Well, here I am. How are you doing?"

"Good, Mathe, busy though," she coolly replied and added before I could get a word in.

"You know Mathe, remember before your deployment to Nam—when all those serious crashes kept happening, I didn't hear from you? You remember, right? When a couple of your squadron mates suffered fatal crashes—as in, died? Again, I didn't hear from you. I was worried sick as names were held until the next of kin could be reached. All I thought was that it was you. I understood you were working your butt off, but Mathe, did you forget how to use the phone? You are such a dope. All I wanted was to know you were okay."

"I'm sorry— unacceptable behavior—am I forgiven?"

"I guess. You keep telling me you're bulletproof anyway. So what's up?"

"Well, I need your opinion on something. How would I look in a Blue Angels flight suit?"

No words from the other end, but I could imagine her face—I saw her smiling from ear to ear but trying to hide it.

"Hmmm—well—drop a few pounds and keep your little friend in check. That might work. What are you saying?"

I love this girl—she never lets me get too full of myself.

"I got a call from the "Boss," Commander Butros.

They want me! The Blues want me. I'm one of the new guys —learning a new way to fly again."

"Wow, Mathe! A dream come true. Congratulations!

When?"

"December, Pensacola—join me. We'll have Christmas on the beach."

"Mathe, you won't have time to turn around, let alone spend time with me. And I can't leave work. They are just beginning to realize I know what I'm doing."

"Please think about it, Rusty."

"I will, Mathe—so happy for you—a bit scared, but happy."

"Me too, Rusty, me too. We will talk again when I know more—and I know you are competent in what you're doing. I'm proud of you. You know that, right?"

"Thank you, Mathe, that means a lot. Now go, flyboy, and call Finn—he will freak out. I'll spend the rest of the day smiling—picturing you in that tight blue suit, or is it yellow? I hope I can concentrate. Love you, Mathe."

"Love you right back, Rusty."

Rusty put down the phone and thought back to the one time she and Mathe had seen the "Blues" perform—six jets, thirty-six inches apart, doing amazing maneuvers at unbelievable speeds—dangerous, exciting, and terrifying. She was so excited for Mathe, remembering the gut-wrenching roar of those engines. Pure duck bump generating power! Damn, and Mathe will be in one soon! Incredible!

Twelve

Big-Tuna

MAINSIDE, PENSACOLA, FLA

I found my way into the Blues pressure cooker—and a pressure cooker it was. Long, hot, exhausting days spent smoothing the good and bad in my "fleet" flying skills.

The learning curve was steep, and the push was on. It took intense concentration and precision to fly the left wing in the diamond formation. But I ate it up—every second. Unfortunately, Rusty was right—no time for anything else.

It was good to see some familiar faces at the first team meeting. My squadron mates from VA-33/Talons were well represented. In addition, Dan O'Shea, aptly named "Mud Skunk" from his Wolverine (University of Michigan) college days, and Al "Taco" Chavez, named for one of his heritage's favorite culinary specialties—greeted me with back slaps and smiles.

Al Cisneros
Blue Angels Pilot 1975-1977

"Take me into my coming of age, into the challenges of combat and the demands of extreme precision flying."

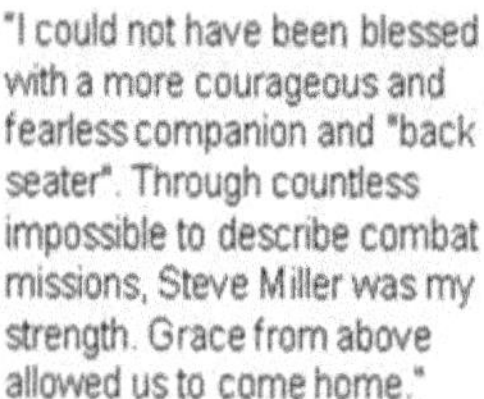

"I could not have been blessed with a more courageous and fearless companion and "back seater". Through countless impossible to describe combat missions, Steve Miller was my strength. Grace from above allowed us to come home."

"Last Dance With Sara"
Mission 154 1973

"She brought me home safely... My War Bird... the phantom."

"Either way...up or down, hard to hold the pose. My third year, flying in the slot...#4."

Before our preflight brief, Dan (Mudskunk) O'Shea cornered me with a question. I immediately picked up on the same smile, remembering O'Shea's rep. from our days on the Raleigh

Our friendship was infamous because we had flown off the Raleigh and the Saratoga on two different deployments. But, as a navy man, he was more than a kindred spirit, and you could still actually visualize the skunkster's DA haircut that was once his trademark before his current occupation.

One of his old school buddies told me his story. 'Everything was going hunky-dory at the high school dance, and we thought we were in like Flynn until that murgatroyd showed up and hung us out to dry. Even in our best bib and tuckers, we couldn't compete, so we didn't even touch the dial. We were hoping for a chance as more poodle skirts saddled up to him. Unfortunately for us, O'Shea had a lot of moxie, and women found the skunkster even when he wasn't looking while the rest of us inherited his leftovers to pick through late most evenings. Our jealousy was on full display. He sure could choke a chicken in the middle of a dance floor."

Despite his rampant social skills and good looks, O'Shea had another side. Even as a Navy man, his liking of Marines ran deep—maybe even more than the navy. He always wanted to fly as one, but it wasn't in the cards. Mudskunk knew being a Marine was serious business. They were a brotherhood of "warriors"—nothing more, nothing less—pure and simple. As Marines, their message to their foes had always been the same.

'We own this side of the street! Threaten my country or our allies, and we will come over to your side of the street, burn your hut down, and whisper, Can you hear me now? We will hold what's left of your heartbeat in our hands.'

He also loved dogs and always talked about his Chihuahua. We all thought it was a bizarre choice. Everyone knew a Doberman or Rottweiler would be more fitting for him, anything that attacks, not some candy-ass dog with big googly eyes. A short-haired tenacious throat grabber—sounded more likely a Marine's choice or at least one with past strong aspirations to be one.

Mudskunk had attended the University of Michigan for two semesters before transferring out to take advantage of the more favorable female student bodies at Michigan State. But, I always found a new way to drive the name of U of M's mascot, "Mud Skunk," hard into him—instead of the real mascot name—"Wolverine." But, today, the tables would turn.

"Hey, Mathe, it's good to see you. Someone finally figured out that you weren't as bad an aviator as everyone thought."

He looked just as I remembered earlier—an impressively rugged demeanor with a long thin face and a pointed "Hatchet" like nose.

I smiled matter-of-factly at the skunkster's dig and his acceptance while my insecurity slowly bubbled up—wondering *w*ho the hell thought that about me.

"Good to see you too, "One Nut."

O'Shea had suffered the same humiliation to his manhood that Finn had endured, the combat loss of a testicle—in radically different ways. The thought of his testicle loss in a strike over Haiphong due to triple-A penetrating his cockpit—always made me cringe. But I saw the real thing when I picked up Finn and carried him to our shot-up rescue Huey.

In time, even without an extra arrow in his quiver, I knew O'Shea would never let us down, flying the eight-ball diamond formation with only seven balls.

"Heard you have something good going on here and thought maybe I ought to see what you guys are up to,"—trying my best to counter his slite cooly.

He smiled demonically.

"You know Mathe, besides your heroic save of Finn that day and Tacos's shoot down—the Talon's first kill—on the same mission, I have wondered about another mission over Haiphong a month earlier. But, unfortunately, I never heard the full story, only that you ran out of gas or something on that mission—any truth to that rumor?"

I hesitated. Boy, this community is a little tighter than I thought—how the hell did he know about that incident?

"So, what happened on that mission, Mathe?"

Remembering that day filled with tension, fear, and rage was never far away, for it, unfortunately, held too many conflicted emotions packed into such a small space in time.

"Well, Skunkster—Yea, it got pretty hot over Haiphong that day. We had a tough time identifying the target after some strange circumstances. That's about the size of it—as I am sure you understand.

Trying to escape further questions, I eyeballed One Nut and frowned nervously to shut it all down with a new tone.

Catching OShea's disbelief, I poked his chest and growled in a schooling, scolding manner in my best-accented godfather's accent, "Listen up, Skunkster! You don't know nutin—you didn't hear nutin, and you don't say nutin—got it!

Our flight lead for the mission was commander capo Sal "Egg Man" Lunchesi, Sammy "The Grave Digger" Luigi Gamberlini, Vincenza Rico "The Butcher" Abruzzi, and myself. We were aptly named "Casino." But, of course, we weren't into money laundering, casino skimming, or bribery—just murder. But, our access to the "skims" was never in jeopardy until that day."

O'Shea smiled back in bewilderment as he caught my direction and played along.

"Jesus, all in the same flight? How'd a substandard white guy work himself into that position with all those dagos? So you were the one in the Mafia Casino that day."

"Yea, kind of—let's say I know some people who know some people!

Okay, "One Nut," I was just the consigliere, the underboss—the advisor to the boss in our section. They called me "Big Tuna" because I handled the money, and the flight listened to me—and respected what I had to say. I made things run smoothly for the boss until that day."

"Big Tuna—Hah!"

One Nut was snickering—ready to burst with laughter.

"You remember our names from our JO (junior officer) days. We called ourselves the "Fighting Foul—Cocks on Top" —created in our spare time to keep everyone from losing their minds while not fully accepting our newbie status in the squadron. You kept asking us about the patches we had made and wore, and we never answered you?'

"Sure do, pard, I remember."

"Well, we were "The Mafia" within the Talons.

"Getting on with the story—Luchesi was a dangerous man and had business to take care of that day—good old bloody killing up north. He was tough and respected in the community. Yes, he was the Boss and had done it all. He knew who to cut loose when they no longer served a purpose. We called him the "Egg Man." But that day, he dropped one too many—and it was his turn in the barrel."

One Nut's smirk widened. "Go on, Mathe, all ears here."

"Okay," I said hesitantly.

"You want to know how it went down? We were talking to Sal on the flight deck after the strike. Umm—well, I don't know what happened to Luchesi. He's gone now, and there is nutin you can do about it."

O'Shea tried hard to contain himself as the Team trickled past into the Blue's ready room for the pre-brief.

Trying to protect my rep, I quickly turned to One Nut. "Looks like I'll have to complete the story later, O'Shea."

"Come on, Mathe, there is more. I know it. Spill it. We got a few minutes."

"Well," I muttered sheepishly and paused, turning to see who might be listening.

"Mathe, from what I have heard, there was guilt to be assigned, so it is not on your shoulder. Nobody's attacking you beyond the mishap—your secret is safe with me, pal. Aw, come on. You can't just drop a bomb like that and walk away!"

"If I tell you, you can't tell anyone!"

His right hand raised a smirk, "Safe with me, pal, I swear."

Sure, realizing too late that this guarantee ensured that my story would most likely now be told to all if I finished. Luckily, the room was filling fast, so there was no time to share this story.

"Okay, Big Tuna. I get it, and I can't wait for you to finish your story. You're not getting out of this one." We entered and found our seats—*Thank God!*

During a pause in the pre-brief, my mind wandered back to the events of the "Mafia Wagon Train" mission.

That damned mission—why the hell did he bring it up? It's a memory I don't want to deal with again. But, like a dog with a bone, he's not going to let go of this one. I looked over at O'Shea again. He was hanging on like a hair in a biscuit—what's with this guy? He wants it all.

I finally shook it off as the brief ended. Checking out the aircraft's pre-launch paperwork and signoffs, I found the smile I had missed as I walked out to the jets. I was alone in my mind until I looked to my side—The Team.

The season was getting close, and it was a critical hop for everyone. This session wasn't like the first time we formed up and walked the line. Today, I treated the hop as if it was our final exam. I was beyond pumped.

Standing in perfect formation in front of our aircraft, our professional line crew waited for us, at attention. Their professionalism girded me, the rookie Angel, to rise to meet their performance expectations. Each salute's snap and pop, walking out together in formation and breaking off, one by one, filled me with pride and anticipation. I had everything to prove repeatedly on each hop as we marched forward in lockstep along the flight line in front of the jets. But today, the jets seemed cleaner than I remembered.

Finally, I approached the number three bird, Angel A-4, coming up on my left—my bird!

As I mounted number three and moved up the cockpit ladder, I was met by my gold helmet perfectly positioned on the windscreen. It hit me with full force. Today had to be perfect—just fast-paced steady squared-away procedures with no fuck ups. I stepped over the cockpit rail and onto the seat.

Thirteen

Trust and Respect

MAINSIDE, PENSACOLA, FLA

Boy, we got a good one going, I thought.

Then the Boss commented over the mic; slowly, methodically, he purred….

"BA Brakes,

Smoke off,

Ease the power,

Lay it on,"

Keep it going, Mathe—I told myself.

As the left wingman, my job was to match the separation between the boss above and ahead of me with the right-side wingman, "*Mud Skunk" O'Shea,* in whatever set maneuver the Boss was establishing.

The Skunkster set up the set and was rock solid—he never moved!

There were lapses in concentration in our first training hops before my total attention to our work was established. Prior, I would have found myself fighting off the images of the mission led by Capo Sal Luchesi, the "Egg Man."

I learned quickly that my survival in this community demanded more than total concentration—lapses were unthinkable now. So we put them back in the box.

I scanned forward and to my right to reconfirm the set separation. Our four jets rolled together laterally. We formed in one direction in a thirty-six-inch aircraft formation, Diamond roll, over Pensacola Beach.

The steady chop of today's unstable air brought the airframe to a constant shutter while I concentrated on holding my position. The turbulent air on our aircraft tried its best to break us from our precise flight paths. It made us work harder to maintain a dependable formation.

It was the second maneuver in our high show series, which each pilot had visualized and practiced enumerable times. And we were so close to showing the perfection that our roles demanded.

In the level flight turn with wings vertical, one high and the other pointed to the ground, I scanned over at "Mud Skunk" on top, to my right, and then caught "Taco's" steady separation to the rear while maintaining my wing set and spacing between the jets. I then concentrated on "flying the boss's paint" while maintaining separation on his wing.

The boss echoed, *'You got to be where you got to be, son.'*

Expectantly, I heard him call again in paused rhythm;

"Cancel,

Roll,

Pause, and then—Turn."

We had rehearsed this pirouette thru the air many times before. Over and over, but it never amounted to the thrill of this day flying together—this tight. I had never felt this kind of exhilaration before in the fleet—well, maybe once on locating Finn in Vietnam. This was altogether different and a complete rush.

I had come a long way from my first flight with the Team. How often had I said to myself—H*ow am I going to do this in this light, slick, slippery jet at these speeds?* But, the physical and mental effort from flying the hard training grind at El Centro had us coming together with this dress rehearsal back at Mainside, Pensacola. So, today might be its proof.

The additional payoff for me was that flying with this Team finally erased any doubts about the importance of working for something greater than yourself. A complete orientation change bound me tighter into the "Team" approach. Confidence in this game was tricky. Coming and going as a pilot's actual and perceived performance ebbed and flowed daily—a common, somewhat human phenomenon. But a human trait that each who flew sought to confirm on each hop for survival. The Blues slowly taught me a new way to walk, a more balanced approach, and today seemed to be the payoff. Finally, I felt part of something as my skill, confidence, and commitment flowered.

I was winning the honor of flying with these guys this morning, and showtime was right around the corner.

I heard Boss's steady purr as we rolled above the Florida coastline in the diamond formation.

"A little Pullllll—then hesitation—More Pulllll," as we sought wings level at show altitude.

And then, like a muscle-bound kitten again, in cadence, he methodically intoned;

"Coming Left, Further Left,
A Little Pull,
A little More Pull,
Smoke On-Pull,
Smoke Off-Pushhhhh,
Ease in the pull,
Ease it Out,
A Little Pulllll,
Take It In,
Smoke On-Pull,
Coming Right for the 360,

Diamond 360 Flat Pass,

POP-POP,

Easing Power."

Yes, we constantly pulled, for the stick had been moved forward in the cockpit. The A-4 was deliberately never trimmed up in our formations. It required muscle by design to hold each set safely.

With the boss's initiation of the Fleur-de-lis maneuver—coming over the top, I tried to slow my heartbeat for its challenge—*and risk.* Initially, I was unsure if I could keep it together each time—but nobody knew. The chance of my screwing up and its consequence thundered through me but lessened in time as we flew this beautiful blossom. But really, who was I kidding? It wasn't like the first uncomfortable Delta formation landing—but much more demanding.

The maneuver pushed my body and the jet faster, in tighter airspace with a smaller margin of error—then closer to the ground. But in time, we worked it out safely. And from the Delta;

"Up We Go,

Ready Break,

Ready Roll,

Split Up."

We rose into the air and abruptly pulled over the top inverted as we split up into that beautiful flowering (Fleur-de-lis) blossom from the diamond formation. We continued the pullover with each jet maintaining a 31-degree nose-down attitude at 3 to 3.5 Gs—trying to make the bottom join into the diamond again. Finally, I squeezed under the leader's airplane with 36" of aircraft separation. Our scheme was to have all aircraft time the join—1500 feet in front of the crowd—show center—two hundred feet above the ground. This maneuver was insane to fly and a real test for me—a manhood separator.

Most who observe this dance never really appreciate the concentration it takes to complete it or the danger it presents if flown improperly. Nevertheless, the boss tested human limits with this one — our extreme dance above the earth.

It had been a long-time dream to be selected for this Blues slot, and I was not going to let go of it—even though doubt about myself occasionally crept in. I became more patient in my flying skills and took the daily verbal beating with increased concentration to meet the high standards of the Blue Angels. Even though I had encountered similar challenges in the fleet, this was another animal. The open honesty that each pilot exhibited—freely admitting flight transgressions in the post-hop briefs was particularly impressive. Ownership of errors by each pilot only instilled a stronger drive to fly to perfection and strengthened our trust in each other.

Each Team member, in stages, learned to check their egos at the door with openness and honesty in our drive to improve. They took personal responsibility for maintaining a safe flying environment. I was even learning to accept criticism without losing it. About time!

The ten weeks of training were drawing to a close. Fatigue and stress had been formidable adversaries, but I did the best I could—and trusted that my future with this team would work out even with some nagging concerns about flying irregularities. I had learned a whole new edge to the word focus. I was more than glad—grateful to be here!

It was a very tight group. We all knew the details of each other's lives—our ability to fly the jet, what made each man tick, and the buttons to drive each other harder. The Team quickly bonded as our flight precision grew. The pre-season workups were proof. There were days when it was hard to keep pace, but our professional reputations would not allow us to take our foot off the pedal—no matter how deep one might be in the barrel.

"Diamond landing," the Boss called.

At the break—tight and precise—each of us buried our sticks into our thighs, found our intervals, and proceeded in sequenced form up to touchdown and roll out. Feeling good about the hop, I smiled on downwind. *We did well today*. The Boss might even give us the nod that we were ready. So even with my few transgressions, the debrief might be OK.

On taxi in—the team's banter slowed.

"Sticks back,

Looks good,"

And then. "Little close to the boss?"

"I'm sorry,"

"No problem."

I wasn't wondering how any of our maneuvers might have missed the mark—but what I might have to face in the debrief.

"Great work today, gentlemen," I heard Boss Butros call out on the walk back.

Pilots and ground flight evaluators took their seats and waited for Boss Butros to start the hop debrief. Today, I was ready for the black criticism and painfully frank burn that occurred when the flight was picked apart by each man, their leaders, and evaluators. But this morning, I felt OK, confident—more than ever before, and almost comfortable in my performance.

Commander Butros took his seat at the end of the table, and before he could say a word, an aide stepped into the room. It was highly unusual for an interruption during this meeting, and Butros scowled.

“Sir, Admiral McCready from the Pentagon would like to speak to you. Will you take the call?”

Butros was on his feet immediately and announced—"Gentlemen, excuse me while I speak to the Admiral in the next office," grumbling his way out of the room.

Hmmm—interesting. McCready’s vision popped into my mind. He had told me about his impending transfer but never any specifics.

Boss was gone for a very short time, and as he re-entered the room, he looked directly at me with a concerned and questioning look.

“Let’s carry on with the debrief, gentlemen.”

Just as the meeting adjourned, Butros grabbed my arm. He gave me that *I think we got a rat in the barn* look, and I braced, expecting the worst.

“Please sit down, Captain. We have something of importance to discuss.”

Butros grabbed a second cup of coffee while I dropped into a chair at the back of the ready room.

Here it comes, more shit rolling downhill and hitting my fan.

“In my discussion with Admiral McCready, he has made a rather unusual request. I can’t speak to the particulars, but he ordered me to tell you to immediately get to the Pentagon. The matter is urgent, and he wants to talk to you personally.

You are temporarily separated from this command until further notice. But do not worry. We will hold your slot open until the time and date of your appropriate reentry back onto the Team. It is a shame that you will not be joining us on our first scheduled show, but I can confirm that your performance has peaked simultaneously with your teammates. Therefore, I assure you that you will be missed and look forward to returning soon."

What's happening? I thought. Hold your spot open—what the hell was he talking about? This is a bunch of bull. McCready again—I thought our conversations were over!

Fourteen

Egg Man Drops One

MAINSIDE, PENSACOLA, FLA

Jumpin Jehosophat!
This really twangs my burston' blood vessels. You better be careful, as there's little doubt that you've forced your guardian angel to take a rest cure.*

Mathe sat in the shadows of the bar waiting for "One Nut." O'Shea. He enjoyed the refreshing cold moisture of the beer glass against his palm in the heat and humidity-laden Pensacola saloon. It was a nice break from a long, hot, typical Pensacola day.

However, his sudden separation from the Team and planned flight out to Washington weighed heavily on his mind. Yet, even in the damp quiet of the bar, he felt a sudden chill, for he couldn't help but reflect on his past.

Damn, I guess this profession is as dangerous as some warned. Today's hop with the Team was no exception and might have ranked right up there against the backdrop of that day in Vietnam. So many pilots and I had felt the trepidation and horror of going feet dry into the North.

I remembered my early training days and concerns like getting blown across the flight deck by a jet's high-pressure tire sidewall blowout on inspection. Pictures of facial burns from our O2 masks carbon mikes catching fire from electrical shorts still haunt me. These early concerns, indeed, were not top of mind anymore. But higher probability accidents, and killers, appeared around each corner—just part of a long list of calamities I had seen and been part of as I grew in the profession. I hoped more serious accidents would never present themselves but realized they would never wane.

Grandpa Pettibone seemed to have it right in his outline of pilot errors and disasters—stories doled for the betterment of navy pilots. However, my chapter with the Blues heightened a new non-nugget concern—not outright fear but the ever-tightening screws of not measuring up in my flying competence.

One Nut found me at the bar, interrupted my daydreaming with a slap on the back, and filled the bar stool beside me. We didn't have much time to visit this traditional navy watering hole, and it was good to meet up. I turned to face him as he smiled, and I thought I caught the same tell-tale weariness on his face that I felt. The Blue's training cycle pace was shrinking what was left of our private lives.

"What's up, Mathe? You look like someone stole your tricycle?"

"Hey, O'Shea, how are they hanging?" O'Shea's face turned a shade of red at the reminder of his masculine loss.

"Sorry to make you wait. I had to chat up that cutie over there."

"Yeah, I noticed. You can't help it, can you?"

"Nope—comes naturally for someone with all my skills and good looks."

"Speaking of skills, asshole. You nearly killed me today. Remember my call out when I noticed your movement up the bearing line, your wingtip inching closer and closer to mine? There couldn't have been more than four inches separating us. We were flying inverted at 400 knots in a rolling diamond. Don't you remember me calling out, "No closer, O'Shea, hold it steady…steadee?"

And with a smirk, “Yeah, sure do.”

“Were you just playing with me—I’m the new guy here, remember?” I thought back to that moment, and I guess I had reached my safety tolerance limit, dripping in sweat, as I made that call to O'Shea.

“You said, ‘No closer, O’Shea, hold it steady,’ and I did. Right?”

“Just making it tight, Mathe, but now that you mention it, I thought I…” One nut glanced to his right as Trader passed by.

“But hold on a minute, Mathe, I have to give Trader a message before he leaves for the evening—more like, clean up a debt.”

I looked over at him as he talked to the barkeep. Our drive for perfection just might kill us. He knew it, too, but had a different, more experienced approach to developing our skills.

How incredible human beings are. Our eyes, mind, and body coordination could tolerate this intense drive for perfection. We gathered the degree of grit, skill, and concentration needed to achieve this level of perfection. And we could block out what could happen—with just one lapse in any of it.

As a team, we had grown in confidence and skill. I finally understood how the definition of perfection related to teamwork—really just trust and respect. But more importantly, striving for perfection was to bring out the best in each other. It was a real goal. We could do no justice trying to define that elusive state individually, for each of us knew it could not be reached. But 4 inches today?

As One Nut turned back from his conversation, "Hey Mathe, Where are you going with this? What’re four inches between friends?”

"O'Shea, we always talk about achieving perfection, and you know that moment this morning really clarified something for me—you trying to be perfect and me doing the same.”

O'Shea caught Mathe's serious expression. T*hat's my boy*—he *hasn't changed a bit. That kind of thinking and flying got him here—well-done, son. It is a shame you have arrived at this state of excellence and must depart quickly. Even so, good work. You are one of us now.*

O'Shea proudly slapped Mathe's back and smiled.

"Mathe, I got it, but damn, lighten up pard. So knock that one down, and I'll buy the next."

"Almost forgot. Maybe you don't know this yet, but you've likely heard. I won't be with you and the Team for our first show. And I won't know why until I get to Washington."

"That McCready call?"

"Yep."

"Sucks. Is this some past indiscretion—who'd you piss off this time? He said with a cagey smirk."

"No, definitely not. I've been trying to figure it out. Maybe it has something to do with that unfinished story—Vietnam—but that doesn't make sense."

"You owe me the rest of that story you didn't finish, man."

I realized I couldn't wait another minute to get my story to him—maybe kill the community's rumor mill.

I called for two more and eyed-balled him.

"Ok. Well, I guess I do—the Wagon Train flight." *Yes—time to come clean.*

O'Shea smiled with a muffled burp as he flexed his shoulders in anticipation.

Egg Man Drops One

"You remember the name—"Egg Man," Commander Capo Genesi Luchesi?

One Nut gave me a blank stare and then casually said as if he could care less, “Oh ya. Go ahead. I’m all ears.”

We had briefed the flight and climbed to the flight deck to man up. I thought I caught the figure's outline from the humid black and wet steam. It appeared and then disappeared in the waves of vapor rolling in front of me. It was “Butt End,” Jolly’s striding outline, my RIO, with his helmet bag and charts ready to kill anything in sight.”

“You know him?”

He shakes his head.

“Let me back up. The mission started with the regular pre-flight routine—the brief that I have covered a thousand times—if this happens, I do this, when I feel this, I do that, you know it—second nature stuff.”

F-4 Phantom

"Yep, know it well."

"I sometimes lose myself when I am gearing up. It's my suit of armor, my lifeline to my steel beast. It's the same gear order suiting up every time. If I miss the slightest thing in mid-order, I have to start it over. The laser focus engulfs my mind and soul and never changes. It just becomes more automatic.

Of course, there are nerves, but as soon as that last buckle clicks, the canopy closes and locks, and I am buttoned down in my seat, a wave covers me, and I am at peace. I know anything can happen, and it usually does, but I am ready. I am one with this machine. I don't have to be perfect. The jet and I together have to be perfect—as one weapon, and when that happens, you know it. So why the hell am I telling you this stuff? You have been through it a thousand times."

Sensing Mathe's trepidation, One Nut piped in, "Yea, I know, Mathe. I do the same fucking thing. Maybe we all do—*so* get on with it."

"I'm not going to bore you with what transpired."

"No, Mathe, please do. Please bore me."

Mathe paused, rolled his head, and released his story.

"There were just too many disconnects that conspired to sink our success. Each one impacted and tightened its grip on our survival. I was in a box, thinking I would not make it out. I was enraged at the causes that transpired to put Jolly and me there. Just getting caught in that situation was almost too much for me to handle—I was better than that!

Crossing the coast, going feet wet, post-strike, at about 400 knots, we staged at the back of Raleigh's wake, glued together at eight hundred feet. I kissed off, grunted under the G-load, and broke hard left, dumping all to set up for the approach, with my heavy breathing adding to the excitement. We slowed, circled up, and slid to the centerline. Yes, my rage and blood pressure were on full display—so high I thought I would pop. The intensity was driven to override the fortunes of the box I had flown in for the last ninety minutes I had to get even. As if I had not done enough killing that day—but, I was not finished. Fury was about to vent."

One Nut frowned slightly and adjusted his arm on the bar top turning the glass of beer in his hand while thinking to himself. *Wow, this guy has a whole other side I knew nothing about. Didn't he miss something like what happened on the mission?*

"I crossed the ramp, and like a pile driver, we smashed onto the deck with an adrenaline-pumped vengeance trembling hand as I firewalled the throttle to military power, and the tail hook caught with a sudden forward whip of my head. No go around —no bolter today!

I wouldn't allow it to happen.

I don't remember the engine spooling up, moving the throttle back to idle, or the aircraft backing up from the arresting wire under tension.

The yellow shirt's signal to raise the tailhook finally caught my attention. After being handed off several times between yellows, I was finally spotted on the deck. My shutdown could not come fast enough."

One Nut looked at Mathe quizzically. *Hell, we do this every day* and wondered what he was covering up—maybe like the whole mission? *He is nervous—going over all the basics, for they both had done the same thing for years. So what the hell was he hiding?*

Michael "Butt End" Jolly, my back seater, was probably hotter than I was and suddenly chirped, 'Mathe, take a look to port, low over your shoulder—at the deck!'

My mouth dropped behind the oxygen mask. The ship's Skipper was there. It would be an understatement to say that I was in awe. Every man on board the ship had the most profound respect for this man. It was more than sincere deference. He was a leader and a warrior. But, there he stood beside my aircraft as I went through the post-mission shutdown—it was more than uncommon for him to meet an aircraft—post-strike. And he wasn't smiling as he looked up at me. *But, what the hell, it ain't like we're making ones bones on this mission.*

I began to sweat in a whole new way—a new kind of tension, different from the normal agitated excretion on each post-mission letdown. As I glanced at him, it was the kind of sweat that smelled of—what might come from him if he found me wanting. I did not want to let this man down.

Taking one more look over the canopy rail—holy shit. There were now three standing there—the Captain, CAG, and the Talon's boss. I caught their commanding stares looking up at me, and I tensed.

Uh, oh.

Quickly dismounting, my stomach squeezed tighter from seeing the entire complement of my world's command structure standing beside my aircraft. I expected the worst."

One Nut caught the hesitation in Mathe's voice in telling the rest of the story.

"Come on, Mathe, keep it rolling—it's getting interesting. What the fuck can you do anyway? It's over now."

Mathe knew better. This community had a long memory, and it was never over for anyone who flew. So your history followed you closely—both good and bad.

"It all started with a series of my unanswered low-state fuel calls on our TARCAP (target combat air patrol) mission. After dropping bombs on the TARCAP Alpha Strike, I joined a sister squadron pilot—Commander Capo Sal "Egg Man" Luchesi. He saw my hand signal when joining him—that my fuel state had gone bingo. But unfortunately, he would not acknowledge my calls. Our TARCAP did not need an inflight refuel pre-strike, but the MIDCAP did.

Now we're getting to it.

He had more than enough JP-5 (fuel) for his MIGCAP mission to make it back to the Raleigh. There wasn't a chance I'd make it home when I joined him with a low-state fuel situation. So it didn't make sense for me to chase MiGs with him—if it came to that. I don't know what he thought when we got the call for the MIGCAP mission. Hell, I was carrying MERS and TERS. You remember O'Shea, multiple and triple ejector racks with bombs, a centerline tank, four sparrows, and four sidewinders. He proceeded to head west as I went to parade on him with another hand signal at around 2.3 (2,300lbs). He then accepted a vector from Red Crown to turn toward Hanoi to intercept MiGs coming out of Kèp before they got to our bombers. Egg Man promptly turned West for the MiG intercept—coming at us, nose on.

One more check of my fuel state told me I was in serious shit. It was the final straw after Egg Man had disregarded my requests for fuel and to leave the flight several times. I had even refused the tanker to complete our run.

As soon as commander "Egg Man" Luchesei reefed his jet North, he called for a mini burner to remove the smoke trail. What the fuck was he doing? I called bullshit. Pushing the throttles to full military power, I threw the stick against my thigh, wrapping the jet up in a 4-g buffeted turn, and creased his windscreen on my 180 hard turn egress due east. The commander snapped.

As my irritation increased, we exchanged words I won't mention now. "Egg Man" kept muttering, "We're here to kill MiGs. Get your ass back. Where the hell are you going?" I didn't respond after that. He ignored everyone around him except the controller.

With 2.1 (2,100 lbs) left in the tank, my concern rose about getting "Butt End" and myself back to the boat. Even so, it could not exceed my rage in this situation—hardly enough JP-5 for the return."

One Nut continued to probe Mathe for answers.

"So, he is nagging you to join him again—knows your status and continues to disregard your fuel state? Are you kidding me, Mathe? I'd be pissed, too! What the hell did you say to him,"

"Well, ok, I said I'd fly with him but would not die for him—and of course, some other expletives were thrown in for good measure. I had used them in a prior run-in with a certain Lieutenant Colonel. But I'd rather not talk about that. There was no way in hell I was allowing him to lead me into that mash-up—just plain stupid."

"You didn't think about going to squadron discreet for a little unofficial discussion?"

"Nope."

This guy has some stones—a set of brass ones. Ain't no quit in this guy, O'Shea thought.

Egg Man kept commanding me to rejoin him, and I gave him an earful on each request. I had enough."

"Yep—I guess I was raging. Not proud of that! After several rowdy multiple SAM attacks and AAA on the way out, "Butt End" and I approached the mouth of the Haiphong with my gauges reading beyond bingo—out of gas!

I made another call for a tanker, any tanker at this point. Finally, a familiar voice heard my distress call and asked about my fuel status. He was driving an A-4, within range, with a fuel cell—thank God.

'Mathe. I got you,' he called—'coming down hard, angels 18. What's your state.'

"1.3," I responded.

"Talk about pucker. Mine had eaten half the seat. I was in it deep. Dago's call back gave me that little bit of hope, though. Maybe we could make it back.

I recognized the voice—our nugget aviator—Ensign Ken "Dago" Evangelista, from our sister squadron on board the Raleigh. I thought he shouldn't be allowed to fly in this airspace with his reputation. But at this point, I didn't care. He was the gas man, and I needed gas. The last time I saw him was not pretty. A vision of him barely hanging onto the O Club bar back in Hawaii flashed before me—slightly conscious from being over-served. Junior said it was some wine from the old country called "Fortissimo."

The posse had finally arrived. 'Hold your heading and altitude steady—Casino 106, this will be close and tight.'

"I caught his jet's shadow over my canopy and then disappear below the nose of our F-4 and suddenly reappeared, from below again, 100 yards right in front of my trail position—with his buddy store fuel drogue coming out. With an intense desire for survival, I drove straight into his dancing drogue chute, and he offloaded 5.6 (5,600 lbs) into my tanks. It wasn't like trying to stick a wet noodle up a cat's ass or taking a running fuck at a rolling donut. Not this time!

"Butt End" and I were going crazy—between relief and bouts of angry rage at our flight lead. I wanted a piece of him with a vengeance, and I am sure Mike felt the same way. Dago's flying skill that day saved our butts with more than enough fuel.

Now we knew we could make it back to the Raleigh. But my anger found its way into my ability to fly the jet as Mike's concern rose over my agitated, erratic air work.

'You OK, Mathe?'

'Sorry, Mike, we're good,' trying to control my irritation with the bind Egg Man had put us in. But, of course, I was mad as hell. Then I heard what I recognized as a familiar voice from the ship, requesting our status.

Was that Captain Sanderson haling me over this channel? Highly irregular, I thought. It was more than humbling but frightening to hear the Captain's voice. He was a true father figure to the whole crew and me onboard the Raleigh. I immediately calmed down. He had been monitoring and hearing it all. Even so, it only slightly countered the payback I wanted to level at Egg Man."

'What's your fuel state, Captain?'

"He sensed my mental state and more—as only a ship's Captain could."

'Three-point two, sir.'

"And then came the fatherly words I needed to hear."

'Come On Home, Son!'

"We trapped, and Mike and I stepped down from the aircraft and faced our futures—three senior officers.

Captain Sanderson stepped forward and told me I was restricted to quarters and to not come out until I heard from him. Uh oh, what's coming next, I thought.

It was getting to bother me. I surmised that the Captain had picked up my extreme and heated comments while we were in the air and wasn't sure that I wouldn't shoot, kick his ass, or throw Egg Man off the flight deck into the ocean—actions I firmly considered even with Egg Man's rank.

I assumed the GAG knew my flashpoint was high and didn't want anything to happen to the commander when he returned from the mission. It rang like my discussion with Admiral McCready after Lieutenant Colonel McVey came aboard—after the Talon's first kill and my save of Finn.

You know the rest of the story—Commander Egg Man just disappeared."

O'Shea had heard that he had gone invisible from the ship. He was not seen again on board the Raleigh—which only added to the intrigue of Mathe's story. Transferred, demoted, de-winged or worse—no one knew.

O'Shea requested another round from Trader Jon and belched. "Mathe, funny you should mention he just disappeared. Do you know where he turned up?"

"Not a clue, but enough is enough of that pud knocker for a while—a real prick, even with all his distinguished battle ribbons."

"Well, you won't ever see him again—he might not be on this planet."

"What do you mean?"

"Even with his stellar career combat record, he was off the radar for some time and then showed up in Pensacola awaiting re-assignment sometime later. So command temporarily stashed his ass until someone could decide what to do with him. He also transitioned as you did to jets from your old rotor community; from what I hear, it was a rough reorientation for him. You might have heard stories about him from your CH - 46 buddies.

The story goes that he had a penchant for flying Hueys out into the desert grasslands to search for and run down rabbits for sport. He would chase those cute frightened bunnies into exhaustion, and when they could run no more, panting in exhaustion, he would slowly, delicately set the chopper's skid down and crush the little fellas—one perverse son of bitch—real sick."

Mathe stared across the bar in amazement, "Wow—never heard that one before."

"Picture this. Soon after arriving in Pensacola, he found his match. Apparently, he got a little liquored up one afternoon and tried to beat the P'cola Bayou Chico Drawbridge. He made it up the rising side but did not make it over—it wasn't a pretty scene. All I know is the commander was in the hospital for a long time. Yep, a one-way ride—bada bing. So, let's go eat some pasta, pal."

Mathe smiled at O'Shea, thinking Egg Man *should be sleeping with the fish.* Then, as he tried not to snicker, he whispered, "Yep, crazier than a hornet in a beer glass."

Mathe took another gulp of beer and looked down the bar with a smirk as if to say, Egg Man and, for that matter, McVey too—*see ya.* Upon leaving, he caught O'Shea closing in on a blond with an impressive rack.

Returning to the BOQ, I packed and did as all good navy men—OBEY. But, I couldn't help thinking about this suddenly lost opportunity to fly with the Blues—the retraining to get up to speed, confidence building from weeks of practice, taking the criticism, and flying the demo as close to precision as possible. I was getting comfortable as focus and trust locked on—synched as a team, then poof—I was gone in a moment—and for what reason!

I had no idea, but it was then off to Washington to see the admiral—for what? As thoughts turned to my TEAM, I yearned to be strapping on my jet for the first show. But, as I buckled up as a passenger earlier, counsel suddenly popped into my head, and I quietly released the words, "Learn the rules and then break them." This sucks!

Fifteen

Lost Souls

PENTAGON – NINETEEN SEVENTY-THREE

One's destination is never a place but rather a new way of looking at things.

I entered the Pentagon lobby and was immediately struck by the Hall of Heroes' presentation. It honored Medal of Honor winners from wars past and those missing in action. It was a powerful reminder of this country's valor and human sacrifice, and I immediately thought of my dad. Was he here?

Told to meet Admiral McCready's aid in the open hallway, I only knew to expect a woman.

"Are you Captain Stone?"

Turning from the names on the wall, a beautiful young female greeted me. You would have thought I had popped out of thin air from her expression. She was a striking blond, maybe in her late twenties/early thirties, with blue-green eyes and a cordial smile.

Her friendly welcoming prompted thoughts of how people seemed to treat me differently after I rescued Finn. And I liked it—I liked it a lot! This new acceptance status driven by the recognition of my actions that day in Vietnam was a good and wholly unique experience for me—in a very tight community.

"Yes, yes!"

I stuttered as she caught me off guard and nodded toward the wall in front of us. "This wall takes your breath away. I was looking for a friend of mine."

"I agree. I never walk by it without being in awe—a hallowed place for sure."

"My name is Evelyn. I will take you to Admiral McCready's office. Do you need another minute to find your acquaintance?" *How did she sense that, I* wondered.

"No, that won't be necessary. I'll probably look for him, *my father,* another time. The Admiral will likely want to move his day forward anyway." We both glanced at the names, and then with a nod and a smile, we went off to who knows where in the building's labyrinth of hallways and offices.

My credentials were reviewed repeatedly as we passed through endless checkpoints. Finally, my appointment was confirmed. What was up with this seeming hyper-security? Something I should know about? A warning of what I was getting into? In my dress service khaki uniform with a tie, I got some strange looks from time to time as she led me toward the admiral's office. What was this about?

Did they know of my mission with Finn, my new medal, or was my lunch stuck to my teeth? Probably all new guys get this treatment. If she knew something, there was no point in asking. I'm sure she wouldn't say—so we discussed the weather, baseball, and how many miles she walked each day.

I had entered the complex from the River Entrance. Finding our way to McCready's office via the stairs, I was struck immediately by marble steps grooved from the footsteps of all those who had preceded me—footsteps of those men and women from the past that had changed the course of war and history for our nation. It was a gotcha moment that I will never forget—an impressive place. We passed a line of offices with the inscribed titles, Secretary of Defense, Secretary of the Navy, and many more—rarified air for sure.

Passing these offices didn't slow her down—she motored along at a fast clip. It was an understatement to say I was humbled and excited to be in the presence of those who wielded so much power and responsibility.

The MacArthur Corridor, with the memorabilia of so many greats, caught my attention. For some reason, the illustration of General MacArthur with his corncob pipe made him seem very real. I shivered at the magnificence and imposing appearance of this hallway of past heroes. My "Blues" attachment suddenly took on a patina as its luster began to fade with the scope of this place. *What did Admiral McCready have in store for me—how could just another pointy-end driver help him?*

The one hundred and sixty yards of warfighter office space followed—those actively making policies, creating missions, and driving the military show spread before me in partially enclosed cubicles.

I followed Evelyn into the admiral's office just off the wing of war fighter cubicles and thanked her for getting me there. I would never have found it myself!

After raising a finger indicating for me to wait, she pushed the paneled entrance slightly open and announced my arrival. She offered her hand and said, "It is a pleasure to have met you, Captain Stone." Taking her hand and thanking her, I bid that lovely lady goodbye as I watched her disappear into this enormous building. McCready's aide led me into his office without facial expression, all business. *OK then, here we go.*

McCready paused and rose behind his desk as he slowly eyeballed Mathew's approach. Then, thinking of all the other Blue Angel pilots he had known—he remembered the line, 'Gentlemen, it's not you the public is interested in—it's the blue flight suit'

But I knew they were wrong in Mathew's case. His persona would be the draw—as much as his Marine uniform. His character would give him a chance to prove himself. His courageous actions and selfless devotion to a shipmate were more than deserving of the accolades he had recently received. *He is the one who shines as bright as a new penny—tight, trained, and ready—not a single wrinkle in his Khakis.* Trying to suppress my smile—*yes, I'm sure McVey hates how he shines.*

I noted Mathew's youthful seriousness in his salute and demeanor—but with a merry glint in his eyes. A unique officer for a Marine, for most others wore masks to protect and hide their insecurities, but Mathew was fully open at just the right moments. He was authentic and would go far because of it.

It seems this young man could survive most anything—his childhood, extreme competition, war with all its pain, and come out the other end ready for more—a professional survivor? But for this assignment, he would have to be tougher than a two-dollar Texas steak. He needs to succeed in the task he's about to be given.

"Welcome aboard, Mathew. I hope your trip went well."

"Thank you, sir. Yes, it did," I said. I faced the Admiral and saluted.

"By the way, did you meet Evelyn, Captain? It's a long way from the entrance, but I assume she kept you entertained. She's not married, you know. Although, who knows why—sharp as a tack, too."

"Yes, sir, I imagine so. But, of course she's a baseball fan, too—loves the Dodgers. But, sir, I'm not looking anymore. I found mine."

"Well, glad to hear that. She must be amazing."

"Yes, sir, she is."

"Have you asked her yet?"

"Asked her what, sir?"

McCready quizzically glanced at me—like I was the dumbest person on the planet—and it dawned on me.

"Oh, no, sir, not yet."

"Well, Mathew, you can't let the good ones get away in my book."

"You've never been married, sir, if I may ask?"

"No, sadly not, Mathew. A broken heart, though."

After a short pause, "I am sorry that we had to take you away from what I am sure was your calling. But, Mathew, being selected for the Angels places you at the top of your profession as a naval aviator. Your profile is quite impressive—rather exemplary across the board."

Mathe suddenly took the face of cloaked humility and smiled.

"Thank you, sir. It is good to see you again."

"But we didn't bring you here to discuss your career profile because it will not come into play on your next assignment. So let's move into my inner office to discuss this."

"Take a seat, Captain. You must be somewhat bewildered as to why you were ordered to meet me today and, more importantly, perhaps why we pulled you out of the Blues—just as your season was starting and your team had become so wired."

My mind whirled with scenarios as I answered, "Well, yes, I am a little confused, sir."

McCready briefly stared at Stone—sizing him up again. Then, with steel eyes, he questioned whether Mathew could handle what he was about to tell him. He knew Mathew always seemed to put himself in challenging situations, which he had not been trained for because he innately knew it was the right thing to do. To top it off, he was truthful, loyal, self-disciplined, and had a good balance between competence and humility. Even though lacking a tad of patience—but was frank.

"I have some new orders for you. The timing couldn't be worse, interrupting your last assignment with the Team, but this is critical. I want you to work for me in the secret service of your country."

"Sir, I'm—I'm not CIA material or whatever. You don't know about my complete past, certainly not everything about me."

McCready leaned across his desk, and I picked up a fatherly look with a bit of prideful sternness and suddenly realized—he did. I was speechless.

"Mathew, you're an intelligent officer, and we both have a very personal stake in completing this assignment—above and beyond our government's motives. Your talents and skills have not gone unnoticed.

So, we have decided to bring you in on a mission of grave national importance. It's not a mission anyone can take lightly, and there is no room for error. But we know you have the ingredients to become successful in this endeavor. So, my only question is: Are you up to the task?"

"I could answer that honestly, sir, if I knew what this is about."

"Do you remember LT Chi Dung Thai from flight school?

My jaw slackened as I warily eyeballed the admiral and launched into the little I could remember about my old friend Chi.

"Ah, yes sir—nice guy, quiet. I believe he was in the Vietnamese Air Force and cross-trained by us. Never could get him to loosen up much—very tight."

"Yes, that's him. Chi completed his flight training with us and eventually flew for the Vietnamese as a combat pilot. We kept track of him. It has been reported that he is suspected to be a communist agent."

"Chi? Are you sure? I could hardly get him to have a beer with us. Really, sir? You mean a spy?"

"Well, for the lack of a better term, yes. But, I suppose you're wondering what this has to do with you."

"Yes, sir. I certainly am."

"We want you to find him, Captain. We think he is in trouble as he recently requested asylum in the US. Your orders are to locate him, learn about his contacts, and, if possible, why he wants sanctuary."

"Yes, sir, I'm glad to help if I can, but I still don't understand—why me?"

"There is much more to this mission, Mathew, that I will explain. But, how you fit into the equation should be clear when I'm done."

I was astonished at McCready's unfolding story as he described Chi's transgressions and suspected treason against our country as a foreign agent.

The information about Chi's past did not match what I knew about him—which wasn't much.

"Stay right there, Captain."

Suddenly, the Admiral rose, walked to the corner of his office, and switched on the television.

"Before we continue, Captain, I think you'll be interested in watching this—something we all have been waiting for—Operation Homecoming. You might even recognize some of your shipmates. We have close to six hundred American prisoners of war returning from Vietnam today."

Mathe stared at the TV in thankful wonder. The moment's excitement was palatable, and he couldn't help but think of my dad. He had never come home. Yet, even though his body had never been recovered from that long-ago war, he could not quiet thoughts of dad as he watched the soldiers and sailors returning from captivity. He knew the Talon's were eating this up—probably a big celebration back in the ready room on the Raleigh. They were most certainly watching this homecoming, cheering and searching for familiar faces.

After departing the Hanoi Taxi bird, each man saluted—some in pretty rough shape, but most grinning from ear to ear, with militarized relief. But I knew each of my old squadron mate's cheers would not dampen the feeling that the war wasn't over. They were still fighting and dying, and there was no natural closure at this joyful moment—not yet, anyway. So maybe this day signaled a light at the end of this long dark burrow.

McCready glanced over at Mathew's enjoyment of the homecoming, which brought back memories of his time as a JO (junior officer) on my first cruise onboard the Saratoga (CV-3) many years earlier.

Yes, my exploits and high jinks were not much different than Mathew's "Cocks On Top" gang of JOs on the Raleigh. But, of course, I knew the "Cocks" story—those did their best to hide their shipboard adventures but were always discovered.

I had witnessed the "Wings Night" on board the Raleigh. The inter-squadron challenge was determining which flyer could eat 75 chicken wings in the shortest time. The betting pool usually grew beyond all the aviators' pay grades. Nevertheless, the skipper of the Raleigh accepted their high jinks as a viable way to beat their operational monotony—a mini moral force multiplier. Their working grind could easily allow complacency to slide in if not for such activities. After all, it was an accepted activity in the growth and stability of a naval aviator—just one of the many. Who would have thought these childish challenges—

to see who could eat the most wings in the shortest time or snickers bars in an hour—would have a morale payoff?

As I switched off the TV and returned to my desk, I moved deeper into Chi Dung's contacts and relationships. Then looking up from the file, I once again stared at Mathew. *Who could be ready for this? I hope he can handle it.*

"Chi has given us information that will turn your world upside down. But, unfortunately, it is not information that has been confirmed, and that is where you step in, Mathew."

Mathe knew something was up, and his posture stiffened as he caught the admiral's shift in his seat with a facial expression change. *How could there be more? Chi, not a nice guy? No way!*

"Captain, this will be tough, so get as comfortable as possible while I explain. Tell me, Mathew, what do you know about your father's time in the military?"

Where is this coming from? "Yes, sir, well, as you know, he was shot down in the Pacific during WWII and was classified as MIA. Presumed dead, I guess. There was no word of him after that."

"How did your mother take the loss?"

"She held it in and never really discussed it—at least with me. She was a sad, lonely woman for most of her life."

McCready looked down at his hands and then at Mathe.

"I'm sorry, Mathew, very sorry."

"Thank you, sir. I am too."

McCready snapped back to his military demeanor and continued.

"Mathew, we have uncovered information that led to your mission's second part. We are still compiling intel, and you will be briefed when the time comes."

I squirmed in my seat. *WTF, I can't deal with this. I should be driving an A-4 right now, getting my ass put through the wringer with the Team. How do I get myself out of this mess?*

McCready was rearranging a few papers on his desk, looking for the file he seemed not to know he held—distracted and grappling with other thoughts.

"I was only recently briefed on this situation, and I have to say the possibility that an American from a prior war might be alive blew me out of the water, Mathew. Over the years since WWII, there have been sightings of men presumed to be lost or dead in China, Japan, and Korea. Some stayed by their own choice—some so lost they did not know where home was. Others are still there, making lives for themselves any way they can—good or bad. Several have been on our radar for reasons I can't go into, but you can probably figure that out. It would be best to remember that what I am about to tell you is not substantiated. So we may be adding two plus two and come up with five."

McCready hesitated, looking uncomfortable, almost tongue-tied, but moved slowly forward.

"Mathew, another individual besides Chi, is of particular interest—not just to the US but on a more personal level. Let me explain the specifics of these sightings. We have a few images and information from locals—as they say—that have been consistent over the years—specifically, a Caucasian in his late 50s with some suspect behavior. Even with the passage of time and poor photo imagery references, this individual could be our man.

These consistent sightings of this male have surfaced again—the American, we think. The unsubstantiated rumor is that this American had been imprisoned for some unknown reason by several governmental agencies of various countries for years. This individual seems to be still alive as of the last six weeks. We think he was a military officer. His specific location is not precise, but we are working on that. "

"An American, sir? An officer? Is there any chance, sir? Do you think it could be? There must be so many other possibilities."

With a pained expression, the Admiral got up and, in reflection, walked to the window, trying to collect himself.

"We are not sure, Mathew, but the descriptions match—even with time."

Then, with a gulp, Mathe's stomach tightened as he tried to steady himself in his chair—a total loss for words. The admiral also stirred quietly, uncomfortably, at his desk. He knew all the incredible things Mathew had done in his youth—and in the navy—activities and performance beyond most his age. All this drive to succeed came from somewhere. Could it be that Mathew is trying to answer the age-old question of whether he is worthy of his father's love? McCready's unease was driven by Admiral Gillespie's caution about alluding to the American's identity in any way, shape, or form—and something else.

Even with the evidence pointing to Stone's possible existence, McCready's soul could not shake the other half of the secret he carried about Mathe's father. His feelings about his government's in-action were more profound than he wanted to admit. He sat back down, looking at Mathew's shocked, confused face.

"Again, Captain, we don't know for sure, but there is a chance. These sightings have been ongoing for many years, ever since WWII. This individual has been seen in China, Korea, and Vietnam."

Mathe perked up again with expectant thoughts of his father.

"Are you sure, sir? How do you know about his whereabouts?"

"From Chi Mathew! And here's the clincher. Chi tells us your father is alive and well and living as a farmer."

"Chi? No, sir, how can this be after all these years?"

"Mathew, all we know is that he is an American, possibly a soldier from WWII. The following documentation will help you understand the nature of these sightings. But unfortunately, Chi might be too compromised to tell us the truth.

"How, where, sir? Sorry, sir. I am, I don't know—blown away."

"You have a right to be, and I hope this is true—that it is him, but as I said, this information is unconfirmed. So Chi may be using this information to forward his asylum quest—making it all up."

Suddenly McCready was called away with Evelyn's announcement that SECDEF requested his presence in his office immediately.

"Captain, stay. We will continue this discussion when I return."

Mathe sat motionless in shock and irritation.

Why would Chi lie? He needs help. Maybe this stuff about my dad is his ticket out. But maybe McCready's right. My dad? Holy shit! He wouldn't have anything to do with Chi. How could he? Coincidence? It has to be just a weird timing thing. Ok, but how does he even think it is my dad, beyond Chi's word, and how is he involved?

The quiet in the office was as startling as his thoughts—hope, sadness, remembrance, and outright irritation at McCready's announcement.

Mathe eyed the office walls, trying to get a grip. On top of this disclosure, he was still having difficulty reconciling his lost Blues slot when he was so close to full acceptance. But he realized that he could only control so much.

He sat, stared into his coffee mug, and then rubbernecked the history lesson around him. He shook his head. Then, while blankly admiring the admiral's career displayed in mementos and art on his desk and walls, his eyes caught the hollowed scene outside the west wing office window behind McCready's desk. What a view!

The Pentagon shadowed a spectacular scene of Arlington Cemetery's rolling hills in the distance—row upon row of those that had given so much. It both calmed and saddened him. Suddenly the admiral returned with an aggressive and agitated demeanor— catching Mathe totally off guard.

McCready didn't seem to notice Mathew, utterly devoid of affect—staring off at the beauty and sadness at the scene outside his office window.

"Mathew, there are some matters I must address, so we will continue our meeting tomorrow morning."

"Yes, sir. What time will that be, sir?"

He gathered papers from the top of his desk and looked surprised by my question.

"Evelyn will inform you, Captain." And that was that. He just left, hurrying to his next meeting.

On the way to his meeting, McCready considered his protégé's bare-knuckled approach, concerned about how it might not work for him inside the Pentagon. But in the field, he suspected his style would be successful—a perfect fit or maybe something else—a chance he was willing to take.

Like many other young men today, he is not so soft, self-righteous, or indulgent. Shirking duty was not in his lexicon. He had paid the price that comes with the service of one's country. Most of his civilian cohorts had undamaged hearts by the loss of friendships. Mathew was different because he had already passed the battle test and survived. This last news I gave him should provide enough spur for him in this assignment.

Sixteen

Playing At Not Playing The Game

SEVERAL WEEKS LATER

They are playing a game, and
They are playing at not playing a game,
If I see they are playing a game,
I will break the rules, and they will punish me,
I must play their game,
not letting them see that, I see the game.

I made my way back to my assigned cubicle with little interruption after another eye-opening meeting with the admiral. In silence, I contemplated my first Pentagon meeting with McCready.

Come on! Call it like it is, admiral—those signals are accurate. It's my Dad!

Working thru the "American's" file, my thoughts wandered back to an incident Finn mentioned early in his flying career. That episode brought up the same feelings I felt after meeting with McCready and my short time working in the "Squirrel Cage." Years ago, Finn described one of his instructors as nervous, with sporadic intensity and agitation. It left Finn almost as unsure of his ability to fly the jet as I now felt about myself.

And I found many with the same nervous unspoken character and behavioral traits working in the Pentagon—the "Squirrel Cage." Maybe they nicknamed it the "Squirrel Cage" or "Fort Fumble" for a reason—

everyone scurrying around gathering nuts. But, most of the time, it left me confused and at a loss for words.

I knew jet flying was essentially an ego-driven, black-and-white vigilant decision-making environment. Unspoken human emotional cues didn't dominate cockpit decision-making. Finn had told me that his naval flight instructor's behavior was not helping him move forward in the program. But, I also knew that Finn hadn't been exposed to many navy instructors, only Marines through the training command.

When Finn received a flight down for failure to meet training syllabus flight standards—a transgression of little consequence in his mind, it made him even more suspicious of his instructor. He then decided to let a Marine, who he trusted, determine his future career on the recheck ride rather than his navy instructor—he wasn't sure he respected or trusted.

I knew both of us initially had enlisted in the Platoon Leaders Class Aviation, instant E5s but that Finn was discharged from the program because of an injury. He then rejoined the navy as an Aviation Officer Candidate. Subsequently, Finn was assigned Marine flight instructors as an ensign because of his past—just fine with him.

So, for the recheck, as an ensign, he asked to take the check ride with a Marine instructor of higher rank than his naval instructor, giving him the down. Finn knew Marines had a rep for straight talk, and he had felt they would be straight with him. He had decided to take the dice roll and let the chips fall where they may—a simple trust factor that might ensure he got a fair check ride evaluation and send a very implicit message, he hoped, to his assigned naval flight instructor.

He felt no middle ground or a gray area with a Marine instructor. There were only missions, objectives, and facts—a straight talk he could take—so he let the Marine decide his future military flying career—whether a final up or down.

In the "Squirrel Cage," I always searched for the truths and the motives for many decisions. There were questions that were always front and center in my mind but never seemed to get answered. Instead, it appeared most spent more time enforcing policy and etiquette than challenging definitions. This behavior reinforced my feelings of not trusting the environment. Moreover, the acrimonious-ladened speak and heavy-handed rank structure overlaid with gray strengthened my distrust.

Was it head games, or were some just slow-witted bigwigs? Or maybe years in this place had taken a toll or numbed them somehow.

They had all passed big tests to be here, so I guess I'll find the best in each and move forward despite all the cross-currents. But maybe it's just my old control thing rearing its ugly head. It hasn't helped me much in the past. So head down, do the work—I constantly reminded myself! But why am I here—to read files and go to meetings?

The navy's challenges, at times, often overwhelmed. But, Admiral McCready had pulled the rug right out from under me.

Somewhere along the line, the Admiral had moved beyond a senior officer of unquestioned authority to more than just an overseer of career—whether I wanted it or not. His influence was pervasive, and now it burdened me somewhat. I realized I was not calling the shots on my future—maybe never had, and it left me with deep insecurity—I wouldn't say I liked it.

With the sightings of "The American," had mom known something and not told me? But, on the other hand, she might not have been told. So the importance of finding Chi might be receding for me even though he was the center of attention in this assignment.

How could my Dad be alive after thirty years? Yet, secretly, I held onto that hope—that he was real and not a ghost. Mom wouldn't talk about him—her pain of his loss forced her into the bottle. They said it was an accident—her car slid off the road and rammed a tree. I will never really know.

So, I again concentrated on the files in front of me—years of pictures, maps, reports, communications, opinions, recommendations—years of information. All of it is referred to as "intelligence."

So I am now in the game I have heard about so often? I guess I have to play their game, not seeing that I see their game.

— · —

Again, my mind drifted off to the past, seeking solace from all the questions I couldn't answer. Then, finally, I returned home to the day I buried mom—in her house on emergency leave from Raleigh after her death.

I remembered being on the living room floor with my parent's life in pictures and mementos. I was staring at the images of their life together—things I had never seen. Had Rusty not come to me, I realized I wouldn't have made it through those four days. She had been way past just a friend for some time, and I was surprised she appeared, out of concern, when she heard I was back from the war for a short time.

Rusty had helped me think through things—get my head on straight. It pained me to see my parent's love for each other, all their good times, all the laughter. But Rusty had found a way to soften the pain of my losses. She had seen the look in my eyes when I discovered dad's medals—never mentioned to me by mom. She had been my comfort, which helped me to let that awful stuff go that night.

And then, after four days of emotional drama and painful remembrance, I found myself lying in bed with open eyes in the early morning of my departure back to Raleigh and the war.

It was not like the first night alone at home when I caught myself looking in the mirror—kind of not remembering who I was. *Could I have lost so much weight—no!* It was very early—still dark outside and so quiet. I had been preparing myself mentally to return.

My ceiling had been the underside of the flight deck, right above my bunk on the Raleigh. And it was coming again. I recalled the smell of the flight deck's hot, spewing, stinky, greasy steam and constant noise. Memories of jets going into burner and their thunderous clawing for the sky for survival—just in case they didn't catch a wire or if they did, their bucking and swerving on the cable after the catch—wanting to run forever into the sky again—just above my bunk room.

I heard the aircraft tie-down chains dragging across the deck in my mind, the bang of touchdowns above, and the catapults smashing to their water stops. In a way, it was more like home than my mom's tranquil house had been.

The quiet had been unfamiliar and had given me too much time to think—for the anxiety and the terror-filled moments I could not calm. I had killed people, and my shipmates had died in horrible ways. Yet, I still saw their faces in my dreams and desperately sought a way to set them aside—to find peace with all of it, even McVey.

The mission into Vietnam to save Finn had brought good things to me. I knew I had done the right thing and was recognized for it. But, with that always came the constant anxiety of that day. It clawed at me continually and ripped out of me in unexpected moments. That last night home had been no different. I had fought to expel my nightmares. But unfortunately, they still robbed me of much-needed sleep.

I remembered the siren in the night that passed by outside and brought me back to the present. I pushed the turmoil of my crumpled sweat-soaked sheets to the side of the bed and remembered McCready's words, 'Chi had told me that my dad was alive and might be a duck farmer.'

Chi said, 'Believe it or not, it was reported that he sells his ducks to those that could afford them in China. So we suspect he picks up bits of information the communists are interested in and passes it to Chi. But, of course, this is uncorroborated.'

Could the American possibly be my dad? It's so impossible—so improbable. But what if it's true? How do I handle that? Why didn't he come home? Dad told mom he would never leave her and promised to return after the war. He loved mom so much—I saw it in their faces—it was in front of me in their album pictures. It just doesn't add up.

— · —

It had been a day, and I was glad to leave the work behind. A severe and no-nonsense aide gives me a lift back to my hotel in DC. I am antsy and can't sit still, so I decide to take myself out for dinner to find something that feels normal. I saw nothing fancy—a little Italian restaurant on one of my runs. It is busy this evening, and there's a wait to get in. So I give them my name and head across the street to sit in the last of the sun.

It's a beautiful evening, all golden, with a soft breeze. As I sit thinking about all the crazy stuff I heard today, I see a little old lady with shopping bags over each arm and a cane in one hand. She's just trying to cross the street, and no one will let her cross. So I get up, stopping traffic on my way to her.

"Can I help you, ma'am?"

"Oh. Young man, how nice of you. I feel like I might be here forever."

"No problem, ma'am. Give me your bags and take my arm across the street, ok?"

"Yes, that bench over there looks pretty good about now."

So off we go. I hold up my hand to stop traffic again. We finally reach the other side, and she sits down with a big sigh, ensuring she has her purse.

"That was very kind of you, young man. Thank you."

"No problem, ma'am, glad to help. Are you alright?"

"Yes, I'm fine. It just takes me longer to do things these days."

She is 4'11" tall with beautiful clear blue eyes and silver-white hair with wire-rim glasses, a bit crooked on her nose…very grandma-like. A stiff wind would blow her away.

She looks me up and down. "You look like a navy man?"

"Well, yes, ma'am, I am."

"My husband was too, but he's been gone for a long time now."

"I'm sorry. How'd you lose him, ma'am, if I may ask?"

"Pearl Harbor. He was on the Arizona. We had only been married for six months when that awful business started. He was wonderful, fun, smart, and a terrific dancer." She winks at me.

"He loved this country and wanted to serve even if it meant leaving me. So off he went. It was the right thing to do, and we both knew it. Life brings us lots of challenges. So many of them, but we do the best we can. Don't you agree?"

The days' anger and confusion just drained away. This little bird of a woman calmed me right down and helped me see thru the clutter.

That's all I can do, just the best with whatever they throw at me.

"Yes, ma'am, you are one hundred percent right. I needed to hear that."

She smiles, pats my hand, and looks down the street.

"Oh, I see my bus coming. Would you mind walking me just down there?"

"Not at all. It would be my pleasure. And ma'am, Thank you."

"Oh no, thank you, young man."

We made our way to the bus stop, and I handed her over to the driver. She slowly turns and blows me a kiss. *That's all I can do, just the best with whatever they throw at me, reverberated again.*

Mick Jagger was right. 'You can't always get what you want. But, if you try some time you'll find you get what you need.'

Seventeen

MIA

SHORT TIME LATER

Mathe had worked late many nights pouring over the trail of both Chi and the Americans' sightings, looking for hope and the truth. He had to be prepared for the briefs and whatever McCready might ask.

He found his way back through the maze of offices and floors of the Pentagon to the Admiral's lair. It became second nature—taking seconds off each trip's time. It was probably still not as fast as with Evelyn, though. Entering his office one more time, he thought, maybe today's the day?

"Captain, good to see you this morning. This has been a long haul for you—an emotional roller coaster. It would be best if we both had all the answers. But, unfortunately, today's brief has been rescheduled, so I want to continue our discussion—about your rescue of Lieutenant Finley.

I also want to clarify the many questions you will ask about your dad and tell you about his disappearance on his last mission—a long time ago—back in nineteen forty-four.

But first—I'm wondering, did you ever question why your run-in with a certain Marine Lieutenant Colonel—on two occasions, resulted in what must have seemed like a free pass? Yet, you stayed on track, maintaining your Marine Naval Aviator status when it could have been flushed down the drain."

Suddenly, Admiral McCready's voice brought Mathe back from his vision of McVey's self-importance—etched in his memory. He bristled at the name and tried to quiet the inferno within—his dislike of the Colonel, but was intrigued and very curious about the Admiral's question.

"Ah—well, yes, sir. I never understood the whole thing—why I wasn't called out—not that I wasn't relieved, sir."

McCready caught Mathe's look and his clenched fists at the mention of McVey. He hesitated—waiting for more. He knew McVey was a highly decorated Marine aviator with serious leadership flaws. Nevertheless, his exemplary combat record was the primary reason for his survival in the Corps.

And then the naval expression "Diode" crept into McCready's mind concerning McVey. Yes, he fit the description of a pompous quasi-officer that had little regard for the opinions of others—his team, an officer who conducts his current in one direction and has high resistance to any other input.

"Mathew, one letter of insubordination in your jacket from one said Lieutenant Colonel with a resultant transfer, and then the theft of one Marine helicopter from the same squadron—the same Colonel's squadron—almost sent you packing."

"At the time, sir, I felt my actions were appropriate even though somewhat unconventional. And, yes, sir, they ran against protocols."

"Well, from what I gathered, you stomped all over Lieutenant Colonel McVey first and then indirectly a second time. I knew about McVey's behavior and decision-making, but your emotional reaction to him has no place in our world."

“I interceded on your behalf with Colonel McVey the first time and told him that someone at a higher level was watching your career. And the second time—well, you know.”

“That explains a lot, sir, but who and why me? Not that I’m ungrateful!”

McCready paused and smiled at him. Mathe caught the admiral’s drift and immediately turned his face away, embarrassed that he had not picked up on McCready’s sponsorship and support earlier.

“Sir, thank you, I don’t know what to say.”

Even though you're a gifted pilot and fiercely competitive, you’re not yet a “hot runner, McCready thought.

“But *s*on, I cannot go through this again with you—pulling strings a third time.”

“Sir, in my defense...”

McCready cut him off like a young pup being swatted by the litter bitch.

"Let's dispense with the bull, Captain. Instead, you might consider this assignment's new visibility and the behaviors you will need to survive in this environment. Your past behaviors cannot be repeated. Your career, so far, is impressive, but you, Mathew, are volatile. It is imperative now for both of us that you succeed. You are now a reflection of me in these halls. A slip-up in this environment can cause wars to start, and a screw-up by you is not an option.”

“I understand, sir. I am much more aware of the consequences now.”

“Do you remember the counsel Finn’s dad gave you several years back?”

“Well, he told us a lot, sir, stories, advice—but he never told us what to do.”

"Let me remind you. I understand you and Lieutenant Finley committed to leading an officer's life, not letting sloppiness slip in—right?"

"Yes, sir."

"Do you remember him telling you to let go of the past—that it will only mess up your future? I stayed in touch with your mom, so I know."

Really? Amazing! I had no idea they even knew each other.

"It is time to let McVey and your other past concerns go—got it? Son, it's time to compartmentalize your emotions. They have no place here."

"Yes, sir"

The phone rang, and McCready took the call.

Mathe swallowed deeply, trying to control himself. With the mention of McVey, Mathe's memory immediately snapped back to his run-in with him while getting his rising hate on, which he tried to tamp down.

That was a shit storm of a day, and McVey is like a sticky booger you can't flick off your finger. I wanted to hold him underwater until the bubbles stopped, and then that day returned.

— · —

Finn was wounded and struggling across the South Vietnam rice paddy, with rounds impacting his feet and more from the tree line. Finn and I had ejected and left our jets in radically different worlds. Both, or what was left of them, were smoking wrecks—his deep in the North and mine just off the sandy red clay perimeter of a Marine airfield. The theft of a Marine Huey allowed me to fly out to rescue my buddy and squadron mate.

Finn heard the chopper over the AK-47 rounds. He limped, ran, fell, and got up to keep going after leaving a small Vietnamese hut to escape his captors—into the rice paddy.

I spit out of the bottom of the low-hanging fog bank, touched down, and quickly jumped for the M-60 door gun. Then, I cocked and pointed the gun toward the tree line with no clear target in sight. I opened up with alternating bursts and kept firing—trying not to let the increasing enemy mussel bursts target Finn running for his life.

"Come on, Finn! Got you! Move, move!" I yelled.

Finn suddenly went forward, stumbling and falling from being hit or sheer exhaustion. I humped the 30 yards to his side after another burst from the 60. Somehow, I reached him, and we stumbled/crawled, arm in arm, back across the paddy. Rounds continued impacting the ground at our heels and into the UH1-E Huey—with rotors still spinning—thank God!

I threw him in the back and got airborne as a bullet smacked through the skin of the chopper and embedded itself just over my helmet into the overhead instrument panel. The Huey didn't shutter like I remembered the CH-46 in past missions.

I recalled one particular mission in the 46. The rotor hub lost sync while my door gunner was blazing away at the usual suspects running from his fire along the trail below. So I set up for an autorotation in a dead bird, and we rode her hard into the ground. But not today, I prayed, in the trusty Huey.

The moisture-laden bird finally popped out of the dense fog bank and into bright sunshine, and I turned around and saw Finn's blood loss on the chopper's deck. It scared the shit out of me.

"Hang in there, pal, hang in there!" Then, suddenly, Lieutenant Colonel McVey's words popped into my head—his face clear as a bell from our earlier meeting.

My imagination brought me to a cold sweat—a snarling, yelling, full overblown apparition, boiling over with rage—three inches from my face. Mad does not describe it. I had returned "his" CH-46 full of holes with rotor blades partially destroyed. The meanness and vitriol in McVey's meager stature were more than I could take. I'd had enough that day and returned his anger word for word—verbally offing him and his pathetic grip on his rank.

— · —

It took me a few minutes to slow my heartbeat as I tried to compartmentalize the anger—just as I had been told.

Lt David E White
Flying the B-29, over the "Hump," China, WWII. He piloted the B-29, B-17, B-25 , C-47, B-26G and B-24.

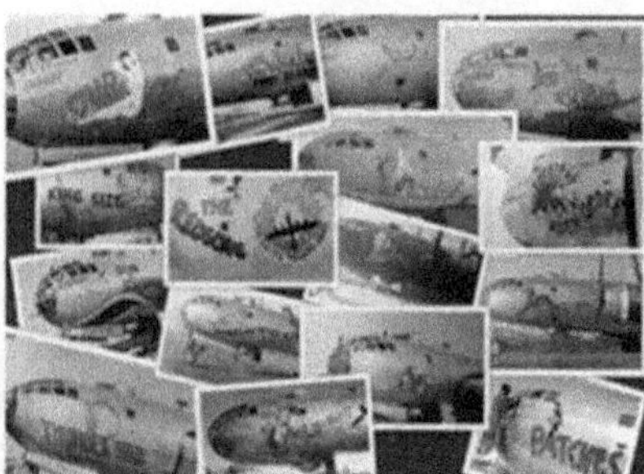

Pairdoba, India ,CBI theater, B-29 base, 1944-45

DEW in a short stay in armor after border patrol duty with Cavalry–then on to the Air Corps.

David and Betty White – Newlyweds 1943

B-17 advanced training - Walker Field, Hays, Kansas - 1943-44

The StarDuster crew prior to losing her from an engine fire flying the Hump in China -1944.

Jim Campbell's crew - MIA

Then, McCready hung up the phone and turned to me, regrouping his thoughts. But, finally, I could not keep myself from asking.

"Sir, why would you intercede on my behalf with McVey? I don't understand."

"Because of your dad and mom, Mathew. Your dad asked me to watch over your mom if anything happened to him long ago. Soon after that, you were born, and your dad went MIA. So I stayed in touch with Elizabeth and also met Finn's dad. I promised him too that I would look after you—and it has been a pleasure. We go way back. I'll explain that in time. But the short of it is that Finn's dad knew you had problems at home, and he caught your angry, rebellious, embarrassed expressions during those times you and Finn met with him. He knew your mom was an embarrassment to you—possibly the source of your angry behavior. You reminded Finn's dad of some of his war buddies—a bunch of mavericks, aggressive, challenging authority, and always getting into fights.

He said you were a real pain in the ass but intelligent and reckless in a controlled way—like some of the guys in his B-29 crew. I know you've had to work hard for everything you've achieved. But, he felt the military might be your answer—he was right!"

God, he sure knows a lot about me!

He continued, almost reading Mathe's mind, "I talked to Elizabeth occasionally and knew what things were like for you."

Mathe slowly sank into his chair—once again floored by what he heard—as his emotional cards hit the table. He thought, *Uncle! I give. Whenever I meet the Admiral, I leave in complete disarray or shock!*

"Well, you are now in a much bigger game than is demanded of an airplane driver. It affects far more people. Your success in this environment will require an entirely different set of skills. You are now a soldier on a new battlefield—a contest that still involves life and death-decisions. I can only protect you so far."

"You mean I'm expendable?" Mathe held his breath, astonished.

"In a way—ultimately, yes, something like that, do you understand? We all are."

"Yes, Sir!"

McCready stared at Mathe's urgency and knew he could not hold back the real story of his dad's last mission much longer.

"Wrapping things up today, let me say this.

We have been tracking the elusive Lieutenant Thai. We have suspected his identity as a foreign agent while tracking his communications to find the ultimate source of his orders.

You will contact Chi Dung Thai, befriend him again, and draw his story out. If you can't, we pull you out. The "Americans" case will take care of itself, hopefully. You will report to me if you learn of the Americans' whereabouts."

"Sir, what is the real objective of this assignment—Chi or the American?"

"Chi is your focus and reason for being here."

"But sir—can you tell me what he has done—why is Chi so important?"

"Captain, all I can tell you is that your assignment is vitally important."

The Admiral knew the real story about Mathe's father, which was radically different than the military version. Time had helped McCready ease the pain of that day—the loss of his friend, Lieutenant William Stone. But he had been there—he knew the absolute truth.

"Let's meet again tomorrow early. I think we have covered enough for today."

We stood at the same time. I waited for him to gather papers, grab his coffee mug, and followed him out the door again—shocked and dumbfounded.

Eighteen

Treachery

THE NEXT MORNING

I returned to the admiral's office for the formal brief. Positioning myself beside McCready and others, I caught the analyst in mid-sentence.

"There are many clues why the Japanese, then the Chinese, held the American for many years.

"Gentleman, why don't we call it like it is? The "American" is my father," Mathe blurted.

"Captain, remember there is no confirmation that the "American" is Lieutenant Stone. And we formally consider his status as MIA even though there is a possibility that he is alive, not a probability it is so. So, the "American" will be our only identifier."

"Do we really think they could imprison an American citizen or, for that matter, a military officer for that long without us knowing?"

"Captain, let me explain. When Japan's hierarchy learned of the American's capture, they contacted their (IGA) Imperial Japanese Army and Secret Intelligence Services (JSIS). They were actively identifying some value in the American if he was Lieutenant Stone—above and beyond his prisoner-of-war status.

We have learned from our sources that "The American" was visited during his Japanese captivity by Baron Hiroshi Oshima, Japan's Chief Ambassador to Nazi Germany. Oshima was characterized as "More Nazi than the Nazis." He was their Asian espionage leader. The meeting occurred in the Hungnam-Chong heavy industrial region—North Korea.

Also, during this time, a Chinese secret society called the Tung Wen was created under Japanese pressure in China to educate political activists. Their activists, lower-level peepers, were trained for espionage—collecting information. We do not know if there is a relationship between them, Chi, and his parents. But, the true nature of the American connection to the Tung Wen is suspected but unknown.

Even though we cannot declare this individual is Lieutenant Stone, our review of intercepts of the Japanese through "MAGIC" has provided many clues. As many of you know, Magic was an American crypto analysis project focused on monitoring, intercepting, decoding, and translating Japanese communications.

The American was eventually passed from the Japanese to the Chinese."

Finally! Mathe gasped.

"Ok, Captain, let's make the assumption—open the possibility that "The American" is Stone. The Chinese Communist Party (CPC) was probably curious why the Japanese held him even for a short period after the war. Or he just might have been forgotten in the transition to peace. But we believe the Chinese suspected he held some knowledge of great importance, and they were committed to ferreting it out of him.

We knew the Chinese inability to use the intelligence they gathered and their inferior operations offices severely impeded their effectiveness in holding and using him in any meaningful way.

But today, let's base our assumption on this little-known fact. Your father, and I do mean if the American is in fact your father, was recruited by the Office of Naval Intelligence, ONI, early in the war. This occurred before he received his designation as a naval aviator. His skill set was essential to identifying, finding, and expanding the US's foresight into new technologies, future weapons (energy) platforms (stealth technology), and early laser technology capabilities. However, his work was classified as secret and only known by US intelligence agencies. As a result, no one knew of his career but us.

We think the Japanese caught wind of his experience from internal US Government leaks and continued to hold him on suspicion of secrets or a capability that was important first to the Japanese and later to the Chinese.

With a dour expression, Mathe fumed but kept it hidden, *blah, blah, blah. They could at least have told my mother—given her a little hope—damn these people!*

"There have been many leads on "The American's" various locations. They have ranged from being held in a prison camp in different Southeast Asia locations to a North Korean cell. There was speculation internally that he was on the loose, escaped, and the Chinese had no idea of his whereabouts. So the possibility exists that he may be hiding from us currently.

According to our intelligence, at one time, "The American" and other captives were marched north to a POW compound near Pyoktong, on the North Korean border with China. In the early sixties, there were frequent sightings of Americans being moved among prison camps. Moreover, after their release from captivity, several US POWs told American interrogators that they had seen Lieutenant Stone alive.

If it was Stone, there is a probability they stashed him away in a prison camp for years. Then, finally, he was shipped to Korea in 1949, shortly after the Korean War began. His last known sighting before the latest one was in Korea—the city of Pyoktong—ten years ago.

Then in the early sixties, a rumor circulated that an American had died of a sudden illness and was taken from North Korea to a city in northern China and then buried. This report seems to be consistent with our suspicions that US captives held in Chinese-run POW camps were never returned when the fighting ended in 1953.

American officials believed this from the earliest days of the armistice that concluded the Korean War in July 1953. We suspect that the Chinese and North Koreans withheld several US POWs, possibly in retaliation for US's refusal to free their POWS, both Chinese and North Korean. In addition, some soldiers chose not to return to their home country for fear of retribution.

Our most recent sighting of an American comes from a POW-MIA advocacy group, which gave their information to the AP. The reported circumstance of an American's death may sound improbable. But the critical revelation—that he was transported several times between prison camps in China and North Korea and finally to a city in northeastern China and buried supports long-held U.S. suspicions.

Moreover, never released to us, wartime Chinese records could shed light on the fate of other U.S. captives who were known to be held in Chinese-run POW camps—but never returned when the fighting ended in 1945 and 1953. But unfortunately, China has yet to provide any additional information.

We have been unable to identify the American that has been reportedly seen. Therefore, the government formally still believes that he is dead."

Gentlemen, the Pentagon has focused more on the related issue of China's management of POW camps inside North Korea during the war, which Chinese troops entered in the fall of 1950 on North Korea's side.

The city of Shenyang was reported to be the American's burial site—formerly known as Mukden. It is interesting because it is far from the North Korean border—often cited in declassified U.S. intelligence reports as the site of one or more prisons holding hundreds of American POWs from Korea. In addition, some U.S. reports referred to Mukden as a possible transshipment point for POWs headed to Russia. We believe the Chinese should be able to account for these individuals.

Now it turns out that China did provide an accounting, although it is incomplete and was kept under wraps for some time. The case of the missing American has been a focal point of a four-decade cover-up by the Chinese government. From what we can tell, the Pentagon has not aggressively followed up, either on this case or hundreds of other Americans for whom the Chinese should be able to account. This news is the first crack in the dike

A top American commander that led forces during the final stages of the Korean War in 1953 gave this account. "We had solid evidence that hundreds of captive Americans were held back by the Chinese and North Koreans, possibly as leverage to gain a China seat on the U.N. Security Council."

Over time, however, U.S. officials muted their concerns out of political insecurity about what they did or didn't know about this subject while pressing the Chinese privately. So today, the Pentagon's stance is that China returned all the US POWs it held.

Some US POWs who spent time in Manchuria have returned to the best of our knowledge. That information is from the Pentagon's POW/MIA office—in a summary of wartime POW camps. But the report he was taken from North Korea to a city in northeastern China and then buried—matches long-held U.S. suspicions about China's handling, or mishandling, of American POWs during and after the war.

So, Captain, do you now see why we have been hesitant to call a spade a spade concerning the possibility that "The American" may be your father?

Mathe gave a contemptuous stare at the analyst and just shook his head.

"Sir, if you read between the lines of your uncorroborated reports, there is enough to warrant an assumption of existence rather than any deniability."

The analyst rolled his eyes and continued as if he did not have time to address Mathe's comment.

"Let us move on, gentlemen."

Academic Espionage

"To add to these concerns were the classified lethal and non-lethal weapons systems programs that were standardized in universities across the nation in the early sixties and offshore, affecting the national defense of our country

Several administrations have continuously been concerned over what U.S. officials render active intelligence-gathering, aided by Chinese diplomats, to collect cutting-edge scientific research from American universities. Many were research projects on war and weapons in ultra-secret think tanks nationwide. What was most disconcerting was the preponderance of foreign nationals employed at these centers without secure and appropriate clearance at the university or with the federal agencies funding the utilization of projects. In addition, intellectual information released to foreign powers was striking. Many classified documents had disappeared and were known to have re-appeared from recent graduates from Korea and elsewhere.

Court documents filed in related court cases have shown that various research areas have been hidden from immigration authorities. In addition, some select student research assistants were on active duty with the People's Liberation Army. Of course, the Chinese Foreign Ministry has consistently denied these accusations of intellectual property theft. But the evidence is concrete, with Federal agents finding research in students' possession to share with their colleagues in China. For example, one Chinese government scholarship student's US research notes turned up in Chinese military documents that allegedly detailed classified research.

Agents found the information in a misplaced folder. Prosecutors see this as evidence of Chinese military affiliation and deception aided by consulate officials. The university spokeswoman has declined to comment on the information found in possession of a Chinese college student. This leads us to a discussion of Chi Dung Thai.

Chi Dung Thai

Now, let's review Pilot Officer Thai's case. Captain Stone, I believe you are familiar with this individual. You knew him from your training days?"

"Yes, I did, but not well. He was reticent."

"In the past, Japanese secret agents, in many instances, were known to be Chinese citizens—foreign nationals with loyalty to Japan. The Chinese eventually went operational with the same structure they had learned from the Japanese—using Chinese, Korean, and Vietnamese nationals as agents loyal to them, agents deemed valuable to their communist policies and agenda as spies.

They also employed university students. They would place them in a host country for a short period—to exploit or, shall we say, steal intellectual capital for the betterment of China.

As I explained, this espionage is still rampant in US academic institutions. Their primary target is research funded directly and indirectly by the US government or US proxies and was deemed crucial to our national interests. And by freakish accident or design, Chi Dung was one of those students who worked on vital research projects at one of our more prestigious universities.

Before entering our navy's flight school, he had his nose in significant research projects. The US Government is concerned about his current location and liaisons with foreign countries. Therefore, he is classified as a threat to the US Government. Unfortunately, I cannot disclose more information than this, but please direct any written questions to my attention. That's all we have for today. Thank you for your time, gentlemen."

I sat even more confused and irritated. Like most meetings I had attended, with oxygen at a premium, today's meeting room wasn't crammed with attendees.

The IDs hanging from each attendee's pocket—CIA and FBI and more, unrecognizable—told me I was a tribal outsider to this culture as the participants lobbed facts and figures to support their contentions. These guys seemed to be picked for their inability to commit their agencies to any firm stance that would answer today's big questions. Moreover, their missions seemed to overlap, and it would take me time to navigate the gaps and differences.

I guessed it was a joint operation. So under the Department of Defense's direction, were these agencies all looking for counterintelligence operators or agents working in the US and targeting US military bases offshore?

They sounded like they were collecting crucial intelligence from multiple sources throughout the country and offshore. Pointed comments and questions told me this was getting very real. How could I impact and support their efforts to identify just one man's whereabouts?

Am I just the lunch bucket guy—the patsy? The fly guy is perceived as streetwise but can get along with most. Or maybe the scapegoat, someone to blame in case all their efforts go south? What can these buttoned-down professionals expect from me? Will this operation expose someone's political cover or worse? How far over my head am I?

The meeting ended, and the room cleared while Admiral McCready hung back—collecting notes and folders.

In a subdued whisper, he said, "Mathew, I had no idea of your father's past, even though we were terrific friends. I'm not sure your mom was even aware of his work for the ONI (Office of Naval Intelligence). She suspected something but never knew anything concrete. I remember her saying his letters to her had changed. She mentioned that he seemed cold and distant and worried about him. Unfortunately, I never got a chance to probe your dad for information on these activities. We will meet again tomorrow morning at 0700 sharp, OK?"

"That helps. Thanks, Admiral."

I was gathering partial answers—and the picture was getting a bit clearer, but I still had many questions.

Nineteen

Convulsive Cultures

ONE DAY LATER

"Mathew, let us continue with my memory of a mission I participated in during the Korean conflict. It had a critical takeaway—that I learned from the Korean culture—and it might help you on your next assignment.

It gave me a more profound understanding of Eastern cultures—Korean and Chinese. I am about to share my first-hand perceptions of the people. Even though my experience is with the Korean people, it led me to explore the Chinese culture and its similarities with the Koreans. During my short time camping trip in Korea, after ejecting from my fighter and hitting the silk just south of the border, I learned some hard lessons about their culture—living with a Korean family for a couple of weeks. They are a unique people but poor, more like deprived and heavily corrupted—a folk culture compared to the rest of the world. Not just the Korean culture but the Chinese, too—they were not all that different from each other during that time.

The ancestral spirit of Confucius is firmly embedded in their political and social dealings—it permeates their culture. So you have to be careful interpreting their behaviors because of this orientation. Don't get me wrong—like us, they respect their elders and authority and understand the importance of family and friendship. However, their solid ancestral traditions and cultural heritage can impede immediately gaining understanding and, of course, acceptance.

It is easy to get into a bind. A family's eldest son seems to hold the cards—the decision-making responsibility. Yet, the family is the most important part of Korean culture. Even though women appear submissive in public, they are more independent than most males in this culture. The family validates them.

Hopefully, you might get to eat rice, vegetables, and meat but don't count on it—they appear to have been a Korean staple but unaffordable for most during that time and today.

As a political and social philosophy, not speaking openly and covering their emotions for fear of hurting feelings pervades these cultures. As a result, there is a rich perception of trickery and hidden agendas. But, these cultures display many attributes we value in the west, like hard work and respect. So, don't misjudge their lack of interaction when they receive information. Information to them is currency.

They can be very shrewd in their dealings with the veneer of goodness. But unfortunately, decisions are very slippery. The Chinese currently hold a monopoly on this behavior, and the Koreans are right behind them. But, above all, remember, if there were one word to describe how this part of the world operates, it would be deceptive.

China is going through another upheaval, and frankly, we can't keep up with the speed at which change occurs in the "East"—alternately opening and then closing to western ways. Generally, I think this folk culture is seeking its path to individual freedom. The population is trying to cast aside the vestiges of one revolution from their past with a surging underground.

Like the Koreans, the Chinese government has many enemies who resent the successful party officials. As a result, they seem to be turning the people against each other, neighbor against neighbor, students against teachers, workers against supervisors—a society turned upside down.

The Chinese Red Guards swept the country with senseless brutality and cultural destruction. It is built on the madness propagated by a man named Mao Zedong. Nevertheless, the possibility exists for a renewed correction from this time of convulsive subversion and withdrawal from the outside world."

Mathe turned in his chair and gazed out his window, and the admiral could almost hear his mind working. Then, trying to decide how much to say, he turned back. Finally, he confirmed his decision by slamming his fist onto the desk.

Twenty

The Awakening

"Mathew, the CIA has recently joined the FBI in admitting there is a good possibility your dad is "The American" and possibly still alive even after all these years—but just shy of total confirmation. This is important! This information stays in this room—between us!"

"Sir, I've heard this, more or less before. So why is this real now? Meetings and briefs, all the allusions and inferences to "The American," reported as dead but may be alive, a spy, a threat, or a farmer? Does anyone actually know anything around here?"

Rein it in, son.

And then, in a somewhat sarcastic tone, "May I speak freely, sir?"

McCready quietly nodded, seeing Mathew's irritation, "Yes, go ahead."

"That's very interesting, sir. Really? My father, sir? What happened? How do they know it's him? Where is he—my father? You know, sir, Jesus Christ, this is horse shit! Is this for real? The Wizard of Oz has nothing on these guys! I don't know what to believe."

McCready sighed as his head sank.

For a long uncomfortable moment, Math sat quietly, holding his breath, wondering if he had overstepped his bounds—realizing his words' possible impact. Then the admiral spoke.

"Son, listen carefully," in a harsh tone. "One step at a time, Mathew. "You know the Bureau is not very forthcoming with information—murky. But, as far as I'm concerned, "The American" is your father. There is no doubt in my mind. But, of course, no one else is willing to admit this might be true. If A equals B and B equals C, then A equals

C. They sometimes don't do math around here very well, only the math that fits their political agenda. So you being chosen for this mission sure makes more sense."

I began to sweat and fumbled for words as a wave of hope swept over me—*along* with its challenge. *It's about time. My father was a decorated veteran with a courageous past—what else has the government held back?* "Sir, how do we get him home?"

McCready reached into his desk and pulled a file from his drawer. It was thick with "TOP SECRET" stamped on the front. McCready could not push it forward toward me while fighting an internal conflict with himself.

"Mathew, this file will explain the timeline of sightings of a man I know in my heart is your father."

I stared at the file before picking it up. I knew he was taking a huge risk. His reputation and probably his job were on the line, but I saw more in his face—sadness I didn't understand. Shouldn't he be happy? *What's in this file? What isn't he telling me?*

As I left the Admiral's office, I turned to say thank you one more time. But instead, I saw more in his face that I could not comprehend.

I closed the office door quietly, leaving McCready to his thoughts as he sat drowning in concerned pain. He knew my dad as a fellow aviator in real life, while I only knew my hero from what little mom had shared—which was not much.

As McCready watched Mathew exit his office, *I had much more to say but enough for today. I'll see him tomorrow. Unfortunately, I don't think he'll sleep much tonight.*

I stepped into the hallway with what felt like a pot of boiling water in my hand. Its heat demanded that I get to my cubicle quickly, yet I was afraid of the contents—like an emergency ejection and finding out it wasn't a parachute in your kit. I understood the place had too many shadows. I'd been here long enough to figure out some of the ins and outs—the rank structure, the turf rules, the quirks, and the agendas of the hierarchy.

But what were the motives, the truths behind all the so-called facts? The Ts never seem crossed, and "Why" answers just fell away.

As I approached my cubicle desk, I felt the heat from the file and was hopeful it held some truths. *But, God, what have I gotten myself into?*

Twenty–One
Masked Anxiety

NEXT MORNING

The admiral sat quietly thinking while sipping his coffee at his desk—his early morning ritual.

With new sightings—reports of Mathew's dad, I knew I would have to come completely clean about the Okinawa mission, regardless of what wasn't written in the original navy after-action report that tragic day back in the big war. Even though I did not know Lieutenant Stone's complete history then, my conscience would eventually drive me to divulge the whole truth—against the government's desire to hide the story.

My vision of that day appeared again—haunting me for many years. I remembered that day vividly, and it all came back.

— · —

On that Okinawa mission, I struggled to keep the Corsair flying as the realization that I was going down took hold. Again, I rolled back the canopy for my ditch into the sea. The ram air was refreshing, and the robust sea scent forced a doubling to refocus on my situation. Tightening the harness even tighter, I turned to search for Bill. But the sky was clear, just empty blue—I was alone. He had shot the Jap off my tail and had temporarily saved my life—and we might have lost him, but I had my hands full now.

I fixed Bill's last approximate position while concentrating on flying my battle-damaged F4U and kept calling out to him repeatedly—with no answer.

It took me a second to take stock of my situation. With temps and pressures rising fast, the fighter seemed to be disintegrating before my eyes. Then, while coaxing the throttle and prop controls, the heat and humidity at a lower altitude finally caught up. Unfortunately, adrenaline was only going to take me so far today, for I was sinking as fast as the Corsair.

Almost to the island, I continued the fight to keep the sweet spot insight—the distance to a firm touchdown with the right angle of attack, driving the airspeed to carry me there without stalling.

It was time to dirty her with the gear and flaps and hold enough airspeed to hit the atoll, for the ground was coming up fast. All I remember was trying to keep the Corsair from stalling on the approach and the heavy metal crunch as I hit the beach. Not much after that.

I must have lost consciousness for a minute or more—I didn't know, and I sure didn't know where I crashed. My head and everything else hurt, and I was very thirsty.

I caught the smell of engine oil, fuel, sea salt, and rotting vegetation as my aching back and neck brought me to semi-consciousness. However, my seat harness had done its job. I was in one piece with minor scrapes and only minor pain, sitting in what was left of the Corsair's cockpit.

The fear of fire pushed me out of the wreck as I half-crawled over the canopy rail and flopped onto the soft hot sandy beach. Just off the beach, a stand of palm trees beckoned me for an escape—relief from the heat and humidity and I hobbled toward them. With my back to the base of a palm, I sat and took stock—first aid kit, survival knife, ammo bandolier, 1911 forty-five revolver, canteen, escape packet, and more in the wrecked Corsair. Again, I looked back at the extent of the F4Us damage and realized how lucky I had been to survive.

One wing lay several yards down the beach, in line with a furrowed ditch in the sand from the aircraft—with sheared-off landing gear and parts spread everywhere. But to my surprise, there was no fire. So my Corsair had saved my life!

While adrenaline drained away, I contemplated my next move as my body started to squawk—just like the seabirds above me who were unhappy with their new invader.

My head was pounding as I searched my body for blood stains and more when suddenly nausea spread like wildfire. I doubled over with a blinding headache—retching where I sat, and then lost consciousness.

I remember clawing my way toward self-awareness and thinking I ought to get to my feet as my eyes opened to two tiny eyes and a small claw waving in front of my face. The sand crab seemed to welcome me, or was it threatening me? Or was it a dream? For some reason, I found myself half in and half out of it in the shoreline surf, lying on my side as it rose and fell away from the beach. Puzzled, I lifted my face from the sand and wondered how I got here as the surf continued to drum away at my body. The sunlight blurred my vision as I questioned who had carried me to the surf line. While trying to scan the tree line, I fought to get upright in the shifting sand. In time, I found myself in the jungle shade just off the beach and still was unsure how I got there.

We were briefed on locations for submarine pickups if we got hit and couldn't make it back. But my background didn't correspond as I again scanned the tree line for the enemy. I thought about a short run deeper into the surf to help with the many cuts and abrasions—not to mention the need to cool my core and douse the pig pen-like smell following me. But some common sense held me back—the enemy must be close. And then reality set in as my knees buckled, and I fell to the sand again. Looking up from my knees, the lagoon stretched out in front of me with a reef no more than 50 yards out with the tropical jungle behind.

I hoped this island and others on the horizon, in the middle of the Okinawa chain, were small enough not to contain a Japanese garrison.

The hot afternoon sun slowly yielded to a few boiling clouds and cooler sea breezes. Then, with a watchful eye, I found glorious relief in the surf. With it came the sting of sea salt licking my wounds, bringing an awakening with more control over my body. I still searched the sky for my squadron mates—no sign of anyone.

But what island was I on, and what about Bill? Was he close by? I kept wondering. I must have been out quite a while and could not have helped him even if he was near. I sure hoped he had survived his dive to the ocean or made it to a nearby island, as I did, or back to the ship

It was reported that after floating in his survival raft for three days and being captured, Bill eventually escaped and made it to a neighboring island.

Recorded conversations with returning post-war prisoners tell us a Japanese troop garrison inhabited the island's far side. He drove them nuts—as a pilot turned guerrilla!

He hounded them and killed them at will for provisions to survive. Eventually, he was captured again, but with a story of his heroic lone survival behind him—he became somewhat of a legend. Even though many admire him, unfortunately, the account has been under wraps in the naval community for a long time—why I don’t know.

Trying to heal from his wounds in the crash and stay alive, he was eventually turned into a Nip slave. He sustained severe mistreatment and torture at their hands and was lucky not to have been executed. At this stage in the war, the Japanese imperial directive was to kill all prisoners of war. Why they didn't kill him immediately is a mystery. They must have seen some advantage in keeping him alive—what did he know?

Reports from men who finally came home after the war confirmed he was taken to a 'Hell Ship' and then ferried to China. It was speculated that he was taken deep into the country's interior. His most likely destination was the prisoner of war camp at Mukden.

— · —

McCready sat quietly with troubled thoughts as his vision of that day slowly released, and he began to ponder his next moves with Mathew.

Twenty–Two
Guilt

NEXT DAY

Mathe could find his way to McCready's office with his eyes closed by now—an all too familiar path for his next meeting.

He arrived early for their meeting this time as Evelyn typed away as if he wasn't there. *I wish I knew what this was about.*

McCready was sitting at his desk shuffling papers as his voice on the intercom broke the quiet. "Send in Stone when he arrives."

He's here, sir."

I nodded to Evelyn and wished her a good day.

"Mathew, how are you doing? Take a seat.

"Fine, sir, just a little whipped but ready to go."

"We have been working on your situation, and I wanted to share some additional information."

"That's great, sir," I responded while wondering if the admiral and his staff might head me in a new direction—and of course, further information about my dad. I had questions too. How were Chi and my dad connected? I didn't believe a single word of their supposed collaboration. If McCready doesn't go there, I will find out for myself. *My dad is a target of my government's duplicity concerns—is this just a straw man? No, just a manufactured crisis!*

"Mathew, your dad was far more than an excellent pilot and soldier. His training went well beyond just flying a plane. Because of his technical and engineering expertise, your father was considered for a critical bombing mission during WWII. Unfortunately, I never could determine the exact role he might have played in the missions that dropped the atomic bomb on Japan. We can only speculate as those files are considered top secret."

Mathe quietly listened but felt the admiral's tone progressively change.

"There are a lot of loose ends, Mathew, but this is what we know for certain. At the time, Bill's knowledge of the Manhattan Project placed him in a select group. He was considered for the mission even though a navy fighter pilot. This might help you understand your dad's importance to our enemies during that war."

Mathew sensed McCready knew more about his dad's past—yet to be explained. *What was it that he couldn't tell me—what was he hiding? I felt that pained hurt in his voice like in my mother, and now I hear it in him.*

"Thank you, sir, but you probably already know I've spent many years being angry with him. My dad had just left us. I don't know how to get past it. I don't want to be one of those emotionally disabled people."

"Son, I know it is easier to be angry than sad. He was the best of us, and I, too, am at a loss."

Suddenly McCready's demeanor changed—no longer ramrod straight, as he sagged in his chair. Instead, his face slackened as if he had just left the room, trying to forget I was there. Then with a sudden jerk, he turned to me and said.

"Mathew, I have another story to tell you about your dad. It's time that I told you the final truth about that day back in nineteen forty-four. I have hesitated to share, for it contradicts what you know or maybe didn't know about your dad's last flight."

"I don't know anything about it, sir, nothing."

Mathe listened to his boss more intently—his pulse knocking to the back of his throat as he quietly, chokingly, gulped for air. He tried to hide his renewed turmoil under an expression of calm.

"Your dad and I had been together eighteen months in two theaters of war. That was close to 13,000 combat hours with 26,000 total flight hours. One night we sat up together, adding it up. I remember thinking, no wonder we're tired. We had flown over 109 sorties throughout the war. With the surrender of the Japanese at Okinawa, our escort carriers were reformed, and squadron VOF-1, renamed VOC-1, was no longer needed in the Pacific Theater. Eighteen months together yielded much success, and many gave themselves selflessly to achieve our goals."

Thinking the admiral's story was finished, I was about to compliment him on a long and rewarding career when he suddenly raised his hand, silencing me. McCready fought for control of his words—to tell a history he had been warned against ever sharing. The US Navy and NSA had scrubbed the mission from its records, and McCready had been sworn to secrecy. But, he owed his best friend's son the complete truth about his father's last days of the war.

So *to hell with the CIA and "State," do the right thing, tell it all, McCready!* "Mathew, this is the real story of your dad's last mission, not just MIA, as your mom thought."

My eyes widened, and my stomach dropped as adrenaline pushed my excitement higher—*years of waiting—just knowing there had to be more. I could see McCready* struggling. This must be incredibly hard for him.

—·—

"Our mission that day was to destroy ground/sea targets, shipping, merchantmen, and Jap island ports. Our flight of four was booking along at 6,000 feet and around 400 knots.

Suddenly I found myself fighting for my life. Where did those Zeros come from? How did they surprise us?

After some tense moments in the air trying to get home, my Corsair gave up the ghost and dropped onto a remote Okinawa atoll.

Putting as much distance between my wrecked Corsair and probable Jap search parties, I stumbled to the second stand of shady palms down the beach from my wrecked aircraft. I looked back longingly at her remains strewn across the furrowed beach one last time. She had served me well. I hoped I would get a second chance to drive another through the sky.

Suddenly, my eyes were drawn to the sea a few miles offshore. The sudden distinctive heavy Japanese machine cannon interspersed with light machine-gun fire shook me out of my stupor. Damn, it was coming from that island across the channel, and my fears of capture ratcheted up.

It took a second for me to pinpoint their target, but their gunfire gave it away. Exploding geysers were directed to a patch of ocean with a small yellow raft. Water explosions erupted in crisscross patterns from a patrol boat. Large cannon bursts slowly walked toward the poor soul floating in the bay. He was in a survival raft that looked like the one we carried in our aircraft for survival.

I could see the figure paddling hard to evade the offshore reef of the neighboring island. I hoped it wasn't one of our squadron mates and prayed it wasn't your dad, our lead that day.

Whoever it was certainly was taking a pounding. There was nothing I could do but watch and pray.

I remember hearing the sound of alternating fire. It came from an element of Corsairs who must have seen us go down. They dove on the Japanese coastal guns and quickly wheeled in a high-banked turn strafing the patrol boat.

As quickly as the Corsairs arrived, their departure signaled a quiet on the sea except for splashing from the survivor's paddle. They had done their jobs. I heard only explosions from the Japanese onshore installation's erupting ammo dump. Success!

They didn't loiter over the yellow raft very long—probably low fuel. The extended legs of our attack profiles were a test and exhausted both the plane and the pilot. We were always figuring and refiguring our fuel—enough to get us back to base or not? We leaned our engines until they were white-hot. Each mission required us to stretch our endurance numbers to the maximum until engine temperatures and pressures told us that the airplane had enough. We didn't have all the bells and whistles you have now.

Many of us never made it back to base, or worse, found sudden death in a ditching or a long-suffering float waiting for the rescue that often never came."

McCready quieted for a moment. His hidden memory stuttered after so many years. It was the first time he'd spoken of this to anyone.

"The small yellow survival raft with its survivor's frantic paddling finally got close to the beach—50 yards from my vantage point. The Japanese were winning the chase, though. The Corsairs had damaged the patrol boat but hadn't killed it. So the boat moved forward as it picked up speed again amid random belching puffs of black smoke from the damage inflicted. I yelled encouragement to the paddler, hoping he could make the beach where I would pull him ashore.

It was a pilot, and he had probably bailed out of his aircraft right after I went down—instead of crashing. Whoever he was, I prayed that he could make it. But unfortunately, I could see no chance of reaching him with the firepower difference. I chose to lie behind the low foliage off the beach rather than risk a shootout with my sidearm. What could I do? I struggled with letting a few rounds fly at the enemy, but they were almost on top of him now. He was one of us, alright. I yelled again, and he heard me. It was killing me that I was so impotent, so fearful of helping him. He was fighting for his life. I was close enough now to hear him. Again I called out, 'Bill, is that you?'

'Hey, McCready, glad you're alive,' he yelled between labored breathing pauses for air as he paddled harder—'coming to help you, pal.'

"Night after night, these words have been my nightmare—those words have plagued me for years. Maybe they reflect the guilt that courses through my veins for not being able to save your father.

He caught sight of my wrecked Corsair on the beach."

'Your airplane looks like shit. How about you?' he hollered between gasping breaths while looking back at the patrol boat pursuers overtaking him. The random seawater geysers from their light machine gun continued to pepper the water around him.

I knew what I had to do but was paralyzed as I took a deep breath and even drew my revolver with the intent to take a few shots but hesitated. That hesitation, or whatever you want to call it, still hurts. So then, weighing my chances for survival with such paltry armament, I decided to either stand up and probable death with my shipmate or lie low.

The Jap gunboat's prow sliced the water toward the raft as if to ram the survivor. Suddenly he stood up resolute, fists clenched, staring at the oncoming attackers for whatever might be ahead for him as the Jap sheered away to a stop within touching distance of the survivor. The patrol boat overtook your dad's raft just off the beach. They pulled him aboard and beat him unmercifully. I heard his screams, and they still haunt me today. The guilt of that experience—your dad, paddling for his life and reaching out to help me and my fear of death overriding my sense of honor in trying to save him has pushed me for years. As a result, I have wanted to do more than is required to support the men under my command."

— · —

I double-blinked, dumbfounded. *Was my dad taken prisoner during WWII? And for all those years! This is insane and so fucking wrong!*

Stuffing down my shock and anger, I got my act together enough to get a few words out.

"Sir, I need to excuse myself—get some air. This news is a lot to take in." *I need to take a walk.*

"Yes, Mathew, I understand. Let's take a break."

McCready saw my confusion and shock. But there was something else, some other emotion he projected that I couldn't read.

"Mathew, I will be here upon your return. We can continue then."

The Walk

He survived after all that shit—you have got to be kidding me. Just move, Mathew, and keep walking!

So I beat feet out of McCready's office and hustled past Evelyn with my head down and stomach grinding. I found the first door in sight and slammed through it. I wanted to scream.

I had no idea where I was going. I got into an elevator and pushed an arbitrary button. Then, with sweat erupting from my forehead with no destination in mind, I walked down the center A-ring on the fourth floor—my mind a mess.

All this time reported as an MIA and known to be a POW was incredible—IMPOSSIBLE! Yet, they kept his existence from my mom and me. What right do they have to do that? God! Things could have been so different.

I walked the halls for some time, trying to keep it together, searching for a quiet place to center up.

Just as I was about to lose my shit, I caught the faces of our military royalty in successive framed, formal caricatures lining the long hallway in my path—cold, focused, with commanding military bearing. At first, I didn't recognize the unknown corridor, but I was caught. Heroes, generals, and aces all doing their best to establish dominance in this clan of wall warriors. One, in particular, seemed to be staring straight at me—a framed famous admiral. He was staring at me with penetrating eyeballs, replete in full dress. I thought nothing of it until the stares of four or five more military leaders on successive walls of the long corridor found me. Their "gun muzzle eyes" slowly drew me away from my pain with an undeniable message—directed right through me. I took several deep breaths and slowed my thoughts.

Their demeanors seemed like my idea of what a bad guy at gunpoint sees before his world explodes—the six bullet heads sticking out of the cylinder end of a single-action shooter—one or more with his name on it

They changed and became dad's eyes—remembered from pictures long ago. They each seemed to communicate a personal message. They told me they had been evaluating me, measuring me—looking thru me perhaps for what mattered.

The feeling was too honest, and each successive portrait's message became obvious.

My anger dissipated, and my hope for my father's existence increased as I moved slowly down the hallway. Then, suddenly, I stopped for no good reason and looked back at what seemed to be their visages rising away from their two-dimensional canvas worlds.

They surrounded me, staring at me, demanding that I take action as the hair on the back of my neck rose.

They seemed to say—'Your mission is not finished.'

Maybe this is what I am supposed to do—find him, bring him home? I finally turned and fast-walked out of the corridor in what I hoped was the right direction. I quickly returned to the admiral's office and sat in front of his desk. *Holy shit, what a day!*

McCready looked up as he caught my entrance. The sadness in McCready's eyes was heartbreaking as he tried too hard to hide his look. But, thinking the admiral's story was finished, I was about to thank him for telling the whole story, just as McCready interpreted my thoughts.

"But son, I had to focus on my survival just like you did with Finn—first in your A-4 punch out and then in the Huey."

I shook my head in acknowledgment.

"My obligation is to honor your father for my past weakness."

"Sir, no need to say more. I understand—it's not your fault. Angrily I thought, *but really MIA and then KIA for all these years? Yes, he is alive!*

Missing in action, my ass—for 30 years? "Screw top secret," I mumbled. *A bunch of idiots are running this place. I keep trying to see*

their point of view, but I can't seem to get my head that far up my ass.
I'm trying to trust our government, so I must have failed history class.

Twenty–Three
Operational

NEXT DAY

I pondered the implications of my last meeting, "The File," and my new career in the Pentagon.

The heavy reliance on PowerPoint decks and slogans was troubling —leading to skeptical analysis and little apparent rigor to challenge the sometimes quasi "can-do" culture.

My concern about the place was growing, and it smelled—a mini-Washington, so watch your back in this two-step environment—hidden under a veneer of self-important militarized boy scouts.

I met McCready the next day, and in a subdued tone, McCready pointedly asked, "Mathew, I am still getting some skepticism—a feeling that you are not all in with us. It's time to discard any lingering doubt. You know you've got to trust somebody, and I am that person now. So stick to our schedule and make it official—make your activities known to me, and you'll be fine. No more treading water about the motives—things you might not know—it's time to light it off. Follow the trail where it leads you."

Nodding, "I understand, sir."

I was getting agitated listening to McCready and sat stone-cold quiet as I weighed my suspicions in light of McCready's friendship and confidence.

Had I conflated my admiration for the Admiral with hope for my dad? Had my distrust of the system amplified it? There is not much I can take from him that you can find as a weakness.

"Your orders came straight from the Secretary of Defense and the Joint Chiefs. So your mission is of the utmost importance. If we are going to avoid war, we need the answers to some questions from Chi. So it is vital that you find him and connect with the American, OK, your dad."

Avoid war? "That's a big order, sir."

"Yes, it is!"

It's crap using my dad to heighten my motivation to find Chi—what next?

"What kind of weapon are we talking about, sir?

The Admiral winced. "You know as much as I do, Captain. However, I am searching for the answers since it will affect your mission and relationship with your targets."

"Sir, this crap about an on a need-to-know basis is starting to piss me off."

"You're not the only one with that feeling, Mathew. Look, son, you joined the navy to become a fighter pilot and rejected the Air Force's offer. You could have been flying top-notch, exceptionally well-maintained aircraft, not navy jets whose quality depends upon parts availability. You probably didn't know that you would be away for months on tedious cruises, not be home for important family events and that you might find yourself in awful squadrons. You never thought that you would be put in situations over your head. And that you might have to manage the troubled navy kid because his hometown judge gave him only one option. You never visualized you would fly in bad weather, day and night, and be scared.

Your current assignment will most likely be the same but different. But remember, the bar's hottest girl wants to meet the Marine aviator, and that bar is in Singapore. So Banzai! There is no turning back."

McCready's picture—its essential truth, brought a sudden smile to my face.

"If it's any consolation, several people in Washington are very unhappy with our assignment. Moreover, some of your superiors seem more interested in protecting their careers than you in accomplishing this mission.

Mathew, we hope you can get us through the door to break Chi's isolation. Renew your friendship with him. We think you have the greatest chance to gain his confidence with your history. He is essential to our technology and weapons programs. So, you will be traveling to his last known point of contact.

Get ready to live on the dark side of our business for a while, Mathew—no-trade outs on your war hero status anymore while you're in the shadows. Your silver star will be of no value to you anymore as you go dark."

"I understand, sir."

"Intel. says Chi is in Shanghai, so report to that department for new credentials. We're sending you to China because you are the right man for the job. Mathew, are you ready for this?"

Mathew suddenly felt the scalding hot splash of coffee he was drinking hit his knee as he gulped at the realization that this was going to happen.

"You're operational now—you ready?"

As I nodded hesitantly, I must have looked pretty much like it felt—a deer in the—well, you know.

"Sir, yes, I am!"

"Do you have any questions?"

"No, sir, not at this time, but I'm sure I will."

McCready stood up with his stone-cold mask facing Mathew and, one more time confirmed my commitment.

"You up to this Stone?"

"Yes, sir."

As I left McCready's office, I realized fully what a mash-up this place was—the classic good vs. evil with a lot of crap attached—honor, courage, and good intentions. But unfortunately, it was all mixed up with deceit and massive egos. McCready is perhaps the exception to the norm. What he's told me rings true as a plan began to come together in my head—with just one key factor missing.

I had no idea how dangerous and, at the same time, helpful Chi's secrets would be to my future and the price it would cost. But any concerns I held were overridden with the hope of confirming my dad's existence.

Twenty–Four
Into The Dragons Claw

ONE DAY LATER

Mathe gave a quick call to his old shipmate and pal Finn. He planned to get him on board for his mission. But, first, he needed help to secure an available jet and depart for Japan with a final leg to Mathe's destination in China—a naval base close to his jump-off point. So their final leg would be to ferry an aircraft from Northern Japan to Mathe's initial destination.

I was excited. It was an excellent chance to fly with Finn after our Vietnam adventure. We were both flight current, with a few calls from the admiral to pull some strings—why not? I realized our good fortune when our schedules meshed perfectly—a rarity in our profession. In Vietnam, we had flown A-4Ms and the F-4 into combat. The F-4 was our ride today, and with it came new capabilities and challenges—not to mention a more comprehensive operation manual to review for the aircraft/mission prep. Nevertheless, we would be ready to go in four days. We flipped for the pilot's front seat, and I won for the transit as Finn, grumbling, buckled up as a pilot turned quasi-RIO in tandem behind me—my "GIB" guy in the back.

After crossing from Hawaii with a second jet in trail for safety, we followed up with our transit to Japan and then into China. Finally, our single jet climbed, over treacherous waters, up to our crossing altitude of FL400 (40,000ft) into the cirrus layer en route from deep within Northern Japan on our final leg of the mission. Then, with the sun showing through our canopy, we arched higher over the Sea of Japan to reach our destination. With a smile on my face, my mind drifted.

In my first discussions with Admiral McCready about the job, I chuckled at my future vision of myself as an agent. Would my role require me to take on a cigar-chomping, rough-bearded, badass persona with a giant bullet bandolier hanging off his shoulder, a bowie knife on his chest, and a Poncho Villa hat? Maybe a trench coat covering a pistol holster and a black fedora covering my eyes would be more appropriate. However, this vision quickly disappeared as I truly understood the depth of the assignment with McCready—the implications for myself and the country.

The night came quickly as I scanned the canopy rail and caught the dark Chinese shoreline in the distant rain and fog-soaked sky. The storm howling down from the North buffeted the jet. Instinctively, I countered the unknown pockets of severe turbulent air with trim, small power, and attitude adjustments while monitoring the AOA indicator for stall awareness.

During our extended flight, my two-hour flight time butt limitation again caught my attention. My ass begged for relief as it alternated between numbness and a not to be dismissed painful low-grade throb. Its pain threshold had exceeded our flight's limit, and it was now screaming at me like the smell of dead meat.

Subconsciously I readied for my feet dry call, our passage from the sea to dry land, as thoughts immediately returned to Vietnam. I've *got to drop these bad habits and memories—I'm no longer in that war.*

We moved further inland thru the driving rain along a ridgeline. It was blacker than night. Then, catching only glimpses of the cliff face off my wing through the canopy that alternately appeared and then was gone, I spotted the dark black void ahead against periodic flashes of lightning in the distance. Cliffs now appeared on either side of our jet and thrust higher as they penetrated alternating thick cloud layers—similar to the topography we encountered in Vietnam.

Any misjudgment could lead us to slam into a ridgeline and disappear in a brilliant fireball of fragmented wreckage. An abrupt death it would be—and for what? So I pushed the PCL (throttles) forward to gain more life-saving speed to trade for altitude if the canyon suddenly ended in a blocking vertical mountain ridge.

The weather drew us deeper into the reason for this flight against my mind, alternating the fear and terror of those war days. I struggled to block out the visions that flooded—deaths of friends in Vietnam—lives snuffed out before my eyes. I labored to compartmentalize them before our approach to the hidden airfield within the mainland—my initial jumping-off destination for the China mission. I was thankful we had survived the war as I fought to tamp down my conflicted emotions while navigating through the black night.

Another explosive lightning strike off his left wing rattled our jet, bouncing my helmet off the canopy and taking me back high over Hanoi again. The vision of bracketed pathways of arched hot lead fireballs with exploding shell bursts searching for my jet in the black of the night took me back to that cockpit box of pain. First, I heard the drum beat of the MiG's spin scan radar, and then the worst—my wingman's jet slowly being torn apart by cannon shells that chewed up his wing as pieces disappeared into the slipstream. Then within seconds, Jamie Tilden's jet was almost cut in half, spewing flame and spitting sparks as it rolled, steadied, and finally nosed up, bending in on itself and stalling.

'Jamie, get out, eject! She's coming apart.' His machine plummeted earthward, and he never returned. He was gone.

Luckily for us, the MiG finally turned away. He'd done enough damage that night, I guess.

I struggled with the pain and tried to shake these visions and fly the jet—to find my new reality. But instead, memories seemed to consume me with fear. Beneath my oxygen mask, I ground my teeth as I had so many other times when the pressure was on to perform—those march-or-die moments that I loved and hated at the same time we're starting to get old—whether in my visions or in real-time.

CDR James D Tilden -"27 years, 7 Seas, 8 Deployments, 4 Different Platforms, 5 Squadrons, Command, Countless friends, only a few Bolters, experiences that will last a lifetime, and I'm still loving every second!"

Couple of gunfighters in desert camo, ready to launch overhead Somalia, chasing bad guys. 2011...Best ever deployment!

Threw out the gratuitous 'Shaka" to start a killer day cloud surfing off the coast of Florida."

Where it all started... a young AW3 Tilden, 1996, first deployment flying the SH-60B as a Rescue Swimmer. Sea Daddy, mentor, and close friend, AWC Joe "Rock" Grossi (right), gave me the tools to be successful my entire Navy career... thanks "Soldier of Fortune" magazine for the photo shoot.

I had fought the sea, the enemy, but the weather was conspiring against us this night with heavy rain and thunderstorms right down to the deck. Finn had been exceptionally quiet on this transit—I guess he had demons of his own.

"How are you doing back there, Finn?

"Mathe, I have a control thing, not flying the jet, and the storm is making it worse.

Now I understand what our back-seaters go through.

I don't like this guy in the hole role."

"Yep, I get it, but we're making progress. So hang in there. I smell the barn."

Finn seems fine, as his comment reminded me of each man's cockpit responsibilities in flying this jet—how important we were to each other's survival. I wiped the stinging sweat from my eyes and questioned myself again in this heightened state of pucker.

Was it the trepidation, the memory of always thinking I would get killed each time I went feet dry crossing the beach into North Vietnam? My emotions again flashed as I glanced down and caught the increased energy of the angry sky ahead peppered with lightning flashes.

"Mathe, I just picked up the weather at our destination—it doesn't look good for an approach—zero/zero. But Pusan East on Korean soil was doable—we can get in." Mathe's mind was accelerating, bringing up options and discarding them quickly to handle this flight challenge. So he refocused his attention in the cockpit and fought his limiting options.

"Ok, Finn, give me a steer—Pusan East it is—what are they reporting?"

With the new course confirmed, I relaxed a bit and smiled.

The turbulence outside caused residue from our F-4's cockpit floor to rise midair and drop just as quickly. It reminded me of a similar experience as a Marine student naval aviator, and I smiled.

— · —

On my first morning in "Batt 1," 0430, my body suddenly flew vertically into the space between our bunks. I rose off the mattress and just as quickly returned. Our Marine DI (drill instructor) wanted to welcome me into his world. He was lying on his back, under my bunk, as his legs thrust my body vertically into the air, timed perfectly as the record needle hit the first note of reveille—launching one Marine "poopy" recruit wannabe. Reveille found me flying in mid-air in a state of WTF, semi-conscious. Sleep deprivation would soon become a constant state in my world. In quick succession, the scene followed several terrorizing expletives of 'move your ass, candidate.'

The magic of the morning was more important as we marched silently to the mess hall in our sloppy new guy formation. I was half-awake, but I remember the salty smell of the air off the gulf and the last of the night's stars. And then a distinctly new scent found me, one probably mixed from multiple sources that I could not decipher, and I excitedly shivered with anticipation and trepidation—in equal measure.

Then the early morning roar of jet turbines warming up on the flight line for the days training evolutions at Ellison came alive, and so did I.

My welcome to naval flight training had done the trick. But unfortunately, that initiation and the continuous pounding of those weeks set up like cement and would never allow me to relax completely—always to be vigilant and ready.

— · —

The storm seemed to give new signals of its displeasure—for our penetration into her hallowed domain. I wondered if they symbolized the individual evil and destructive forces awaiting my arrival in China.

Ah, here we go again, I thought.

But, even with my naval aviator superstitions, I knew it was time to dismiss such notions and concentrate on the approach to the city.

I rolled the fighter over the razor-backed ridge that cut across our course and picked up our flight path directly into a gorge that led to the middle of a river valley. We had escaped the mountains and weather and intercepted the pre-set course to our destination. Or was my demise awaiting me as our wheels finally touched the Pusan runway?

I cracked the canopy upon landing, and the heat and humidity hit us like a hot wet wall as we dismounted our bird. *How hare-brained was this mission anyway?*

As I started to say my goodbyes to Finn, I hesitated as I picked up the overwhelming stench of the place. It caught us both off guard as we keened the air looking for its source. Then, while eyeballing the perimeter for line support to help direct me to transport inland, Finn suddenly grabbed my arm.

"Hey, Mathe, we're here now. Don't you think it's about time you share a little more explanation about your assignment? Hell, I wouldn't have babysat you through that storm and missed the chance to ask you what's going on for nothing. I know you're in the Pentagon, but I think I deserve a little more. Don't you?"

"Finn, I'm glad we got to do this, and thanks for our help in securing the aircraft and taking the time to join me."

"No sweat, Mathe. I probably would have flown thru that mess better than you did, but it was great doing this together—getting into the air and flying with you again, even though it was in the backseat. The last time we did this, I was a bit of a mess."

Mathe smiled and thought, *Survival—yes, it was always there, a constant, hanging front and center and around the edges of our friendship for years.*

I stared at Finn and was torn. *How much can I share?*

"You know I can't tell you much. This is Pentagon shit, and whether I like it or not, I have to respect the secrecy attached, but there is something I would like to talk over with you when I get back."

"I'm open to that, Mathe—give me a call when you can carve out the time. You know where I am for at least one more week."

Mathe was silent, turned his head away, then back with a different look.

Finn, with an expectant look, "Mathe, hold on a minute. So you are you, man. I've known you forever. Where's that edge?"

Finn had seen it before. Mathe's demeanor and voice weren't right. His voice seemed to betray carefully restrained insecurity. Finn searched Mathe's eyes. *Was he part of the Pentagon's butcher's bill with this assignment?*

"The reason for being here is none of my business. That's not what's bothering me. I've never seen you so unsure of yourself. The skepticism surrounding you is shining through. I'm not sure you are all in with what the navy has thrown at you. But you still believe in yourself. I know you too well. Finn picked up on Mathe's struggle for words."

"Well, I ah… Ah"

"Your boss, Admiral McCready, seems more than just your boss. I sense your respect for him, but you seem out of your element, pal—may be over your head? What do you think?"

"What are you talking about?"

"From what you have told me about McCready, he knows the end doesn't always justify the means. He seems to know a positive outcome isn't, well, a good thing if the methods used are dishonest or harmful to others. He wouldn't lie, cheat or steal for an advantage, right? You believe he is a fair-play guy and not a win-at-all-cost temperament. So go on and make sure to fly McCready's paint. You have to trust him and, more importantly, trust yourself. I know you can find your way around just about anything. I'm standing here because of you. I have not served in the Pentagon and don't know the impact of the system, but it doesn't have to change you. Ok, Mathe, that's all I have to say."

I smiled at Finn's allusion to the Team's paint reference to hide my concern about the hidden truth I thought I had masked.

And my thoughts momentarily returned to my work at "Fort Fumble." The mountains of forms and reports that piled on my desk daily really told me it wasn't so much how good you were, but it might be the amount of paper one produced was the critical metric. My teeth ground harder with the thought. McCready's words then reverberated as I slipped back into the mission,

'He not in Shanghai—Chi's last reported position was now in Xi'an. So, even though we have provided you with a process to communicate with us, our agents will track you. But, they will not intercede on your behalf while you are in-country.'

Finn picked up on Mathe's loss of focus and dropped the subject.

"But Mathe, I did want to tell you what happened on that day back in country during the war."

"No need, Finn, we made it out."

"Really, man, I need to get it off my chest. You were more than there—so please indulge me."

"Go, Finn— hit it!"

"Well, I swung wide off the target and called strike for a steer to the ship. The jet hadn't burped even though we were holed out from AAA until all hell broke loose. I scanned the instruments, searching for weaknesses. There was no engine surging, just the steady hiss of escaping air from the side of the cockpit and the expanding circle of moisture around the shrapnel holes in my flight suit's nether regions from the anti-aircraft artillery."

"Finn, you don't have to tell me this. I brought you home, remember—man, boy do I remember."

Finn waved Mathe off and continued.

"I kept trying to figure out a way to clamp off the holes—to stop the hot blood dripping from my groin but couldn't figure it out in the moment's stress.

I remember you guys calling me, which kept me moving forward—maybe even alive—and then the damned fire enveloped the jet.

The last thing I remember was thumbing the trim button on the stick as I tried to stay awake and work through the options to stay alive. I was sweating in the growing gray tunnel and knew I was going out.

Funny, I kept nudging the power control lever forward on the dead engine, searching for the nonexistent few percentage points of thrust to stop the sink rate—just in case. But the PCL gave me nothing, the jet was dead and on fire, yet this did not compute until it finally did, and I ejected. I didn't understand. I guess the blood loss was the reason."

"Finn, that's enough. You handled it the right way at the right time. There will be a day to do that. Then, we can share it again if you need to."

"Mathe, I know that, just like the Blues, you have had to work hard at building your trust with the environment inside the Pentagon—kind of like your dad did in the Pacific with his squadron mates and you with your Angel teammates.

Have faith, Mathe. You'll be ok. Whatever this is all about, it will work out for you. Just don't forget who you are."

His words began to sink in, for I realized I was still myself and not a tool. My negative perceptions were melting away. Finally, maybe, I might actually learn to trust the "Fort Fumble" environment with its unexplained ethos and contradictions of shadowy intentions. McCready is a good man, and he must see something in me. Finn's warrior words were undoubtedly a good reminder of why I was here.

Finn sure had my read—and he hit the nail.

We separated with a warm handshake on the flight line, and I hustled to find my new path into China from Korea. The truths of my new occupation would soon become clear.

This mission would not be like kissing your ass goodbye when your luck ran out in the air—but a new set of unknown threats. I just hoped the fear wouldn't ambush me.

Twenty–Five
The Operator–
Living The Lie

SEVERAL DAYS LATER

I made my way into China with a discreet insertion into a local Chinese coastal town—and the mission search began.

Finn would piss himself if he could see me now.

No military uniform for me. Instead, I have been given a standard peasant outfit—baggy pants, a loose-fitting shirt and jacket, sandals, and one Asian conical farmer's hat (rice hat) that looks like an umbrella. One good thing is that it hides the 38 strapped around my chest.

As long as no one looks closely at my face—which they don't so much here, I'll blend in—more or less. But 6' 2" sure says a lot. Oh well.

My papers say I am a farm inspector working for the government, giving me the freedom to go from one village to the next without suspicion. But, so far, no one has asked to see them. I suspect this charade will be short-lived, for these people are brighter than I imagine, and it is just a matter of time before I am exposed in one way or another. I've picked up a bit of the language, a few words to acknowledge, asked a few questions, and mostly understood bits of the answers. I feel like I have become part of an alternate universe—and I guess I have.

It rains on time every afternoon. You could set your watch by it if you had one. And humid, Jesus! It is like swimming thru the air.

I was driven farther into the mainland to meet my contact for my drop-off. The noise, poverty, and squalor added to the stench of the place. It was more than overpowering as I tried to break down the smell to understand it. It was laced with the unspeakable fetid smell of unkempt bodies, rotting food, and a mixture of smoke and human excrement—all mixed with many cooking smells. I was in another world—*you better get used to it.*

Cheng Tu Peasant

The town's dock area and shipyard were a vibrant old-world merchant sector. Trying not to stick out too much, I walked, searching for the target's exact location I'd been given. I cut down a side street among a bustling activity center as the fish market's merchants and struggling locals carried their wares to and fro to their stalls and unknown places. There was palatable anxiety in most faces, and an insistent necessity to their shouts for recognition as money exchanged hands and adrenalin rose—in haggling over prices in many stalls. Their unfamiliar tongue seemed to ooze fear and ramp up their anxious cries for recognition—as if everything could be taken from them in a moment—and most certainly had—from their history. Was it my insecurity, or were informers and spies watching idly around most corners?

I'd catch an occasional glance or a few people observing me with no smiles in their undercurrent of whispers. Instead, their suspicious demeanors and nervous ways told me to stay alert and keep a low profile.

I covered my nose, tried to blend in, and occasionally slipped on the slippery tacky surface of the enormous complex, heaving with activity. It was probably a combination of fish guts, chicken poop, and god knows what. I moved between back alley garbage piles, small delivery trucks, and hand carts. It was all so different, so foreign—this parade of somber locals and the penetrating rich smells of a foreign culture. However, occasional inviting aromas that crossed my path were quickly overridden by the stench of dung. I began to question my viability of surviving the harshness of this peasant culture.

My search had already taken me to several cities and rural communities. With each tentative step forward in my search, I slowly adapted to this new world—but without success in finding my target—Chi.

In each city and village I queried locals, with limited language ability, for his location. He constantly disappeared—as if he was watching me. I knew he was close again, yet he had disappeared for the third time. He is running, but from whom or what? I have chased this phantom all over Northern China, Vietnam, and Korea. What the hell is with this guy? I'm not the enemy, and what does he have to do with the "American."

The search for Chi had been exhausting, with more dead ends than I cared to admit—and this night was no different. Each dead end brought with it the uncertain feeling I was being watched but by whom I could not discern. These cues were everywhere, a glance my way, longer than usual, and then quickly hidden, sudden quiet on my approach to small groups, suspicious turn-aways, and then back glances with prolonged discussions upon my retreat. Paranoid? Maybe so.

While trudging a trail leading to the next village, my mind meandered back to what seemed to be a similar predicament over the Pacific during my time off Yankee Station. I had completed the mission with shot-up NAVS and COMMS and was separated from the flight.

— · —

Lost on a black sea night without a horizon, I sought the safety of my ship with my marginal dead reckoning skills. The Saratoga had to be close, just as Chi was now—but where? The Chinese villages would not give up their secrets in my search for Chi, nor would the ship divulge its location that night. If I could not find the boat, my survival was at stake, and certainly, failure to find Chi was not an option. The negative consequences were too significant for my country.

Way beyond bingo (low fuel state) in my A-4, my eyes strained, searching for the boat that night—for any signal to lead me home. The dead black night was messing with my senses, and my survival box was rapidly shrinking. For most, the night is never really black. There are always lights or a distant glow that give hints of safety—from something. But not that night—no light, no reflections, just blackness and the feeling of penetrating loneliness that took on a new dimension.

Everything had conspired against me—a turbulent seascape, low fog, and the loss of my wingman over the target with COMMS out of commission. The thought of an ejection over this cold black sea—was not a pleasant line of thinking—survival down there—very iffy.

Unlike my search for Chi—that black night in the early morning hours, there was one natural but unrecognized element that could unknowingly save my ass from a watery grave. I had descended thru a broken cloud deck with a moon glowing through vertical chimneys of light from the high cirrus to the fog bank below—with its rain and visibility of less than a mile.

I was about to give up on staying dry when I caught it out of the corner of my eye—a twinkling on top of the sea below. It was a shimmering fluorescent image—green and blue luminescence off in the distance. It was a sparkling direct line on top of the black ocean. Not understanding the surreal animal spirits it represented, I bent the stick in its direction and followed in hypnotic wonder—a virtual pathway pointing the way. Leading to what, I wasn't sure. It was the only concrete sign of hope I had—some form of life in the black night. Unfortunately, I was out of options as I followed its line.

The natural fear of my jet's complete fuel starvation brought intense focus. My bird was not destined to fly much longer. At first, I didn't recognize the significance of the pathway. I just hoped following it would lead to safety. I was hungry for the shelter of the ship—searching the night for her safety—to set my jet down on her deck and be done.

The luminescence formed a straight shimmering pathway beckoning me to follow. It appeared as my savior cut out of nowhere. But, this was no "kiss the wind and know it will love you back" night—for this night's sea sirens were menacingly reaching for my jet—seeking to pull me down. Searching the horizon, I thought I was hallucinating. Finally, as I descended, I spotted a glimmer, or was it the ship at the end of the yellow brick road—a tiny distant smear of glowing red on a rainy night. Yes, SARA, at last!

A mile and a half from the ship, rain flowed over and around the canopy as I struggled for a clear view ahead. Then, finally, I caught the translucent glisten again, and one part of my piloting concerns fell away—now to get aboard.

I searched for the life-saving glide slope but couldn't pick up the meatball. And then, out of the torrent, my strained eyes caught that friendly meatball's helping hand. It pitched off the bottom and then the top at a quarter of a mile. The sea state had put the ship out of control as I took the average of the ball's movement, spotted the deck, and petitioned a higher power.

Instinctively becoming the stick and rudder aviator my training dictated, I searched for the on-speed number with trim and power adjustments to meet the indexer reading.

My jet's wheels finally banged onto the dark-adapted red glow of the ship's flight deck. The jet wiggled, struggling against the ship's restraint to fly, a signal I was hooked—caught a wire. Finally, I was safe, and I realized this kind of excitement—the night—really was ok. *Ah, thank you, night sea creatures!*

That natural wonder of this chemical process—the plankton's organism bioluminescent was caused by the ship's props disrupting its current state. It churned and excited the algae resting just below the surface and created a lighted road home directly to the ship. Thank God!

— · —

Sitting by the side of the road, I knew I was lost. The threat of night was no more, though. So far, the search had turned out to be more like a series of targeted village cold calls—going nowhere. Yet, somehow I was still expecting a clear path to my destination, just like that black night over the sea. But, I pressed on to find Chi, just as I had found the ship that gloomy night, lost over the ocean.

I was now a tourist in a cross-country, village, and roadside hunt for Chi. The challenge was to avoid each of the many roadblocks and checkpoints. Finally, rounding a bend in a rural area in the province of Shaanxi, I saw the communist party patrol vehicle blocking the road ahead. It was not a bad spot for a roadblock with a clear vision in all quadrants for miles. It provided them with a clear picture of surrounding hills and fields but provided me with only one avenue of concealment—a line of trees a mile to the South.

I froze low behind a small hillock and caught a group of communist Cultural Revolution believers in the beams of their vehicle lights, interrogating and beating several travelers. With each blow, a woman trying to balance small loads on her head struggled to keep her baskets of produce and rice from tumbling out onto the road—without much success. This activity might have saved me, for they couldn't see me pass by just off the side of the road through the glare of their lights. Quickly exiting the road for the shelter of the high meadow grasses, I hunkered down until it was safe to move again. Crouching behind a small hill, I found my way to the distant forest tree line edge—concealed from the eyes of the patrol car parked across the shoulder of the road.

They were looking for Chinese counter-revolutionary spies and renegades—trying to cleanse the class ranks—as if these peasants, beggars, and vagabonds along the road hadn't enough to worry about in their hopeless upside-down lives.

These gritty peasants deserved more. Their economy, or what was left, looked like it was in the process of imploding. There were shortages everywhere. The disenchanted and diseased people were rampant—lying on the side of the road or shuffling thru their days bent over—each a hollowed-eyed shadow without much hope for tomorrow. Some lived in thatched grass and mud sheds, and many, ulcerated and emaciated, just roamed the fields for food. I was told many ate mud and sucked on tree bark to exist. Those who plied the road with enough strength to approach were left to beg the travelers.

Even though still lost in my search with no luminescent road for guidance—I looked for cover to rest again in a stand of trees—a real aberration in these times of denuded trees cut down for wood and bark. After sleepless nights in the forest, I awoke, brushed the dew from my clothes, and continued my search.

Passing through the area, I came to the lip of a hill, and another small village spread before me. It seemed to fit the description of the town where I would find Chi. I hoped this wasn't just another in the endless leads heading me nowhere. *Just maybe this could be it.*

I moved closer to the village and down a long steep hill before crossing a street to the front of a small tea shop. My curiosity peaked at the number of villagers milling around a flatbed truck offloading or selling vegetables. Moving closer and slumped over, they still saw the truth—a foreigner. Several turned to stare at me. They were fascinated by this tall round eye walking their village streets. I crossed over to observe their activity when a voice from behind caught my attention. "Mathew, is that you?"

And I turned to face a tallish, haggard, scruffy-faced tattered oriental—not the blue luminescence of my past yellow brick road, but my destination, my target—Chi? I judged him to be about my age, but the coal-black intensity of his eyes looked familiar. Could this be him after all the searching? I was unsure and didn't know what to say.

"You have no idea who I am, Mathew?" His eyes regarded me with nerveless intelligence—calm and utterly expressionless.

"Chi, is that you?"

His dark eyes twinkled.

"Yes, Mathew. You were my friend, my only friend during our pilot training. Your friendship helped me through the training when so many sought to end my pursuit of becoming a pilot. We were very much an unwanted minority in your navy. So what are you doing here?"

"Yes, I know, I remember, Chi. I was glad to help when I could."

"I know you have been looking for me, but I didn't know why. These are dangerous times. I have been trying to evade contact with you, Mathew, but it is no use playing this charade anymore. What do you want from me? How can I be of assistance, Mathew?"

Before I could reply, Chi launched into a commentary of seeming excuses and dodges laced with richly present insecurity. So I let him run on. He finally slowed down enough to ask a few questions—but I had to say, "It is good to find you, Chi."

He smiled and talked at light speed again, covering his tracks with limited specifics. He was too willing to share himself with me—maybe McCready was right about him.

"My family lived in the south during the big war. But, my parents rebelled against the land reforms of the communist party during the revolution. As a result, the party requisitioned my family's land—they had no choice. As the country descended into violence, my parents were forced to participate in hideous crimes against the people. You probably know it as the Great Leap Forward. They were part of a local militia and took part only to survive the beatings and torture of ordinary people—beaten into submission.

Early on, they were outcasts in a party they hated and were openly despised by many of their neighbors. They gritted their teeth and carried on under the unbearable truths of their conscription. They parroted the party line for years to hide their pain and survive. The country seemed to develop two personalities—two completely different psyches—two ways of behaving and thinking. One was private with friends and confidants, and the other for public party lines. People began to fight deception with deception—lies with lies.

They kept my family in indebtedness for years. We lost our freedoms, and I knew they would kill my family if I didn't comply with their wishes. I was initially open to working with them, for they supported and educated me. I had nothing, and they helped my family. But now, I can't go on—running. For years, I ran scared as an operative working for the Chinese communists—disguised as a Vietnamese national.

They trained and groomed me, and I became what they told me to become. I didn't have any other way out with my family under constant threat. I had to comply. It was painful living with this shadow of deceit hanging over my head and the fear that any misstep would cause my family great harm."

Christ, are you kidding me? His was so open. This is too easy. His trust or maybe insecurity had opened him like a can of worms—but why? Had my endless pursuit forced his hand—a decision he knew he had to make—or was he threatened and close to discovery?

"I always wanted to be a pilot and found my way into the Vietnamese Air Force early in the Vietnamese conflict. They gave me a Vietnamese identity knowing it could take me into the US military. Their reach was far and wide.

The Vietnamese and the Chinese taught me much. Their training before I met you was extensive in the craft of an agent. They even sent me to an America University where I became a research moll for them. As a result, I was familiar with much of the hands-on work with some of your government's later nuclear research and other sensitive areas.

I remember you befriending me in flight school in Pensacola—when most wouldn't. It was always hard not to tell you the truth about my life, but I was scared of being found out. Your last name instantly brought up memories of an American soldier, a POW with the same name I was exposed to in my training with the communists. I often wondered if there was a connection."

What? Jesus, an American with the same name? It's true! All true!

I fought to listen and not interrupt him. I let him continue his story in earnest—apparently, he needed to open up. I had to draw out his complete confidence in me as a rekindled friend—but the news of my dad almost forced me over the edge.

"I need to tell you about a meeting with several POWs held later in the war in Vietnam. I think the Vietnamese—letting me talk with these men and observe their torture was to see how I handled this type of situation and, of course, maybe conditioning me on what could happen if I broke or chose to cross over. I didn't think prisoners suspected anything. But it was shocking.

The POWs were suffering and probably as scared as I was. Still, many were defiant in their stand to take terrible punishment without divulging who and what they knew—not answering questions directly. I learned that many had come from different conflicts—prisoners from many other wars.

Three, to be exact."

Christ, this is unbelievable, and we did nothing to find them except ask questions, swallow the Chinese lies, and believe all their crap—and these guys just left there to rot.

"Their torment had taken much out of them both physically and mentally. It was horrible to see firsthand. Finally, I just couldn't hold back anymore."

"Chi. did you ever hear the name Lieutenant William Stone?"

"Yes, I remember the name well. I knew him from multiple meetings and kept track of him. He was an older American pilot—yes?"

Chi saw the look of shock on my face. "So the same name does mean something?"

"Chi, he is my father, and I have been looking for any word of his location. Do you know where he is now?"

"Perhaps, Mathew. Six months ago, I heard he was not far from here—maybe an hour's walk."

My eyes widened with his news. *God, if this is true.*

I probed Chi for new details and what might be honest and realistic appraisals of my father's location and information on others. He opened up like a good book. I was developing a renewed comfort level that exceeded our past friendship. All this still flew in the face of McCready's evaluation of the man. He seemed to carry an innate pride in his country and its people and was courageous and forthright in his distaste for the communist party—firm in his desire to stifle their plans.

He mentioned he was married, and his wife and children must have served as de facto hostages against his defection. I hoped our discussion wasn't cloaked like the rest of the Chinese society—two faces of truth and only one spoken conveniently—for expediency. This man didn't seem to have a bone of deceit.

Then he dropped the bomb I suspected was coming. He wanted something from me.

"Yes, but Mathew, his exact location will come with a cost. But, of course, if I divulge his location, I will have nothing to bargain with. I will need your help to save my family."

I hesitated as the Admiral's words crept into my head. 'Watch out for the conditional bribe—the one we will not be able to satisfy or control.'

In my preoccupation with Chi, I never saw the man watching us from the edge of the street across from the alley. As "One Ton's" words reverberated in my mind, my ears caught the quick successive hiss and rap of three bullets that sang out over our heads. They found the wall just past the tea house entrance behind me. I was caught entirely off guard as my adrenaline rush flowed, my world blurred in slow motion, and fear took center stage. We both scurried deeper into the alley and hid behind extremely smelly crates. God only knew what was in them. I grabbed Chi's shoulder and made him crouch next to me.

"Chi, tell me now where I will find him. Are you sure about the village? I'll do everything I can for you. Just tell me where to look." As I felt for the 45, hidden under my thin, flimsy coat.

Hell, I haven't used one of these things since Quantico. But, as I scanned the distant street—*looks like this would be the time.*

Chi, in stunned surprise, caught the ambush before I did, pointed to a side alley passageway as a way of escape, and yelled, "Run, Mathew, I'll be right behind you." So I turned and ran—running hard for a considerable time before seeking refuge in the town's winding streets.

Was someone trying to kill Chi, or maybe me? Who was taking these potshots? Were they a warning or just an amateur?

I looked around, hiding in a doorway, searching for Chi. He had seemingly disappeared. I asked myself if I should turn and find him. Then, two more shots immediately rang out, and I found their mark close to my head.

Well, that pretty much answers that question. Ok, then. That's it!

I had plied the roads over half of Asia as a partially disguised national trying to fit in. But instead, one of us was into something more profound than I realized, and the ambush was proof.

In an alley—targeted, swell!

Trying to catch my breath, I stopped running again and found shelter in another back alley doorway.

Then, out of the corner of my eye, four raggedy but intense and determined Chinese with automatic pistols in hand slithered forward about 10 meters from my hiding place.

My heartbeat was beyond jacked up, but my hand was steady as I pulled the revolver out and pointed it. I had no choice. I bought this thing in Shanghai. *I sure hope it works.* I fired, and their apparent leader took one pistol bullet in the forehead, then the second went down similarly. They were killed instantly. One fell forward and the other to the side while inhabitants walking in the alley scattered—howling in fear.

One woman held two infant-size bundles in her arms and waddled faster down the alley screaming, trying not to drop them as she hustled for her life. The other two assassins just disappeared into the evening.

My Chinese peasant's outfit hadn't obscured me from suspecting eyes. The brim of my hat could only hide so much, and it looked like my quasi-cover was blown. I was still a Caucasian, no matter how you cut it.

My shock at having killed up close for the first time in my life weighed heavily. Dropping bombs from 8,000 ft is different than shooting someone only a few yards away. I had killed someone deliberately with my own hands. Oh, God! I sought out the bodies of my assailants and searched them for any identification. Finding nothing of value, I humped further down the alley, leaving the incident's turmoil behind. *What about Chi?*

I hadn't slept well in weeks, and my brain felt wrapped in wet cotton. My eyeballs rebelled from a feeling of being sand-papered. Should I double back to find Chi again and probe him for my dad's exact location? After finding refuge in a small bordello and relative safety, I hid for several hours as the reality of what had happened walloped me. Then finally, the fear kicked in.

I slid the chain on the door symbolically to hold back what happened in the impossible situation I had been placed in. I now had become a legitimate member of the US intelligence network with the killings in the alley. I thought better of returning to the area where Chi and I had met. I was learning this craft the hard way, and now it was up to me alone to survive this brush with death and complete the mission.

I hated the word "victim" for its reference to most that would not tolerate accountability or gave in to others to control their futures, circumstance, or environment, and more—the weak and the soft by nature—VICTIMS. Yet, this term fits the description of my plight—a situation I would never acknowledge with this word. I didn't want to admit the helplessness, but the thought had crossed my mind as I fought to control my bowels—to lose the dread of it.

Finally catching my fear, I remembered the Admiral's words.' You ready for some adventures,' he said as he kicked back some hair of the dog in his office. 'But Mathew, this affair might not have an end. Are you in for the duration? Remember, self-power is inherent—battle with your mind—stay in the zone. I would have given up many times, but your mind must continue the will to win—the training—to reduce risk and maximize your chance for survival—it's a contrary learning process for most—just a reminder Mathew since you already passed this test once.'

Easier said than done, I told myself. *I'm not going to let this situation drive me. I will pilot my way out of this shit—no one else. I'm in an outside Cuban eight, pulling 5-6 negative Gs and running out of forward stick. This "Blivit" situation could kill me—no red out on this one!*

I knew our people (the good guys) were here. McCready told me they would know where I was most of the time. But I had no idea who they were—maybe that's a good thing. I didn't know. I was new at this spy shit!

Am I the target, or maybe it's both of us—but why? Even with limited experience, I knew what could happen on this mission. This hunt was getting out of control. Am I being played? Here I was, in it deep, hiding out in a small bordello room somewhere in China.

I laid back on the bed, more like a cot, staring at the ceiling, pondering my next move, when Rusty's beautiful face flew into my head—and the wanting of the only woman I ever loved. God, I missed her—her mouth, perfume, and smile. She'd have this mess figured out in no time. The blood pulsating in my body drove the sweet vision of her. The heat I remembered when our lips touched and more came flushing back. Or was it the varied and demanding carnal sounds from the bordello's rooms down the hallway reverberating through the paper-thin walls? *Damn, what a woman...have to talk to her.*

The open window did not affect the heat within the room. Lying on the bed, still fully clothed, I listened to the sounds of the city and distant wailing sirens—and kept seeing those two dead bodies in my mind. Sweat is my only companion this night.

I turned restlessly and drifted off into half-sleep as my teeth ground in desperation. I floated throughout the night, working scenarios of what could be—trying to solve the roadblocks that danced across my mind. Then, seeking solace, I drifted back to the one thing that provided comfort from the confusion and overrunning fear. The blood in my brain drove the sweet vision of her as loneliness and trepidation sought to take hold.

God, she is more than a fine woman—intelligent, level-headed, and passionate. I remembered our first time together, in the moonlight in my old room at home. What a night! Vague visions of our lovemaking brought me back to the reality of who I was and her need always to please me. But, when I'm with her—exploring each other, I am a different person, and oh, her desire to make me happy with that gorgeous body. Damn!

I just react to stuff. She thinks things through—arrives at answers that include the consequences—no bull in the China shop stuff. Being a nurse, her body knowledge, specifically mine, amazes me. I have no control with her. The heat I remember when our lips touched, and more came flushing back—her face and auburn hair blowing in the breeze.

We are so different in our love. Of course, she needs to talk more than I do, but I love listening, watching her face, and hearing her voice. She slows me down and makes things last—much better that way. Then, my constant drive for sex against her more sensitive approach and requirements completed my dream smile. Oh, God! This is getting nowhere.

I would have cherished her chatter in this night of foreign smells and sounds. But, instead, I turned restlessly in half sleep as my eyelids flickered in dream desperation. In a gauzy haze, my fingers would search out the gun on my side in the middle of the night, and I would take comfort as I fell back into the disquiet of my rest.

I startled myself awake in an unfamiliar room. With the sounds of an unknown city, I rose from the bed—drenched in sweat. Forgetting where I was, the heat quickly provided the reminder.

And just as quickly, the wave of fear ambushed me again. I had felt it in Finn's rescue and sticky situations in the air several times, but nothing like this. My lack of knowledge compounded my helplessness as I realized I was entirely out of my element—a newbie again in this job.

What a shit storm. My high-wire act might not have a safety net if I screw this one up. I should never have taken this assignment—I don't know what I'm doing. I've got to get back in a fighter—it is the only thing I do well. I have to get out of this.

I sat up on the end of the bed, wanting only one thing. *I don't think she knows how much I love her because I mostly only think about myself. I've got to tell her. I want to marry her, but I suck at these sentiments—about how I feel about anything. I'm a pissy difficult person to love—I know. I have to find a way to call herg..*

After a few days, I made my way to the only known safe house in the area for a communications link. Knowing better, I picked up the secure SAT phone to reach the only absolute security I knew and dialed Rusty's work number. After a lot of static and odd sounds, a voice answered.

"Nurses station, second floor, nurse McKenzie speaking. Can I help you?"

"Rusty, it's me."

"Mathe, is that you? You sound like you're in a tunnel."

Then, frantically Mathe blurted, "I shouldn't be doing this—a call to you on this phone."

Rusty quieted and felt Mathe's sudden urgency as her concern quietly bubbled up. Something was wrong!

"Ok, Mathe, you can't tell me where you are or what you're doing. I get it. Just tell me you are alright."

"Rusty, I love you! Will you marry me next spring—on Pensacola Beach? Ask anyone you want or no one at all! I can't stop thinking about you. Please say yes."

"Calm down, Mathe. What's going on?"

"Well, many things, but this call is the most important."

"Do I have time to think about this?"

"Well, no."

"Well, if you're serious about this, here are my terms. When you get your sorry ass back here, you get down on one knee and ask me properly because this phone doesn't work for me. And, you love me for the rest of your life—no matter what."

"Well, OK! I can manage that. But I can't talk much longer. You have no idea how happy I am to hear your voice—no idea."

"Mathe, I love you too. But, whatever weird stuff you are doing, please be careful and come home. You are very important to me."

"I'll do my best, fiancé Rusty. You are my home—take care."

"You too, Mathe, take care, and I mean it."

Twenty–Six

Red Ice

A SHORT TIME LATER

I felt like a new man, clear-headed, relieved, and happy. Now I just had to get this thing done. My thoughts returned to the threat of the mission. *Could the Admiral be right about Chi?*

And then McCready's quiet plea echoed in my mind. 'It is my fault your dad is gone, Mathew. For that, I am sorry. I'll do anything to help you find him. I am so sorry you never got to know him. I will help you save him.'

Thank you for your guilt and support, Admiral, but no, our country has misjudged both Chi and my dad!

And with that insecurity out in the open, I realized it was time to talk to him. After getting shot at and separated from Chi, I knew the only direction I could take was to find both of them.

"Mathew, it is good to hear from you. Have you made contact with Chi? Where are you, Mathew?"

"Sir, I'm in a brothel—the best place I could find quickly under the circumstance. I had to get inside somewhere fast. I had money. My appearance didn't matter to them. They didn't care, and yes, I have. I thought I'd lost him a few days ago. I want to explain his situation and motivations to you as I see them."

I sensed McCready's alarm at the turn of events as I told him of my pursuit and Chi's story of generational terror under the communists.

Chi told a believable story about his work as an interpreter over the years at various prison camps—a go-between for the captors and the multiple countries that held them in bondage. And yes, Chi did remember an American pilot left behind in terrible condition from a distant war.

"Sir, Chi said he thought his release was in a small village in northern China and told me how to find him but not specifically where. But, in our discussion of his whereabouts, we were ambushed in an alley, and Chi suddenly disappeared."

McCready perked up and paused, concerned that Mathew had expressed no reason not to believe Chi—he did not think he was a traitor. However, he knew there was more to Chi than just the Chinese Communists' involvement, and he was alarmed for Mathew.

"Mathew, Chi is all that the government thought, and I will set plans to take the pursuit over. You have done your job well, so plan on returning to the US. Unfortunately, as a result, the American matter may have to be put on hold."

I was in disbelief and blurted out, "But, sir, Chi was genuine in his story of the threats to himself and his family," as my thoughts returned to my meeting with Chi. Probably overstepping my boundaries, I had promised to give Chi and his family repatriation and protection—even knowing the Communists would pursue his treachery and bring the full force of the military. Having second thoughts, I was not sure I wanted to get caught between what I had promised Chi and the reality of my government's most likely response to Chi's request for asylum—the complete rejection of any support I had promised. But I was convinced that the repatriation of my dad from China had to happen.

"Where is Chi, Mathew? What did Chi tell you?"

"Sir, we are in the Shaanxi Province on the outskirts of a village called Yan'an, and sir, he had a lot more to tell me."

"Go ahead, Captain. I'm listening."

"My discussion with Chi and his description of his journey back to where he grew up showed me how he fell in with the communists. He is not a Chinese Communist ideologue but was conditionally bribed into agreeing to go undercover for them.

Initially, he welcomed their support to help him bring his family out of the severe poverty they had been in for years—it was a way for them to live a better life. However, he eventually realized commitment to their expectations had become harder to rationalize. His family was in real peril for the support they had accepted. His espionage became a difficult pursuit of endangerment, and he said he began to lose himself and his family. He seems to have been stripped of everything that has made him safe and comfortable. He has had enough of living in an upside-down world—where good is evil, and evil is good.

Sir, I believe he wants out of the party and China now and safety for his family. I think we have found him at the right moment in time. He is scared for his own life and theirs."

I hesitated, waiting for the admiral's response to my disagreement with his perception of Chi.

"Go ahead, Mathew."

"Sir, in addition, Chi told me that if his parents didn't comply with the demands of the Japanese during WWII, they would be killed. His father had witnessed the Japanese depravity of the Chinese citizens. His father had no other choice but to cow to their demands. He was the primary driver in the jailing and assassinating of those Chinese cells/factions in his region who sought to overthrow the Japanese occupation of China. Keeping their family alive meant taking roads that conflicted with their values. As a result, his family was perceived as traitors to their own country.

In time Chi's parents grew into very successful entrepreneurs in the truest sense—running several small village enterprises but were always viewed as enemies of the state by—depriving the legal livelihood of the working class.

He said they called them "Capitalist Zhū (pigs)" by the local cadres and suffered pained humiliation at their hands to make them pay for the sins of their capitalism. Finally, the family was forced to pay reparations and gradually slid into poverty again, driven by unemployment.

Chi told me he saw freedom in the Party, and his willingness, he thought, to serve the new China surely would be rewarded—which it was in time. However, that so-called freedom was eventually taken away from his family. Chi was forced to commit intolerable acts to appease his handlers, just like his parents in the war. Though unwarranted, his parents absorbed the party's second round of intensive re-education strip away.

Even so, Chi's higher education, combined with his father's allegiances during WWII, drove Chi's visibility among the local communists throughout his early years. So, he followed his father's early course and played two ends against the middle. First, the party became his surrogate family. It was a way to clear his family's name and ensure some form of acceptance and remuneration for them to survive. He was eventually singled out for indoctrination as a communist agent and sent to Vietnam as a pilot in training working for the NVA. It provided a quick entry back into the US for his pilot training and who knows what else. The Marxist philosophy and teaching of Mao became his forced God."

"Look, Mathew, we know the Japanese held Chi's father in great respect for his work contesting Chinese communist resistance cells during WWII. Yes, he was a Japanese mole, but the perception of Chi and his family as traitors to the Chinese people still runs deep. And you're right. It probably was not warranted. But there is so much more. Likely, he did not choose his allegiances, but this is beside the point. Chi is steeped in his father's lore with commitments to many with suspect motives.

Listen to me, Mathew. Hear what I have to say. I have trusted you in our line of work—that is very rare for an asset. So you don't need to trust me—but just listen to what I'm saying.

He is dangerous. It is not that I doubt your conclusions, but I, like many others, do not trust Chi and the seeds he has sown. Did he mention anything about his research work while he was in the US or pirating technologies from US universities?"

"Well, no, sir."

"Mathew, your recent discussions and the alley incident tell me the level of danger to Chi and yourself. His past activities tell me his support comes from many wishing no good for our country. Please stand down with your communications with Chi until I get back to you. I understand your concern for his well-being under the circumstances."

I didn't believe McCready but searched his words and tone for his truth. There was no sense of evasion or untruth, and I wondered why McCready might think honesty is not synonymous with truth. *Could he be lying? No, just lousy Intel.*

McCready considered giving him a choice to fly back on anything he could get his hands on or take a military transport stationed in Japan. Consider maybe even taking an airlift shuttle for the long over-water flight to his final mainland destination—it was his choice. Then he thought better of it, weighing his next orders for Mathew.

"Above all, remember your tradecraft—you are more than a Marine pilot. So, Mathew, let's discuss your options in two days. Stay where you are."

"Yes, Sir."

Twenty–Seven

Decisions

A FEW HOURS LATER

The faint lights of the city passed into my tiny room thru the half-closed drapes of my hideaway. But unfortunately, it also brought the steaming heat of the streets that interrupted more than just my concentration. As sweat poured, I rolled over my conversation with the Admiral that had ratcheted up my tension. Then, alert to detect reverberated sounds and noises that might signal those in the outer hallway who had discovered me, I pondered my situation and speculated on outcomes.

Fighting my momentary insecurity, I pep-talked myself like so many times before. *Ok, I am in this for far more than just intelligence collection. So what if it's a fluid and unstructured environment with abounding unconventional attitudes? Even though I have limited human espionage skills and the technical abilities that go with the job, I am confident in my ability to ferret out an espionage agent. I can and will determine fact-based intelligence from inference, speculation, or opinion. The direction I will take now is clear. Even though it was more than just me against me now, I will overcome these obstacles to achieve my mission.*

The politics of the CCP seemed to change daily, and I knew McCready would discern the truth in my vision for Chi's future—the one I had willingly committed. If it were to be, he would see past my error and allow me to survive and grow in my operational contributions to our end goals.

I wanted to believe Chi, but could I trust him? I wasn't sure what the admiral and the analysts had shared about his past. But, the chance to find my dad—oh well. I liked Chi and tended to believe him but hesitated to disclose all I knew about him to McCready—that contradicted the admiral's intelligence reports. My rising fury from my conflicted understanding of Chi's persona only emboldened me to find the truth in him.

I had been through a grinder in my search for Chi, and my belief in Chi's innocence was undeniable, even with the withering opinions of McCready. But I knew I didn't want to cross the admiral—to let things get out of hand, for I thought McCready and the US Government would have to find a way to support Chi's asylum. Was it a proper long shot in this political environment? I felt slightly sabotaged—but stand down from this assignment when it was all coming together—no way!

Twenty–Eight

A Foot In The Bucket

A SHORT TIME LATER

McCready pondered his discussion with Mathe, with all the conflicting thoughts at odds in his mind.

Before his call-in, he thought Chi's trail was colder than a morgue freezer. Mathew has his foot in the bucket and can't get it out. He's a real pisser.

But a conflict with more than one significant international power on this mission was a huge concern. Mathew and Chi had narrowly escaped the assassin's efforts. But Mathew wanted more—to get his dad to safety. He had poked in every nook and cranny of villages across China, exposing himself. I knew his life was in jeopardy. This was the kind of game you frequently lost just by playing. Even with Mathew's effectiveness in finding Chi and, most likely, his father, the thought of mission continuance was frightening. So I told Mathew we might have to pull him out.

We picked the right guy, but maybe we didn't train him well enough. So we concentrated on the identification of trouble and avoidance. But he was prepared to thoroughly and continually protect himself with lethal force if necessary—and shoot his way out of what might come. Maybe his hourglass was glued to the table. There was more to this than we previously communicated, with the possibility of a Russian intrusion.

Mathew had achieved a modicum of rapport and trust with Chi in a brief period—or was it something else—Chi's need to get his family out of the country was intense.

Mathew took it upon himself to make an unauthorized verbal agreement that he would help Chi. Unfortunately that could become a shared risk for both of them because I can't guarantee their safety. I hoped Mathew understood the many broken promises US agents had made in similar situations and their disastrous consequences.

Chi had guts and seemed honest and devoted to his people and family, not the CCP. He communicated a lot with Mathew. But, unfortunately, he was probably putting both of them in more danger.

What drove Chi's traitor motivations—pure ideology, compromise, ego, or a grudge? It was indeed survival now. Mathew would not abandon Chi regardless of what happened. He is not that kind of man—regardless of orders. Then there is the drive to find his father.

There were deeper truths I had hidden from my protégé, including my honest relationship with Mathew's mother. My honor would dictate full disclosure with Mathew even if Mathew did find his father.

Although successful to date, the natural consequence of Mathew's actions in my mind went beyond the surface. It would have a powerful effect on some very touchy relationships in the government and beyond. Truths would be exposed in finding and helping Chi, possibly leading to prominent US leaders being tried for their past actions. But, on the other hand, it would not protect the political reputations of many in Washington. So Chi had to be dealt with very carefully while I fought the frustration of my operational limitations.

Gathering accurate, verifiable, and sustained intelligence was one thing, but this was now spiraling into actions that seemed beyond the political will of many, with the downside falling directly on me. The bureaucratic fight was getting nasty, but I was ready and resistant to the many who sought to subvert this operation—I would push harder.

Though damning for many, my internal report would show that the political threat did not outweigh the risks. Above all, I had faith in Mathew.

McCready remembered a discussion—when Mathew told him he always felt like the Lone Ranger. 'He mentioned he would make his own decisions—that he felt like he did not need to show his cards to anyone.' I reminded him that he was alone and yet on a team.

'Yes,' he said, 'still a team member—but with barriers.' Nevertheless, he was learning fast, and his practical and pragmatic iconoclastic behavior would push him to grow and become the leader I knew he had not yet recognized in himself.

He did have a remarkable talent for pissing off all the wrong people by doing the right thing. So, yes, his tenacity, intuition, and high intelligence were assets we could use right now. Unfortunately, they were in very short supply in Washington.

Twenty–Nine
The Duck Conductor

YAN'AN, CHINA

The day was overcast, with a slight sporadic drizzle. As I looked east, the sun was doing its best to burn off the cloud layer above.

Then peering over the bamboo fence on the hilltop at the fields below, I tried to find something familiar from Chi's village description.

A high-angle view showed me a wide area of squat earthen huts separated by dirt alleys with market stalls in the middle. It was buzzing with people, carts, animals, and you name it. Without suspicion, I had reached the small peasant farmland and village outskirts. Although, after all I had been through in my search for Chi Dung Thai, being told my dad was here was almost more than I could take. It all seemed so unreal. But the village was just as described by Chi Dung.

'He will be right there, Mathew,' he recalled Chi saying while pointing to the National Geographic map a few days earlier—just a pinprick on the map—Yan'an, in the province of Shaanxi.

'See, there it is, that small village to the city's southwest. You will find his small farm there. He frequently sells his prized ducks to restaurants that cater to those who can afford them and, I suspect, offshore markets. Also, look for him in the town, a few miles down the road every Saturday and Tuesday selling his ducks to the local food distributors. But mostly, he is on his small farm.'

I had no reason to disbelieve Chi. He had more than just skin in this game. My desire to finally see my dad had overpowered any cause for concern for Chi's credibility, rational or otherwise. The reality of meeting him was just too strong. Again, Chi's words resonated in my mind.

'You will find him there, Mathew!'

So my trek continued as I skirted the market and kept moving into the farmland beyond.

I fingered the heavy coin in my pocket given to me by Admiral McCready as thoughts of my dad's history and a sudden gastric disruption rolled through my mind and body. The grumbling in my stomach caused by the local food's digestive disturbance, coupled with the oppressive summer sun, was sucking my life. The fried scorpion and black beetle soup diet were wearing as I looked for shade to quench my thirst.

But shade would have to wait as I struggled to hold it together, trekking down the side of the hill to the meadow below.

I remembered my agreement with Chi to help his family leave the country if I found my dad. Chi's future hung in the balance. Why would he lie?

The figure of what appeared to be a non-Asian exiting a farming hut caught my attention. A small neat hut with a porch and a large pond full of squawking ducks were right in front of me. But, the fields beyond had rows of crops I didn't recognize. If he lived here, he sure was thriving by the standards of abject poverty I had witnessed in this country. The unmistakable shape of an apple tree standing outside the front door might be the cue.

As I drew closer, my heart jumped. I could not distinguish the man's facial features yet, but I knew something. With raging expectations, I quickened my pace, descending the hill.

It had to be him—much time had passed. Will he know me?

Worry spread through me. I never dared to believe I would see my father.

Mathe caught his irrational thoughts and tried to hold them in check. *But, hell, he doesn't even know I exist.*

Hesitating—I remember others I had mistaken for my dad in the last month. I focused on his flock. He hadn't seen me yet as I caught the wave of motion surrounding his feet. He was holding a long pole in the air and waving his arm as if he was the conductor of a strange, noisy feathered, quacking orchestra that spread from side to side in front of him.

With a tiger's eye now fixed solely on the figure at the far end of the property, I reached the base of the hill approaching the farm.

As the peasant directed his whole plumy mass toward me, I took in his tattered clothes, slumped shoulders, and slight limp. Then, as the wave of squawking at his feet moved closer in tight formation, the ducks' excitement became louder as it matched my own. As Chi Dung had predicted, it had to be my father, ducks and all. I now saw the round-eyed farmer, and he saw me.

Oh my God! Here we go!

The flock moved with him as he approached me, and I focused—trying to remember the details of every picture I'd seen of him. Then, finally, they parted in my path, coming down the middle of the road. Was he real, or was it the shadow of a father I had built in my mind? I was afraid of what he might have become. As my expectations took over, I realized I didn't care who he might be. I just wanted this man to be my dad. I swallowed his visage, ate it all up—as a memory of him from pictures in my mom's scrapbook—just like those ducks ate—everything in one bite.

Age had not erased his appearance—this peasant's essential character. His body was bowed from age, farm labor, and years of harsh captivity. My hope grew. He held the pride of who he was boldly, even with his aged frame. As he came closer, the glow in his round eyes showed just as brightly as I pictured them in my head.

I approached the farmer, the "American," my dad, and held out my hand, but the farmer stared at me vacantly. He was mute with surprise. Then, I thought I saw recognition creep in as his face filled with conflicted emotion. He gave me a smile of surprised pain and then confused acceptance. He did not speak, but his eyes told me what I so badly wanted to see—that he innately sensed a recognition of me. But, was I fooling myself—for how could he know me? I wanted him to be authentic, which was beyond excitement and expectation. How can someone you've never met feel so familiar? Didn't fathers wish for their son's admiration?

Was he filled with shame from the guilt of not knowing his true family? Was I the actual apparition from his past that had haunted him as he had me for so long? We studied each other in silence.

Don't rush this, Mathe.

His eyes were kind and questioning, and it was hard not to yell out— Are you William Stone?

My god, an older version of me!

It came over me. He was more than a specter.

I had so many mental conversations with him. Finn would be beside himself. He knew how much this meant to me.

For a moment, Mathe allowed his thoughts to take him back to his last annual mountain meeting with his friend in the northern Italian Alps. The place was special—their domain—a place Mathe and Finn understood and had traveled often with and without each other but never alone in heart and spirit. The mountains had always given them one more chance to meet and touch the tall air of their high-altitude worlds.

He and Finn had drawn strength from their beautiful, energizing mountain meetings. They knew each other too well—they were a part of each other. They were the two sides of the same coin.

The farmer searched my face. Finally, his head dropped to his chest, and he nodded slightly, seeing the likeness and so much that was different. I was the foreigner in him. Then he straightened his posture to stare at me with little understanding. He was part of this world now, and it saddened me.

My idealized vision slowly disappeared as the profound truth in his presence shone through. The fact was—he was genuine and standing before me. Yet, I continued to struggle with my emotions. I had carried pieces of my dad for years and wanted this to be real. I still wasn't sure what to say.

And then—a tear of recognition ran down his furrowed right cheek.

I blurted out, "Your name is William Stone, right?"

In a pitch-perfect Chinese dialect, he hesitantly spoke.

"Yes, that is true, but let us sit."

Though still not believing, my eyes I followed him toward a stone wall that bordered his farm. We eyed each other furtively as we walked, smiling now and then to keep things friendly but somewhat distant.

Perched on the rocks with the swarm of squawks enveloping our feet, I told him how beautiful his farm was, and he asked if I was there to buy some of his ducks.

"No, I'm not here for ducks." *Oh God, can this be real? Where do I begin? I have so many questions for you, though—about your past.*

His wrinkled, leathery face held so much sorrow and regret.

"I didn't think so." He lowered his head but then suddenly peered off into the distance as his surrounding ducks closed in as if forming a halo of protection.

"I thought that was all behind me by now."

I didn't want to hurt this battered version of him but thought, *I'm sorry, I have to know. I have dreamt of this for so long.*

"Does the name McCready mean anything to you?"

He looked at me with confusion and shock—written all over him.

"Yes. But?"

All I can do is smile, for it is so hard not to take this older man into my arms and cry.

Lord help me—keep it together.

"He is my boss and mentor. Although I didn't know, he always watched my back—just like Elizabeth asked him to do."

He then turned to me, searched my face and hands, and looked me in the eye.

"Elizabeth? Elizabeth, who?"

Of course, he doesn't know she is gone. How do I explain that?

"My mother's name is Elizabeth Stone—from Pennsylvania. A beautiful woman who missed you until the day she died."

Again, that same confused, mournful look.

"She's gone? How?"

"In a car accident several years ago."

"I see—I'm sorry," as the realization of her passage sunk in.

"I am, too."

A breeze rustled leaves in the nearby apple tree as the sun peeked from behind clouds. Was it a signal for us to realize the moment's importance?

The look on his face is beyond description. I could feel his wheels turning and words trying to form in his cotton-encrusted mouth. He slumped a bit more and almost fell off our perch as I caught him with my hand on his back—steadying him against the realization of the possible truths of our meeting.

I am actually touching my father—incredible!

"She must have told you. She was my mother, and you are my dad. I was born on December 3rd, 1945. Didn't she ever tell you?"

Finally, I couldn't hold it anymore, "Why didn't you come home?" She needed you badly. I needed you to."

"Did you call me dad? Who are you?" He was so confused.

I paused slowly and said, "My name is Mathew Stone."

He gazes at the countryside and slowly says, "I did come home, son. I did. It was the first time I could leave this place freely without scrutiny," he exclaimed. "So I entered the US under a supplied ID and began my search. I had missed her for all those years. Her vision had kept me alive during some horrible times. The memory and the good times we had together kept me going. I yearned to see her again. So when I could finally leave, I traveled back to the farm I left before the war. It was in severe disrepair. The fields were fallow—they hadn't been worked for years. I searched for family and knocked on doors, but everything and everybody was gone. I even tracked the farm's records and could not find any mention of her. It was like she had just disappeared.

Eventually, I thought she had probably accepted my death and moved on. It had been a long time. I didn't even know that you existed—that you were born. I just didn't know. So, I returned to China to make a new life."

He turned to me, searching my face for acceptance. All I could do was nod my head. I still didn't understand.

"The Japanese imprisoned me in China and passed my confinement on to the Chinese. They never told me anything but kept asking me questions about my past until I broke down. It went on for years, and my loss of reality became a problem for me—I lost track of everything—time, my wife, the US—everything. The Chinese finally released me to a local village family that nursed me back to health. I had been in captivity for over 15 years but was unaware of my lost time. The family that adopted me had a daughter, and we eventually married.

It was almost as if that family had chosen me—for this to happen. I was attracted to her, but not in a sensual way. Her support and encouragement helped me heal. I gradually became accepted by the family and the community. It took a long time to be accepted. There seemed no reason to return to the US again. I had a new family and a new life. I even found a way to make a small living from farming ducks.

The US had changed so much, and I didn't recognize anything friendly or comfortable anymore. I am so very sorry." The sadness in his eyes broke my heart.

"I was messed up after all those years in isolation, deprivation, and torture. I lost hope of ever seeing your mother. I had nowhere to go until that Chinese family took me in. After that, I did not know who I was anymore.

I was imprisoned for years. They wanted information from my work with the ONI. Looking back, there are so many projects. It might have been the laser or stealth technology I worked on for the US. I never divulged anything to them. Of course, I gave them snippets of misinformation as I feigned borderline insanity, which always seemed to satisfy them for short periods. But I was losing it and was unsure how long I could carry on.

I did not know the war had ended. The Chinese were still unsure what I knew or had divulged and continued my imprisonment. Based on their perception, I surmised that if the Japanese had kept me in a special prisoner status, the importance of what they thought I knew should also be valuable and important to them. And the cycle continued. Gradually, their patience wore thin, as I was almost a useless incoherent mess to nearly everyone by that time. Finally, they pushed me out into their world, hoping I would disappear or die."

He paused and suddenly blurted out, "If you were thinking of me coming home now, I can't. I've done things I'm not proud of, and I don't think you will like me." He took my hand and held it so tightly my fingers turned white—a*ll this time, all his pain and sadness.*

I saw dad's pain and felt sorry for him—that he had missed so much of his life. He had let down those who loved and missed him terribly. Yet, there didn't seem to be a way of getting him out. Did I need to accept that this was his home now?

To have come this far and actually found him—alive—God. Of course, I should be happy beyond words, but selfishly, I wanted him in my life, every day, for as long as possible. I wanted him to be at my wedding, love Rusty and Finn, spend time with McCready, and maybe hold a grandchild. Was it too much to ask for—to have a quiet life, safe life with people who cared for him—his blood? How could I make this happen? *Shit, I can't breathe.*

Thirty

A Boys Hero Found

As my father quietly rose from the rock fence wall, he motioned me to walk beside him—and we walked.

I looked over at this withering image of a man, my dad, and a quiet peace filled me. The peace that comes from finding him. I was somehow more complete.

"Dad, I have tried to make you proud for many years, even though I didn't know you. Really, I have tried. I looked up to you—you have always been real to me, even though we have never met. Mom suffered your loss for years."

"I'm sure she did. My memories of her kept me alive for a very long time. You have made me proud, Mathew, by just finding me and loving me. It was all my fault. I let you and your mother down for not knowing. I am sorry. I hope you can understand. You found me, and we are no longer strangers. We have a second chance, and I hope you can forgive me."

Tears rolled down my face. I could not help myself. All those years. All that pain. All that lost time. I wanted a father so badly.

"I created expectations in my mind. I wanted you to be proud of me even though you weren't there. So I tried to complete the vision of what I thought you wanted me to be—to achieve. Finn, my best friend, and his dad helped a lot, but it wasn't the same. I have lived in your shadow for my whole life. But right now, this is good enough. You are my dad, I'm here for you, and that's all that counts."

He smiled, "I am so thankful you have found me, son."

And then, I couldn't help it and whispered.

"Please listen to what I have to say, dad, and carefully consider what could come next for you. Your country would like to provide you and your family with an avenue back home and will do everything possible to alleviate your situation. I'd like you to travel home with me. Arrangements can be made quickly. I know everything about you from mom's albums and our abbreviated discussions about your life together. I have chosen a career that I thought you would be proud of, and I know people who want you back. Would you like to make a go of it back home?

Knowing I had crossed orders now, out on a limb in more ways than one—there was no turning back. I knew it might not end well for both of us—but I felt it was the only way.

"I still love you, dad. I want you with me. Don't you think it is time?"

He looked me in the eye, straightened himself up, and took a deep breath.

"I admire your courage coming all this way to look for me and the danger you have placed yourself in. But I cannot leave. The project is now more important than ever. If I leave, it will fail and have repercussions around the world. If I'm gone, people will die as the project will impact many."

What was he talking about? What project? Is this real, or has he lost it? No, He'd never do that!

"Do not worry about this matter. It will be better. You will be safer if you do not know the details. But, unfortunately, I have to stay. I have no choice, son."

I stared at him and felt terrible. He was confused and a little angry. *Am I getting used? Was he really in with the communists?*

I tried to make sense of his words. His response was like nothing I'd planned for in my head. As I pushed to hold back my frustration, I wanted to beg him to return with me. I had pictured our lives together a thousand times. How could he even consider not letting me get to know him? It was unfathomable, and the confusion and disappointment were overwhelming.

I looked around, remembering what I'd seen in the last several weeks: poverty, fear, and loss of hope. Had he been duped? Was he a victim of all that? What had he done to stay alive? I turned to him. He put his hand in mine and then abruptly snatched it away. I felt like I had been dropped on my head. And then…

Thirty–One
Disillusionment

"Dad, what project?"

It was like a switch turned on in my father, as if his dyke had finally broken. He now appeared in front of my eyes in utter confusion and pain. The insanity of his years of imprisonment flowed like a waterfall. He stuttered and stammered as a confused stream of his tortured, broken thoughts drifted out of his anguished, sweating face and into a confusing stream of consciousness.

"Old men, women, and children—what are those people doing to their world? They were hands on my arms, holding me back from my life, and they wouldn't let go—things were not what I expected. Then, finally, I understood that the enemy was something intangible, not the people. Still, the people were—these people are the enemy, they are all the enemy—I had begun to understand that nothing had changed—my friends were killing my friends—I began to realize what I had been told. What was going on in China was nuts. They had their finger on the trigger, and the bead was on me somewhere.

My sole purpose in life was to stay alive and get out. But, oh, the questions, I don't want to know the answers. Things smelled bad. I smelled terrible and hurt everywhere.

The questions that began to present themselves were too much to handle—I peered into the darkness of my need to save McCready on that atoll long ago, and then the frustration of not getting to him again was ugly. I could not make sense of what had happened to me. I needed to understand it—it was like playing gin with 30 versus 52 cards."

I stared at him in disbelief and realized that my dad, at this moment, had gone haywire. His deck had been shuffled pretty hard over the years.

"The reasons for me being here were disturbing—they hated me, I destroyed them—I could see my impact was minimal and was primarily negative. What happened to me in that village was nothing like what I believed. The Japs, Koreans, and Chinese were all the same. The war went on at the same pace regardless of what we did. I was happy to be alive, excited, and ambivalent but afraid I'd get a dear john letter. She was the focus of my life, and I thought she had taken a hike—I didn't know where I would find her when I got out.

Thank you for your years of service. Maybe getting some pension money would be all she would receive. 'But, you should think of the others who didn't come home.' They would say—'you have been programmed—have felt uncomfortable and endured—so have a great life—see ya.'

McCready's words crossed Mathe's mind, 'Many POWS were triggered by repetitive patterns after being drugged and electro-shocked to wipe out their memories. But instead, behavior patterns erased for 30 to 40 years by the communists usually returned with a vengeance.' Today I was the trigger.

"You OK, dad?" Thinking he was batshit, borderline gone at this moment. "Try to calm down. It's OK. We are OK. The war is long over."

He took a few deep breaths and rubbed his eyes as though he was getting rid of the pictures in his head.

"No, it is not son! It's such a mess—all my fault. My head doesn't work right. Sometimes I don't know where or who I am, and sometimes it all comes back. I wanted to get out on a freedom bird to fly away. I ceased to think about why I was here and what I was doing. But, I'm

OK—feeling I don't deserve to return—I feel bad because of the whole thing."

My disillusionment with my hero, my dad, was almost complete with his ramblings. It was compounded by the unrevealed motives of my superiors, my resultant distrust of them, and now dad's state of mind. The only thing that saved my sink was the need to fix this—to get this man the help he needed.

My government will not leave him here again, nor I.

Thirty–Two
Razor Blade Allegiances

PENTAGON

“It is good to see you alive and healthy today, Mathew, after what you have been through in China.” He recounted the story Mathe had transmitted about his brush with the shooters—probing for more knowledge and insight.

“I have been around battlefield types and seen those fellows scared shitless. Of course, they had every right to be, but then some stick their noses in thinking they will never get hit, acting as if they were bulletproof, and believe me, in time, they die—the hard way.”

Mathe stared at McCready, puzzled by his statement, as he had no choice but to let him roll.

“You stuck to the plan, followed orders, and the fact that you might even have been afraid to die is an asset versus those that go independent and get their comrades eventually killed for their driven, misplaced, unauthorized courage.

Our fear is quite different in the cockpit, but we all share that moment when we hesitate to lean into the target and disengage from our course—the proper course of action in the plan because of our more personal fear—but you stuck to the program and called me. I take actions by those operators who endanger others personally and turn them into dead sticks in reassignment or worse.”

McCready paused to gauge the impact of his statement before leaning in as Mathe remained silent.

"You know, we all dream up the hero we want to be when we're young, and some spend their lives trying to live out that ideal, and even more so when we build that idol from actual personal imagined perceptions of who or what we think they were. Maybe your drive to find your father and his strengths and failings were so you could accept yours. His emotional and intellectual DNA is there; you have probably touched it through this mission.

But, before you provide your full debrief, I think it is time to share the back side of Chi's life story. We purposely kept you and others out of the loop to cover the real motivations for your mission. But, with your successful probe into the whereabouts of Chi and the striking find of your father, the CIA will now take over Chi's future. But, first, you understand that any venture that deals with double-dealing, treachery and spying wouldn't be straightforward.

Chi became a leader for the communists and traveled the country, establishing revolutionary networks. He followed the Lin Biao movement to power. Chi was channeled into the Vietnamese military and ordered to flight instruction in Pensacola as an unsuspected Vietnamese pilot. We had lost contact with Chi after Chinese students were instructed to enter education relocation from the US back into their country.

Since WWII, we have tracked his family and communist party espionage activities.

Remember, we spoke of Chi's father and mother as moles for the Japanese during WWII. But at the same time, they were also building formidable intelligence networks of sympathetic Chinese informants. They supplied their US contacts with information on Jap troop movements and supplies and performed dangerous field assignments in their region. Yet, as far as we can tell, they were never uncovered by the Japanese nor turned.

"So, they were operators for the Japanese?"

"Yes, they were pictured as traitors by the people, called renegades, and worse by their fellow citizens while at the same time doing field intelligence work for the US. It must have been a hellish life walking the double-edged razor of two allegiances.

It became even dicier for them as the communist-led government sought to expel the Japanese imperial forces, including US personnel collaborating with remaining Japanese troops at the war's end. Their visibility became more important to us with the murder of Captain John Birch, an OSS intelligence resource. His murder by Chinese communists blew our intelligence gathering, and his network had to be saved and resurrected. I won't comment on how its integrity was maintained,

But Chi came into our picture years later. Their son Chi has been an agent for the communist party before his graduation and departure from Pensacola NAVAIR training. We did not know that he played two roles with two different allegiances, like his parents. Current information has been received on Chi and his family—information leaked by sources close to the Chinese communist government and the Party.

"Two different allegiances, sir?"

"Yes, Mathew, I am getting to that. Recently our sources indicated that Chi is a team member that assassinated a high-level Russian government official. In addition, Chi has had extensive special military training, combat experience, and security and intelligence service experience above and beyond what he learned in the US.

Lieutenant Chi Dung Thai became a special agent for the Chinese communists for his courage during difficult times for the regime. As a result, Chi worked for the Communist Party early in his career.

As a student at the University of Chicago, funded by the US government and supported by a cloaked US agency, he kept a low profile while working on multiple projects at the University. However, he was clever enough to sneak under our radar. Yet, his work on some of the most critical defense projects still affects us today. His ties with the communist party were discovered later in his collegiate career. He was a student agent for the CCP in pure espionage and theft.

Unbelievably, Chi and others like him handed over top military data on the radar used to down American planes early in the Vietnam War. And yet he flew for the Vietnamese against the very weapons he assisted in helping the North build. His work became a genuinely invaluable asset for the communists. It was a clever idea for them to send Chinese nationals under a Vietnamese cover to our best universities and get them access to critical research being conducted.

From our point of view, a new kind of stupid appears to have been running or overseeing these kinds of research programs—for these educational research programs are rift with covert operators.

As you have sensed, his priority was never wholly dedicated to achieving communist goals.

As the disillusionment with his handlers grew over time, we saw an opportunity to turn him in our direction. Eventually, he became a high communist officer while secretly working with the US. But there were many indicators that he was not what he appeared to be. US officials became dubious. His efforts cost the lives of several communist agents and helped us destroy many of their sectors of influence. Even so, there were mixed signals. We suspected he might have been "doubled"—

found out and forced to supply us with disinformation to survive. To make matters worse, he recently broke contact in China, which has become problematic for him and us.

The Chinese were very concerned about the Soviet threat. Russian agents were the culprits in that gunfight you were in—not the Chinese. We know the Russians are trying to break the peace in the region, increasing the Soviet threat to China. The Chinese felt the US could moderate the area by offsetting Soviet aggression. We are not sure if Chi has been compromised yet by his handlers, but something is up.

You and Chi were attacked by members of a Russian cell in China. They were supported by other elements that provided their field team with logistical support to carry the attack, hoping to kill both of you. There is the possibility that they know of Chi's status as a joint Chinese/US operative. It is unclear whether they knew of Chi's defection plans or were trying to erase him for something even more critical."

"So the Russians are also culpable, sir?"

"I wouldn't rule out anything, Mathew. We think you were caught in an international conflict with roots deep into the China-Russian relationship. Our sources tell us that the Russian assassin(s) knew precisely the dates and times of Chi's movements even though he was constantly on the move—as you know. As soon as the skirmish was over, the Chinese communist party had a team waiting for the Russian convoy that had captured Chi. They opened fire on the convoy outside of the city.

Within a short period after your second meeting with Chi and his disclosure of Lieutenant Stone's specific whereabouts, we have confidential reports that Chi was caught in a vehicle that was detonated after your conflict, resulting in his death. But this is just conjectured with new pieces of the incident.

Even more alarming, internal Russian communication links report that Russian assassins were killed during a secret operation to capture Chi—their highly-valued target. But, subsequent reports indicate the Chinese saved him during this operation. Very mixed messages but expected from biased ideological and propaganda-driven cultures.

Above all, his status remains unknown even with our high intelligence penetration of the Chinese security services. You knew him, and he knew that you made a big difference.

We sent you to find Chi and possibly confirm his loyalty and nothing more.

All your predecessors have failed, and your success now demands that you report directly to me and no one else. They now know a new player has entered the equation.

In other words, you should not communicate with anyone about your activities. The politics of your success compromise the positions of many within our government.

We are constrained from participating in activities or discussions with any foreign government concerning Chi Dung Thai. Therefore, it's time for you to stand down.

I am far from prescient about our foreign relationships. Still, I suspect that some parts of China and the US economies will rely on each other in the future, so we do not want to threaten the potential for a strategic alliance. Remember Nixon and his first baby steps to normalize our relations?

There is no measure of how much your actions in this regard might have affected unwanted visibility in the region. We only suspected a slight downside to your search. But, again, your successful activities could create a political nightmare for many in our government. Sorely warranted, I suppose and possibly causing a furor in some circles.

Communications with Chi have become quite a hot commodity within the party structure. I want you out of it for your safety. Don't ask me how or who is involved, but the CIA is now on the case. The FBI is all over my ass, so I agreed that the CIA would take over from here. I know you're invested now, but it is time to stop your communications with Chi. I am reassigning you. Chi's days may be numbered if he is alive, but your dad's story is another matter."

Mathew thought back to the meeting with Chi and wondered what would have happened if he had shared Chi's whole story with the Admiral—how their fates would be different. Mathe couldn't tell McCready the full story of what Chi was about, for it would jeopardize his chances of getting him and his dad out alive. Instead, Chi asked Mathe to find some specific INTEL on the Communists, which he knew would allow them to convince McCready and others of his innocence and therefore protect him and his family.

"But, sir?"

"Let me spell this all out for you. Mathew. Chi has studied the mindset of those he has aligned himself with. He has been feeding us misinformation for some time, but he did not realize we knew his treachery. He pretended to change his allegiance to keep us confused or at least to muddy the waters, but his true allegiance to the communists never wavered. Many years ago, his recruiting by us might have been a calculated mistake and could bite us in the ass."

Mathe wrestled with how much to tell him. He knew McCready was a man that could not be easily misled.

"Admiral, what I didn't mention was that even though Chi's life wasn't the life he imagined—I mean the killing, sabotage, and more—

he said that if we couldn't get him and his family to safety, he would go to work, and it wouldn't be pretty."

"Captain, what the hell is he talking about?"

"Sir, I don't have any idea—but it appears to be a threat if I don't deliver."

"Mathew, we will keep this strictly confidential—for your dad's sake. Chi used your dad for reasons we cannot mention. They might both be under pressure from the communists. He knows something about your dad that I cannot disclose. We need to know what he knows. So we cannot underestimate him."

" But sir, what are our intentions on getting my dad out."

"Let's take one step at a time, Mathew. This is complicated stuff. We have to go inch by inch. It's not that I don't trust you."

McCready paused. Mathe could feel the intensity as he leaned forward, looking Mathew directly in the eye. The sudden stiffness in his voice punctuated a renewed boundary.

"Captain, I'm not happy with this outcome either, but we have this mission directly from the CNO. This is what the President wants. You are dismissed."

Thoughts about his dad flooded Mathe—his long-term suffering in China and his strength to escape and avoid capture while evading the Japs on that tiny island in the Pacific during WWII, his eventual torture when caught, and all those years lost; in captivity for what?

To hell with them. This is about Dad!

Thirty–Three

Pensacola Beach

Blue Diamond over Pensacola Beach

God! What a day it has been! I've gone from being a nervous wreck to being happier than I ever thought I could be.

Maddy has worked one miracle after another. Even the weather has been perfect. Pensacola beach usually has way more than a stiff breeze. But, today, she has calmed herself down.

After far too many beers and much raucous shit last night, Finn rousted me. Coffee, aspirin, and a run put me back in order.

Rusty insisted on my officer evening dress uniform, so that's the attire for today. But I have to borrow a dress sword from one of the boys. I couldn't justify purchasing one for the little usage it would be given. I've only talked to her, not seen her, for three days—something about bad luck if I did.

Yeah, that's right. I'm not single anymore, thank God!

The little chapel on base, watching her come down the aisle on her Dad's arm—damn. I am one lucky SOB.

There we were—Finn, One Nut, and I standing up front, trying to act like adults, and I chuckled—*three guys and only four nuts.*

I do, and another I do, and then it was off to the beach.

Picnic tables, coolers, kegs, tents, grills, a huge, loud boom box, and kites flying everywhere. The aroma of grilled steaks, gumbo, and shrimp told me the party was on. But lookout, throw in a few Marines with those two enormous sheet cakes the size of a runway, and I knew someone would be wearing one of them before the afternoon was over. Somehow all this stuff got hauled over the dunes to the beach. Thank you, Maddy, Trader, and Joe Patti's.

All our favorite people—well, almost all of them are having a great time. Even McCready was yucking it up in his buttoned-down fashion with Rusty's mom.

His presence brought me back to our recent meeting and his challenge.

'Mathew, you have the skills we need to win wars. You may have already helped start one without even knowing it. So, what do you want, Mathew—what do you want from us? It certainly isn't security. No one wants a war, but wouldn't you like to be in it if there is one? I know what's coming down the pike. If you think about it, you do, too.'

My mind instantly pivoted to Chi and my dad. What would have happened if I had disclosed Chi's whole story? I might not be here—McCready would not have brought me home. I couldn't tell McCready all that day—too much for our country hung in the balance.

Suddenly McCready and I were interrupted by the roar of a lone Angel making a low pass over the celebration that capstoned our party. Then, with heads tuned to the sky, the jet suddenly banked in burner and beat feet back to the base on his "post-maintenance test flight." One Nut assured me he had invited the team to our wedding celebration, and they would join us on the beach—post haste.

One Nut had zeroed in on one of Rusty's nurse friends. But, of course, Rusty had warned her, so I'm not too concerned.

I danced with my girl, pinned my wings on her, and told her not to plan on much sleep tonight. She grabbed my ass and said, 'hope you can keep up with me, Marine.'

The sun started its slide, and the sky softened in color as bonfires were magically lit and blankets and coolers were moved close to the fire. Kites finally came to rest in the sand, even as the music rocked—but softer. I tried to take in every detail of the faces around the fire, laughing and enjoying each other. I looked back at Finn and Maddy wrapped around each other looking exceptionally happy, just as I felt. Catching the twinkle of the first star to appear this night—it just couldn't get better. Feeling Rusty's arm wrap around my waist and quietly squeeze, we found our truth together. Rusty caught the tear in the corner of my eye and held me tighter, with no words, not wanting to upset my feelings as we found our way, in the quiet of the moment, down the beach.

Looking back, I see the admiral walking in our footsteps toward us. I assume to say good night, but he asks Rusty if he can borrow me for a minute.

We continue away from the festivities down the beach without a word. He then stops and takes in the sunset, the waves, and the distant people around the fire.

"It's been a great day, Mathew. Thanks for including me."

"We both wanted you here today, sir. Thank you for coming."

"Looking back on your excellent work, I am sure you have found some level of comfort with the Pentagon process, which probably at times seemed like a house of mirrors."

"Yes, sir. But can I ask you a question?" McCready gave Mathe a steely look, less than a mentor, more admiral.

"Sir, why haven't we brought my dad home?" The admiral's nervous tick suddenly reappeared under his left eye, as it had many times in past discussions, as he softened, hesitated, and then stammered, "I haven't wanted to…I need to…well, I don't want to spoil…."

"What is it, sir? You are making me nervous."

"Ok, then, Mathew, your dad is in serious trouble. So you have to go back."

Momentarily hesitating, I looked up at the darkened sky while pulling the coin he had given me from my pocket. I caught the admiral's smile as it rose in the air and made my vow—not waiting for the coin's decision.

Thank You!

If you enjoyed the book I would be grateful if you would consider posting a review on Amazon.com or on the source of your purchase.

Your positive review will help Amazon get the book in front of more people who also might enjoy the novel.

Thank you again for reading True Blue!

D Stuart White

Acknowledgments

The book is a work of imagination inspired by historical events and true stories. I have departed when necessary for the sake of storytelling, except for the most significant historical figures of the time. Several veterans of WWII, Korea, and the Vietnam conflict offered comments and narratives to develop this novel's storyline and flesh out fictitious characterizations.

I have tried to be mindful of the historical record and reflect on the actual experiences of those who participated. For those that might wonder, my father's keepsakes and files revealed much about the times and his involvement in WWII, not to mention the depth of devotion and love for his life partner, Betty White, in Tall Air. True Blue was woven with actions that reflect multiple families and individuals into characters that reflect specific timelines in the 40s thru the 70s.

The True Blue storyline was aided enormously by several people. I must thank them; the Candler and Matthews families and specifically LT W R Candler, LCDR Darwin "Dart" Kinney, CDR Jamie "Tilly" Tilden, Al "Taco" Cisneros (Blue Angels Pilot 1976-1977), LT D E White, and Captain D R Matthews. If they had not shared their stories, I would not have mine.

Eternal thanks go to my family members and friends who served as early readers. Without their encouragement, I would never have imagined writing my second book. Thanks to A D White, Aaron Helander, William Finnicum, Ward Lamphere, James M Sharp, LT Daniel Heming, Captain "One Ton" McCready, Mike Jolly, Nabin Karna, Pat Kilkenny, Robert Varney, Penny McCready, Robert

Johannes, Tom Patterson, Jack Haughton, and David Aretha, Award-winning author, and editor). I am indebted to them for their support.

The many friends, authors, artists, historians, bloggers, broadcasters, pilots, and executives pivotal to my research can't be left out: D D Smith (Author - Above Average: Naval Aviation the Hard Way), ADM Hamlin Tallent (Author - Weenie Kleegan), Peter Chilelli, Tyler White, ADM R. A. Hopwood Author - The Laws of the Navy), Nick "Ditch' Suppa, LtCol Robert McVey, John R. Doughty Jr, Joe Heywood (Author, Covered Waters; The Wolf Who Saved the Deer), Thomas R Combs (Author - Flight Line), David P. Wagner (Author - Death in the Dolomites), Class 69-07, Captain Richard M. Saunders, Frank DiKötter, Eustace L. Adams, PT Deutermann, Marshall "Pappy" Coulter, John "JJ" Miller (Blue Angels Pilot 1976-1978), Bruce "Squire" Davey (Blue Angels Pilot 1977-79), and Keith "Casey" Jones (Blue Angels Pilot 1976-1977)

And Ann White, my wife, with her many contributions and endearing patience seeing me through.

Angel Echelon

History of the Blues Angels Flight Demonstration Team

76 Years of Aviation Excellence

In 1946, the Chief of Naval Operations, Admiral Chester Nimitz, had the vision to create a flight exhibition team to raise the public's interest in naval aviation and boost Navy morale. In the 1940s, we thrilled audiences with our precision combat maneuvers in the F6 Hellcat, the F8 Bearcat, and the F9 Panther. During the 1950s, we refined our demonstration with aerobatic maneuvers in the F9 Cougar and F-11 Tiger and introduced the first six-plane delta formation, still flown to this day. By the end of the 1960s, we were flying the F-4 Phantom, the only two-seat aircraft flown by the delta formation. In 1974, we transitioned to the A-4 Skyhawk, a smaller and lighter aircraft with a tighter turning radius allowing for a more dynamic flight demonstration. In 1986, we celebrated our 40th Anniversary by unveiling the Boeing F/A-18 Hornet. In 2021, we transitioned to our current aircraft, the Boeing F/A-18 Super Hornet, and celebrated our 75th anniversary.

In 1949, it became necessary for the Blue Angels to operate a support aircraft to move personnel and equipment between show sites. These support aircraft include the Douglas R4D Sky Train, the Curtiss R5C Commando, the Douglas R5D Skymaster, and the Lockheed C-121 Super Constellation. In 1970 the team received the Lockheed Martin C-130, affectionately known as "Fat Albert." In 2020, "Fat Albert" transitioned to its current platform, the C-130J Super Hercules."

The Laws Of The Navy

By Adm. R. A. Hopwood, RN*

Admiral Hopwood's "Laws of the Navy" was published in a British periodical on 23 July 1898. It has appeared in the United States Naval Academy's "Reef Points" for several years and is well-known throughout the Navy.

Now, these are the laws of the Navy,
Unwritten and varied they be;
And he who is wise will observe them,
Going down in his ship to the sea.

As naught may outrun the destroyer,
So, it is with the law and its grip,
For the strength of a ship is the Service,
And the strength of the Service the ship.

Take heed what you say of your seniors,
Be your words spoken softly or plain,
Let a bird of the air tell the matter,

And so, shall ye hear it again.
If you labor from morn until even,
And meet with reproof for your toil,

*A Royal Navy captain who later rose to admiral, the following poem -- a bit of rhyming advice; the poem's salty particulars cannot hide the essence of good advice for young hopefuls, whatever their sphere. Admiral Hopwood's words are all-encompassing and timeless.

'Tis well that the gun may be humbled
The compressor must check the recoil.
On the strength of one link in the cable,
Dependeth the might of the chain.
Who knows when thou may'st be tested?
So, live that thou bearest the strain!

When a ship that is tired returneth,
With the signs of the seas showing plain;
Men place her in dock for a season,
And her speed she reneweth again.

So shall ye, if perchance ye grow weary,
In the uttermost parts of the sea,
Pray for leave for the good of the Service,
As much and as oft as may be.

Count not upon certain promotion
But rather to gain it aspire;
Though the sightline may end on the target
There cometh perchance the miss-fire.

Can'st follow the track of the dolphin?
Or tell where the sea swallows roam?
Where Leviathan taketh his pastime?
What ocean he calleth his own?

So, it is with the words of the rulers,
And the orders these words shall convey;

Every law is naught beside this one:
Thou shalt not criticize but Obey.

Say the wise: How may I know their purpose?
Then acts without wherefore or why.
Stays the fool but one moment to question,
And the chance of his life passes by.

If ye win through an African jungle,
Unmentioned at home in the press,
Heed it not. No man seeth the piston,
But it driveth the ship nonetheless.

Do they growl? it is well. Be thou silent,
If the work goeth forward amain.
Lo! the gun throws the shot to a hair's breadth
And shouteth, yet none shall complain.

Do they growl, and the work be retarded?
It is ill, be whatever their rank.
The half-loaded gun also shouteth,
But can she pierce target with blank?

Doth the paintwork make war with the funnels
And the deck to the cannons complain? Nay, they know that some soap and freshwater
Unites them as brothers again.

So ye, being heads of departments,
Do you growl with a smile on your lip?
Lest ye strive and in anger be parted,
And lessen the might of your ship.

Dost deem that thy vessel needs gilding,
And the dockyard forbears to supply?
Put thy hand in thy pocket and gild her --
There are those who have risen thereby.

Dost think in a moment of anger
'Tis well with thy seniors to fight?
They prosper, who burn in the morning,
The letters they wrote overnight.

For many are shelved and forgotten,
With nothing to thank for their fate,
But that on a half sheet of foolscap
A fool "Had the honor to state."

Should the fairway be crowded with shipping?
Beating homeward the harbor to win,
It is meet that lest any should suffer,
The steamers pass cautiously in.

So, thou, when thou nearest promotion,
And the peak that is gilded is nigh,
Give heed to words and thine actions,
Lest others be wearied thereby.

It is ill for the winners to worry,
Take thy fate as it comes, with a smile,
And when thou art safe in the harbor
They may envy, but will not revile.

Uncharted the rocks that surround thee,
Take heed that the channels thou learn,
Lest thy name serve to buoy for another
That shoal the "Court-Martial Return."

Though a strong armored belt may protect her
The ship bears the scar on her side;'
'Tis well if the Court should acquit thee --
But 'twere best had'st thou never been tried.

MORAL

As the wave washes clear at the hawse pipe,
Washes aft, and is lost in the wake;
So shalt thou drop astern all unheeded
Such time as these laws ye forsake.

Take heed in your manner of speaking
That the language ye use may be sound,
In the list of the words of your choosing
"Impossible" may not be found.
Now, these are the Laws of the Navy,
And many and mighty are they.
But the hull and the deck and the keel
And the truck of the law is -- **OBEY**.

DON'T MISS THE EXPLOSIVE ACTION OF NAVY PILOTS IN ACTION OVER VIETNAM

Tall Air

An Epic Story of Friendship, Family, and War – In The Sixties.

First Book in Series

Join Mathew Stone and Jonathon Finley in their heroism and sacrifice as they reach for *Tall Air* throughout their lives. Tall Air's pulse-pounding combat sequences focus their heroism as Navy fighter pilots on each other under fire and the sacrifices of their loved ones and country.

Thrilling, tragic, and funny in the extreme, Tall Air is highly readable and an irresistible and authentic account of an extraordinary friendship—heartfelt with fear and pride.

D Stuart White's Articles, Editorials, Posts – LinkedIn

- Build PR and Sales Enablers - Ask the Right Research
- Crisis Preparedness Could Save Your Organization
- How to Build Effective Direct Marketing Propositions
- Fill the Holes in your Sales Force's Digital Communications
- A Reluctant Hero
- How to Build a Fund-Raising Campaign by Leveraging your Senator's Inner Devil

- Bad Day Flying the "Hump" in WWII
- First Steps to Profitability – Reorganization
- The Best and Worst Direct Marketing Creative Strategies

- How To Improve - Corporate Performance, with 500 personnel (staff & field) performing duplicate tasks
- Fighter Pilot and Corporate Human Factors in Project Management Leadership.
- How To Profit From Non-Profit Alliances - Case Study
- Learn 12 Key Automotive Branch & Business Center KPI Growth Strategies - Case Study
- How One Automotive Mfg. Mitigate Their Quality Swiss Cheese Accident Trajectories

- Auto Dealer Sales/Service Underachievement Dashboard
- Developing Payoffs in Non-Profit Organizations
- What Part Do Human Factors Play In Project Management?

CPSIA information can be obtained
at www.ICGtesting.com
Printed in the USA
LVHW040159010623
748607LV00004B/69